TRAPPED!

He wondered what sort of a woman she was, reading alone so close beside the sea without marking the approach of the hungry waves. Then, before he could think further, there came one large wave rushing and tumbling in mad glee. It merrily dashed into the young lady's lap, wetting her book and sending her flying back from the spot in alarm. And then it calmly seized the white silk parasol and hurled it out on its retreating arms, a toy upon the billows.

He took two strides into the saucy waters and brought the dripping thing to Maria. "Please, let me carry it home for you," he said as she reached her hand for the sunshade. "Your cottage is nearby, is it not?"

And so, quite against her will, Maria walked the length of the beach to her home with a stranger, her dress wet and bedraggled, her borrowed parasol and book carried by him, wishing fiercely that she could find some way of getting rid of him before they arrived. . . .

Grace
LIVINGSTON HILL

AMERICA'S BEST-LOVED STORYTELLER

LONE POINT
AND THE ESSELSTYNES

LIVING BOOKS®
Tyndale House Publishers, Inc.
Wheaton, Illinois

This Tyndale House book
by Grace Livingston Hill
contains the complete text
of the original hardcover edition.
NOT ONE WORD
HAS BEEN OMITTED.

Living Books is a registered trademark of Tyndale House
Publishers, Inc.

Library of Congress Catalog Card Number 94-60951
ISBN 0-8423-3858-6

Printed in the United States of America

01   00   99   98   97   96
 9   8   7   6   5   4

CONTENTS

LONE POINT

RACHEL HAMMOND sat by the open window with her Bible on her knee. The muslin curtains did not blow with the breeze, for there was no breeze that hot morning in June. The air seemed breathless. Rachel had put her pretty room in order, finished all her little morning duties, and now had sat down for a quiet minute with her Bible before she began the day.

Her sister Maria, two years older, sat in the adjoining room, her door open for all possible circulation of air. Indeed the door between the sisters' rooms was scarcely ever shut by day or by night. But Maria was trimming a hat instead of reading her Bible. Not that Maria did not read her Bible, for she did, but she never had a set, quiet time for doing it as Rachel had.

The hat was a white sailor and had been very stylish and consequently very expensive earlier in the season, but now the mass of people were supplied with millinery for the summer, and poorer people were enabled by the great reduction in prices to indulge their taste for pretty things. It went very much against the grain with Maria Hammond to have to wait until late for the pretty to buy with careful hand and long-hoarded savings, for until recently she had been used to buying when and what she pleased since she could remember. Maria had taken more bitterly her father's change of fortune than any of the other members of the family. The others had looked on the bright side of things and cheerfully told each other how good it was that matters were no worse; that the father had not fallen ill physically under the heavy burden that had been placed upon him by the fraud of a trusted partner; that the dear beautiful home where the three children had been born was saved to them, with a little—a very little, it is true, but still a little—with which to keep things going; and best of all, that all the creditors had been fully paid. But Maria could only see the dark side. From a rich man, who was able to do what he pleased, and who intended soon to build a home lovelier even than their present one, and who could afford to place his daughters in the best society, her father had become a poor man. Thus to her the present home had lost even the charms which it had possessed before she looked forward to the finer one.

This present home was by no means an undesirable one. It was located on a quiet, pleasant street where the neighbors were staid and old-fashioned, people of fine old families. It was built of stone in a comfortable manner, with ample room and broad piazzas, vines peeping in the windows in summer, and lawn enough about it to give the feeling of plenty of room. It was in the plainest end of a fashionable suburb, but it was not fashionable. The house had none of the modern twists and turns which art and fashion have decreed shall adorn the modern handsome dwelling, and for this reason Maria despised it and pitied herself for having to live in it. A look of discontent had settled down upon her pretty white forehead which was gradually but surely changing her expression permanently.

"Oh, dear!" sighed Maria, as she jerked a loop of white ribbon into place behind the many cheap white wings she was arranging on her hat. "What's the use of fussing and fixing up things to wear after all? There won't be a place to wear them except church, and all the people we know or care about will be out of town by another month. One might as well wear one's old duds after all."

Rachel looked up from her Bible, through the open door where she could see her sister at work.

"Oh, yes, there will be plenty of places. Don't be so disheartened, dear," she answered brightly. "How pretty that hat will be, 'Ri! It looks just like you."

"Does it, indeed?" responded the elder sister. "Then my face must be badly snarled up, for this ribbon is. I can't get the right twist to it any way I put it. I do wish I could afford to take it down to Haskins' and have it trimmed by our old milliner. It is awfully vexatious to have to do everything one's self or else go without. But I'd be willing to do it myself if we could only go out of town for a little while, Ray; it's so horribly plebeian to stay in the city all the year round. Everybody else is going."

"You forget, 'Ri, we don't live in the city, we live in the suburbs, and plenty of people stay all summer in the suburbs. Some people prefer to take their trips away from home in the winter, you know. Look at the Adamses and Monteiths, they don't go away at all, and even Mrs. Burbank told me the other day that they didn't care to take any vacation, they enjoyed their home in the summer so much."

"Oh, yes, I should think they would. They have a park surrounding them, a great, cool house with plenty of servants, all the guests they want, and are up on a high hill besides, with plenty of shade about. Besides, it's nonsense for them to talk about not going away. They are hardly at home two weeks in succession all the year around. Mrs. Burbank and Tilly spend a week at a time at Atlantic City every time they sneeze or have a headache, and Mr. and Mrs. Burbank took a trip to California last winter, while Tom and his aunt went to Florida. When they don't run up to New York or out to Pittsburg for a few days they go up to that sanitarium in the mountains for their health for a month or take a trip to Bermuda. I don't know that I should care either about going away in the summer if I only knew I could go whenever I pleased, and what is more, knew that everybody else knew it. I tell you, Ray, the hardest thing to bear is to feel that folks are saying we can't go anywhere now, and pitying us! I just can't stand it," and Maria threw her half-finished hat on the bed beside her and lay back on one of the snowy pillows in a discouraged attitude.

Rachel by long experience with her sister knew that it was of no use to argue with her, so she tried to cheer her as best she could, sighing a little regretfully as she closed her Bible and came into her sister's room. She had been reading the verse, "For me to live is Christ," and she wondered wistfully if she would ever know what that meant, and wished that Maria felt more of the spirit of it, so that her life would not seem so hard to her.

"If you want to go away so much perhaps we might go to the same place Marvie Parker told me about yesterday," said Rachel, seating herself on the foot of Maria's bed and resting her chin thoughtfully in her hand.

"No, thanks!" said Maria promptly and decidedly. "I don't think I should care for any place where Marvie

Parker goes. I don't see what you find in that girl to attract you, Ray. She is the dowdiest thing I've seen in a long time. Her father is nothing but a clerk in his brother-in-law's store. There are plenty of nice girls for you to go with without choosing her for a friend."

"But she is nice, 'Ri," said the younger sister, her eyes flashing bright in her eagerness to defend her friend. "You don't know her or you wouldn't talk that way. She is very bright and has read and studied far more than either of us. The whole family are very bright. I never enjoyed myself more in my life than I did the evening I spent with them last week. She has a brother just home from college who is as full of life as can be, and Marvie is the sweetest girl I know, next to you."

"She may be sweet enough," answered Maria, ignoring the earnest compliment, "but she is not of the same social standing with you, and it is a great deal wiser and pleasanter not to try to upset the world and drag people out of their spheres." This with an air and expression of long experience with the world.

"Well, I think you might wait until you have known them before you judge them; but listen. Let me tell you where they are going. It sounds very interesting. The place is an island right between the bay and the ocean, not very wide either, so you get the view of both. Marvie says it is beautiful there, and the sunsets are so gorgeous. It is a real, old-time beach such as you read about, with no boardwalks and no merry-go-rounds, and everybody does as he pleases, and lots of bathing and boating and fishing and sailing. I think it would be delightful. Marvie says there are cottages down there for seventy-five dollars for the season, just think of that! They are not fine, of course, but are real comfortable, with big rooms, and lots of corners and shelves and places to fix up. I think I should like it immensely."

"Now Rachel Weldon Hammond, what in the world do you mean?" said Maria, sitting upright on the bed and looking at her. "Seventy-five dollars for the season! The very idea of our living in a cottage that costs only seventy-five dollars for the season! You must be crazy. Why the cottage the Johnses lived in last year at Atlantic City was twelve hundred, and even the Pattersons paid a thousand. I think you are nothing but a child, in spite of your seventeen years."

Just then a servant came to announce that a young lady was in the parlor to see Miss Ray, and Rachel with a bright spot on each cheek went down to find her friend Marvie.

It was not until dinner that evening that the subject was renewed. Maria had spent the afternoon in town hunting among the bargain tables and had come home thoroughly tired. There is something in a disappointing day of shopping which particularly exasperates some people's nerves. Every subject that came to Maria's mind seemed to be productive of discomfort. At last something was said about Rachel's morning caller. Then Maria burst out:

"Was that Marvie Parker here again? I think she is rather running things into the ground. Mamma, do you know what kind of a girl is getting an influence over Rachel? I think the friendship ought to be stopped. She isn't in our set at all, and Rachel will feel most uncomfortable in a year or two if she makes a special friend of a girl like that, whom she can't invite nor go with, of course, when she gets old enough to care about things."

"What is the matter with Miss Parker?" questioned Mr. Hammond, turning his sad gray eyes to his elder daughter's face. "It does not seem to be a good reason for objecting to her merely because she is not in your set. If she isn't in, bring her in; that is, if the set is worth her coming. If it isn't, it might be a good thing for Rachel to have a few friends outside it, in case of an emergency. Miss Parker ought to be a good girl. Her father is a fine man, and I used to know her mother years ago when we were children. The girl ought to be well brought up. What is the matter with her, aside from that senseless notion?"

Maria's face grew red. She did not like to have her father against her, neither did she feel fully prepared to face his keen eyes or his searching questions. She was on the point of reminding him that she and Rachel were no longer in a position to say who should or should not belong in their set, and that their own footing there might at any time grow insecure, but she remembered just in time to save herself this disgrace and her father the pain of such a remark. Instead she flew at once to some defense of her own statements.

"She may be a good girl, papa, I presume she is," she replied; "but you will surely acknowledge that she is putting queer notions into Ray's head. Why this morning she actually confided to me that she would enjoy going to some out-of-the-way place, on an almost desert island, where the Parkers are going to seek solitude for the summer, and live in a shanty at seventy-five dollars for the season. Just think of it! I don't know where she thought even the seventy-five dollars was to come from, with the railroad fares and all, but she would really like us all to go. Did you ever hear of such an idea!"

Rachel's fair face had grown rosy red during the conversation. She was an exceedingly sensitive girl, and shrank from being the center of observation, even in her own family, and now as the glance of father, mother, and brother were turned upon her, she could scarcely keep the excited tears from rushing into her eyes. But she tried to smile in answer to her father's encouraging look as he asked for an explanation.

"Why, papa, I didn't really say I wanted to do it," said Rachel, her cheeks flushing redder, "I only said I thought it would be real nice. And of course I'm perfectly happy where I am. But if we were to do it I suppose we'd have to in the same way that the Parkers do. They rent their house here, and they get two hundred and fifty dollars for the season for it from some people who have to stay in town on account of business all summer and have to be at their store at seven o'clock; so they couldn't get in from far away from the city in time. Marvie said her father knew a lot of men who wanted just such homes as ours for the summer, where they could bring their families out of the rows of brick houses. I thought maybe there would be some one who might want our house that way, and it ought to bring more than the Parkers', because it is larger and has more ground and is on a nicer street. But I didn't really mean ever to say anything about it, for 'Ri seemed to think it was all so dreadful that I didn't mention the renting of our house."

Rachel dropped her burning face from the exclamations which she knew would follow.

"Rent our house!" said Maria aghast. "Whatever can you be thinking about? Are you crazy? I guess we have not quite come to that state of disgrace!"

"My dear child!" exclaimed the mother, not so much in horror as astonishment at the new thought. "How could we have people using our carpets and our dishes?" There came a little distressed pucker between her eyes, showing that the idea was not an impossibility to her after all and she was really considering it.

"And what did you propose to do with father and me, Ray?" asked her brother Winthrop, who was a little older than Maria and in business with his father, struggling to bring back the name and fame which the former firm had lost through the treachery of one of its members. "You know we are obliged to be in town at a set hour every day, as well as some other folks!"

Rachel's cheeks flushed anew at the implication that she, the quietest member of the household, had taken the family affairs into consideration and assumed to make the plans, but she answered shyly:

"I hadn't thought it all out, but Mr. Parker and his son go in to town every day. Marvie said there was a train leaving the island early enough to get here before nine, I think, and there are special season tickets for business men, so it doesn't cost much, and the store closes early during the summer anyway, doesn't it? But I didn't mean to plan. I am happy where I am. I wouldn't have said a word, only 'Ri was worrying because we had to stay in town all summer, and I thought maybe mother would enjoy the coolness by the shore."

"She is nothing but an absurd child!" exclaimed her sister. "Papa, surely you are not going to encourage her in such plebeian notions. I'm sure I'd rather die respectably than go away for the summer in such a disgraceful manner." And she sat back in her chair with a sneer.

"My daughter," said Mr. Hammond, looking straight at Maria, "I am ashamed if a child of mine has come to the place where she can say such a thing as that. You do not mean it. And as for this 'notion,' as you are pleased to term it, it is nothing new to me. I have long thought that I could save a good deal and make matters mend in our pecuniary affairs much more quickly if I could rent this house. Indeed, I had an offer last week of four hundred dollars for this place, stable and all, from now till the first of October. The reason I declined the offer was not on account of any such frivolous and unworthy motives as you have expressed, but simply because I knew of no cheaper place where my family could be comfortable while the house was earning the four hundred dollars."

"I should think not!" put in Maria with red, excited face. It meant a great deal to her, this question of fashion, and what her little world of "they" would think and say. It meant all that she now cared for in life, though she would not have believed it if she had been told that this was true of her. But her father went on in his calm tone:

"Now if the Parkers have found a place for seventy-five dollars where they can be comfortable, I should think we might do so as well. The Parkers are respectable people and used to having the necessaries of life, at least, if not all of the luxuries. I should think it might be worth the looking into at least. Don't you think so, mother?"

And the wife, with a troubled look at her eldest daughter's face, and a sigh of longing for the cool air of the ocean, assented that she thought they ought to make inquiries, at least.

Maria, with tears of chagrin in her eyes, suddenly left the table, and Rachel, whose tender heart was sorely distressed at having been the cause of the trouble to her sister, went soon to her own room, where for once she found the connecting door between her room and her sister's closed, and upon softly turning the knob a few minutes later she discovered it was also locked. This was something that had not happened since the two girls were very little and first had rooms to themselves, and Rachel could not keep the tears back. She betook herself to her Bible for comfort and through blinding tears she found it, and resolved to try to make Maria happy that summer no matter what happened, seashore or home, heat or cool breezes, pleasure or disagreeableness. And so she slept.

2

MARIA HAMMOND was a girl of very determined nature. When she liked or wanted a thing she liked or wanted it intensely, and bent all her energies to get it. What she disliked she was equally persistent in opposing; and when it happened, as it often did in her life, that her plans and desires were frustrated, it took a great struggle of will before she could give up and yield to the inevitable. Even then, should the least chance occur, she would try for her own way again. She insisted that it was not her own way, however, which she desired, but merely to have things right about her, and as they ought to be; and that if the way were another's and it seemed right to her, she would be just as eager to have it as though it had been her own. With such sophistry did she excuse herself to herself and to others for her persistency and headstrong, stubborn willfulness, and because of a discontented nature, which was always desiring the unattainable, she was constantly in trouble.

When she went to her room after her stormy speeches at the dinner table the tears of anger, defeat, chagrin, and disappointment swelled into her throat and eyes. Locking her door, she threw herself on her bed in a torrent of weeping. It is true she had attained the years when young ladies are supposed not to weep violently, unless for some great grief of life, and she would not for the world have had any one, even a member of her own family, see her thus; but her nature was so uncontrolled that when it burst out upon her in this way she could but give way to it. Moreover, in her eyes very little things often seemed important, and thus it came about that what to another might simply be an annoyance to her became a great and overwhelming grief. It was, as it were, her very life that was in the balance. For what else was life to her but the good opinion of the world? And so Maria lay upon her bed crying for a long time. It was not merely what had occurred at the dinner table which caused her trouble, nor even the prospect of spending the summer in a most unfashionable retreat, though that seemed to her mind very unlikely, even after what had been said by father and mother, "For surely," thought she, "their reason will see that it would be dreadful, simply dreadful"; but it seemed to her a sort of climax of all the disappointments which had come since her father had lost his money. In consequence, she mourned and cried and pitied herself, and perhaps pitied the rest of the family a little with what heart she had left after her own need was lavishly supplied. By and by she grew more calm, and then there came to her a shadow of her religion to question why it could not help her in this trying time, for she had a religion, this stormy-natured girl, in spite of all her will and her fear of what "they" would say. And with the thought of her religion came the reflection of all she had meant to do to help in the church work during the summer, of the class of delightfully bad little boys she had promised to take in the Sunday-school; of the young people's meeting she had promised to lead; and of the tennis picnic in the park she was planning for those same young people, which was to close in the dusk of evening with a short prayer meeting under the trees, and which she hoped would do much good. Then she told herself it could not be that she was to be removed to an out-of-the-way place where there would be no possible opportunity for anything of the kind when she had planned to do so much. Thus she magnified her own projected goodness until she seemed a very martyr.

Now such a nature as Maria's is not one which long remains under a cloud. She began to persuade herself by and by that things could not possibly be as bad as they seemed about to be, and to silence her own uncomfortable conscience, which was beginning to reproach her keenly for the way in which she had spoken to her father and sister. She resolved with a large sigh of conscious martyrdom to go to her father the next morning and tell him she was resigned to being a hermit if it would conduce to his financial comfort. Having thus resolved, and being comforted by the thought that if she pursued such a course her father would by no means be likely to accept her sacrifice, she went to sleep.

Meantime the father and mother had been holding a consultation. Money matters had been coming to a crisis during the last few weeks. Business was very dull at the store. Mr. Hammond hoped if he could tide affairs over until fall that he might be able to weather the gale. He now felt that a serious talk with his wife was necessary, though she was such a frail little woman that he always spared her all he could because she took every burden at twice its weight, and went about with her face sad and anxious. The result of this talk, however, was that Mr. Hammond took his breakfast a half-hour earlier than usual in order that he might stop in and speak to his friend Mr. Parker on his way to the office. And so it was that Maria did not get an opportunity to speak to her father until evening.

It was just as the dinner bell rang through the house, and Maria, hastening down the stairs that she might speak to her father as he entered the dining room, heard her mother's voice speaking to him as she passed the door of the library. She spoke with an anxious sigh: "Yes, it would be very nice and just the thing. I would do it in a minute if it only were not for the girls' sake. I hate to do it when they are so opposed."

And her father's weary tones answered: "It is Maria that is opposed, not both of them, remember, and things are as they are. Maria may come to worse trouble if we do not do this."

"Yes," said the mother sadly; "but Maria is the oldest, you know, and just at the age when everything of this sort makes so much difference to her. It might hurt her future life, my dear."

"Nonsense!" said her father rather sharply, although he felt the truth of what his wife was saying, keenly enough. "If Maria's future is to be hurt by the fact that her father rented his home to good, respectable people for a few months, and went to a quiet, unfashionable place to stay during that time, I think it had better be hurt. It seems to me that friends who are affected by such things are not worth the having." But he sighed again as he came down the stairs, his face wearing a careworn expression.

Maria's heart beat fast and the tears came into her eyes. She had not realized that she was making her loved father so much trouble. Her impulsive nature at once forgot all about any personal sacrifices, and rushing up to her father, she drew him into the door of the sitting room they were passing, and throwing her arms about his neck, begged him to forgive her for all she had said, and not to mind her in the least in anything he wished to do, that she would try to be as helpful as she could.

And so it came about after all that it was through Maria that the Hammond home was rented to a family who would pay well for four months' use of it, and the Hammonds themselves migrated to the seashore. It must not be supposed that Maria was changed all in a moment. She had many evenings of weeping over the inevitable, but the memory of her father's weary face and her mother's anxious tones was sufficient to keep her from demurring any further to the family plans, and it was only to her sister Rachel and her brother Winthrop that she permitted herself to grumble. Winthrop had long ago said that his sisters were well named: Rachel was like a ray of bright sunlight everywhere, always cheery, never cross, while Maria, or 'Ri, as they all called her, "always took things awry and kept a wry face much of the time."

"I say 'Ri, do let up a little, can't you?" said her brother one day when Maria had finished one of her sarcastic speeches about their summer outing. "It's too late now to give up, so you'd better make the best of it. Where's the Christian fortitude I hear most church-members talk so much about? Can't you summon up a little bit to help you through this vale of tears? I'm sure you've taken every grain of pleasure out of this summer that it might possibly have contained for Rachel and me, so do be satisfied, for you surely can't wish father and mother to suffer."

This somewhat caustic speech from her usually good-natured brother sent Maria to her room weeping. The days had been very hard for her even before this. She had endured, in imagination, the heavy trial of coming home to find her room treasures spoiled by ruthless alien hands.

She had pleaded that certain necessary articles—necessary to the thorough furnishing of the house—be put away under lock and key, but had been made to understand that this could not be. She suffered a great deal while clearing out her bureau drawers and closet and all her little private "cubby-holes," realizing how in a few days these places would be filled with some other girl's belongings, and she felt that when she returned she never could feel the same toward the home-corners again after strangers had called them their own. She had also been obliged to help in packing cushions and cretonne draperies that could be well spared from the home, with curtains, pictures, screens, and a few such things as were considered essential to make the summer cottage, to which they were going, habitable.

This had also gone much against the grain. To think of having to spend one's summer amid things that were merely fit to put in a bedroom! It was humiliating. If they were to have a cottage, why couldn't they at least have it look comfortable, cheery, and furnished with taste? Maria was the artist of the family, and so had been called upon to select the draperies they should take, but when her mother found that Maria's choice would be to carry silk-chenille portiéres and satin embroidered sofa pillows and a plush hand-painted screen, she was obliged to do the selecting herself, or quietly put it into Rachel's hands, for Rachel had been down to the little beach cottage. Her friend, Marvie Parker, had invited her for over a Sunday, and her father thought this would be a good opportunity for some member of the family to judge of the fitness of the cottage for their abode. It is true Rachel had hitherto been considered the child of the family, but her judgment was usually good, and her father and mother felt her to be a much more unprejudiced judge than her sister would have been, for Rachel would tell not only the best but also the worst, which Maria would not have seen at all, had she desired to go as much as her sister did. So Rachel had accepted the invitation, much to the chagrin of Maria, who told her that if she did this she would open the way for the Parkers to be entirely too intimate with them for the summer, a thing she, for one, did not intend to countenance. But Rachel, having the consent of father and mother, went and enjoyed her two days immensely, coming home with glowing accounts of all the pleasures in store for them, as well as an accurate description of the cottages for rent. They were rough, she admitted; not finished inside except for a high facing of heavy manilla paper. The ceilings were high, reaching indeed to the peak of the roof, and thus giving the rooms a lofty appearance. She felt sure that Maria could make of the parlor or sitting room, or whatever they chose to call it, a perfect summer bower, and the rooms, though few, were all large, indeed quite spacious for a place so cheap. It was all on one floor, with a wide piazza for hammocks and a view of sea and bay. But when Maria—a slight interest awakened for the moment—began to select silk and velour portiéres, Rachel laughed and then looked troubled. She saw endless difficulties in making her sister understand.

"They will look incongruous, 'Ri," she said. "You ought to have gone in my place and then you would know just what to take, for you always know how to make things fit; but really I should think some of that pretty printed burlap we bought to make cozy-corner cushions for our bedrooms would be just the thing."

"If I had gone," said Maria severely, "I should probably have brought back such an account as would have made the family understand it was no fit place for us to live in. However, you seem to be having everything your own way this time and I suppose we will take what curtains you say. I wish with all my heart we were not compelled to spend the summer entirely in a burlap atmosphere. I didn't suppose things would be quite so rough."

And so had Maria gone on, fighting every step of the way, contesting every inch of the plans that were made, until all who asked her to help were glad to see her go away and leave them to finish alone.

Poor Maria! Don't be too hard upon her. Her heart was very heavy during these days. She discovered a day or two before they flitted to the shore that the place selected was but a mile from a fashionable summer resort of which she had often heard as being at the very height of refined and aristocratic summer haunts. She also discovered to her dismay that the De Veres, of the West End of the city, who were very wealthy and literary and cultured, had taken a cottage there. Now Maria had met the Misses De Vere and their brother some three or four times at various social functions, and she felt that their acquaintance would be worth cultivating. But she knew she should shrink into herself with shame if they discovered her whereabouts and came to see the kind of place in which she was summering. She had really taken quite a liking to those young people, and it was hard for her to think of them as looking down upon her. Why she did not feel that people who would look down upon her because of the house in which she lived were not worth her caring for, is hardly explainable, unless it was because she knew that she should look down upon any one similarly placed, and so judged them by herself. She had listened to a bit of talk between George Parker, Marvie's brother, and her sister Rachel, wherein he described some of the cottages at Lone Point and told how the Spray View people laughed at them and called them

"Lone Point Barracks," and all sorts of funny names. Maria's spirit writhed within her as she pictured to herself Roland De Vere driving by their cottage some day and laughing with other strangers about their home. The blood crimsoned her whole face, and she resolved that by no word of hers should the De Veres find out where she was to spend her summer, even though she missed many a pleasant invitation thereby.

One more experience Maria had to complete her wretchedness before they left for Lone Point. She had been with her sister on some last errands prior to their departure from civilization for a time, and just before they took the car for home, stopped at the public library to secure a store of books for summer reading. It was while they were waiting at the desk for their cards to be marked, that Roland De Vere, with his arms full of books, stepped up to them and touched his hat. Maria introduced her sister, of course, and the three walked out together.

"By the way, where do you spend your summer this year?" asked the young man as they paused at the corner to wait for a car.

Maria's cheeks grew rosy. She never could keep her face from telling tales which she would rather were untold, but she caught at her presence of mind and answered:

"Papa is talking of the seashore somewhere," rather vaguely, and then looked eagerly to see if the car were not coming.

But Rachel, not noticing her sister's vague response and not understanding in the least its intention, turned in her eager, girlish way and said:

"Why, yes, we're going quite near to where you will be, if I have heard aright. Are you not going to Spray View? Your sister told a friend of ours. I hoped I might meet your sisters this summer, I have heard so much about them, and Maria is quite in love with both of them. Our place is only a mile from there, Lone Point; do you know it?"

Maria's face was crimson now. She motioned violently to the car which was still half a block away, and telling her sister the car was ready, never even turned her eyes to see what Mr. De Vere was thinking. She had so often rehearsed in her mind how under such circumstances his face would grow astonished, and he would utter a very expressive "Oh!" and turn away, that her imaginings became a reality to her, of which the true scene which followed was not able to efface the impression. So with a vexation and embarrassment that amounted almost to an agony she stepped out into the street with the other waiting passengers, thinking to prevent all further conversation.

This, however, Mr. De Vere did not notice. He was entirely taken up with talking to Rachel. His face lighted with pleasure and he said: "Know it? I should think I did. It is a delightful little place. I had a good friend there last year. I hope we shall see each other often. You go to-morrow, you say? How pleasant! We go the first of next week, and sooner if mother can get ready. Good-afternoon, Miss Rachel; Miss Hammond, good-afternoon. I am glad there is a prospect of our seeing one another often this summer."

He touched his hat; they stepped on the car and were soon speeding away. The car was crowded and the two girls had difficulty at first in finding seats, but as they neared the suburbs the passengers grew fewer, and Maria found opportunity to seat herself beside Rachel, who in blissful unconsciousness of her sister's state of mind had been letting her eyes dance and her heart rejoice in the innocent pleasures in store in the possibilities of the summer. Maria had been bottled up for nearly twenty minutes and the vials of her wrath had not cooled during the process. She always showed her feelings to their full extent in her face, so Rachel had a sudden and unpleasant awakening from her girlish dreams.

"Rachel Hammond!" said Maria, trying to lower her excited voice so none of their fellow-passengers could hear, "I should think you might learn to keep your mouth shut occasionally. I never introduce you to one of my friends but I regret it bitterly at once. It seems as if you might be old enough now to know how to behave."

Poor Rachel! Her sensitive face flushed and she roused herself at once to remember what terrible breach of etiquette she had been guilty of, but could think of nothing. She dreaded one of Maria's tirades beyond almost any experience that came into her life, and was constantly studying to avoid them, and perhaps as a consequence she was the one who had to receive the larger number of them.

"What did I do, 'Ri?" she faltered, and if Maria had not been too angry she would have been touched by the pitiful quiver of the pretty, sensitive lips, and the grieved, troubled look of Rachel's large eyes.

"What did you do, indeed! You little tattle-tale! You need not tell me you don't know, for you did it just to annoy me, you know you did, or else from some high and mighty notion that you would rebuke me for not telling everything I knew. You will have to learn that it isn't necessary to tell all you know in this world in order to avoid telling a falsehood. Why was it necessary for you to explain fully to that elegant Mr. De Vere in what a humiliating state we were to spend our summer? I should think things were being made uncomfortable enough for me already without that being added. I shall simply die of shame if they come over to that horrid little place and find us rusticating in a cowshed. I think you have fully overstepped the mark this time. You have chosen your friends and I have a right to mine. I shall ask papa to let you know hereafter that you are not to interfere with me and my friends."

Maria had grown angrier as she talked. She had kindled her imagination during the silent ride with fancied scenes of meeting between herself and Fannie De Vere at Spray View, until she scarcely could contain herself. Rachel's fair face grew almost white at her sister's words. She tried to explain, but Maria was in no state to be reasonable.

"But, Maria dear," she pleaded, "I didn't dream I was saying anything unpleasant to you."

"Then you must be very blind," snapped Maria. "You certainly must have seen from the way I answered him that I would have bitten out my tongue sooner than have him know."

"But I didn't, 'Ri, indeed; indeed I didn't dream of such a thing! I was only delighted for your sake, for I thought you would have some company, and he seemed so pleased about it."

"Oh, yes, he was pleased!" sneered Maria. "He's too polite to let anything else appear, but he's probably laughing in his sleeve this minute. You needn't worry. We shall not see either him or his lovely sisters at all this summer. As soon as he said he was acquainted with Lone Point I knew what to expect. I heard a man from Spray View talk about Lone Point the other day, and they don't consider the place fit for Spray Viewers to wipe their feet on."

Poor Rachel quivered under her sister's upbraidings, until when they reached home she could bear it no more and went to her room to do an unusual thing for her, have it out with her tears. And then she went to her Heavenly Father with her little bruised heart and found comfort.

3

MEANTIME Roland De Vere was walking down Walnut Street reflectively.

"Strange," he said to himself. "What could have been her reason? Was she ashamed of going to a quiet, unfashionable resort? She was angry with her sister for telling me. I could see that. Her face struck me as being a very intellectual one when I first saw her, and a pretty one too, but I didn't notice that discontented curl to her lips. However, I have never seen her in the daytime before. Gaslight makes a wonderful difference. It is not so good as I thought at first. But that other face is like a flower. The younger sister must be worth cultivating. I did enjoy her frank eagerness. Fannie would like her. I mean to take her over to call as soon as possible after we get to the shore."

How Maria's eyes would have opened in surprise could she have known his true feeling. It is a pity that some inventor could not give us a little instrument for divining occasionally what others really think of us. It would sometimes save a world of worry. But how careful we should then have to be of our own thoughts of others. Perhaps some one greater than Edison will arise one day who will search out the hidden law that governs thoughts and let us look into one another's hearts, and then how much better—or how much worse, alas—we shall be! For surely the kingdom of heaven will be near at hand when men's judgments of one another are kind and loving.

The Hammonds' journey to Lone Point was taken on a Saturday, for then they might have the escort of father and brother and their assistance during the day in unpacking and arranging their belongings for the summer. Maria looked sadly about on familiar objects as she walked toward the nearest station in the early morning. She felt as if she were going out of the world, and that when she returned, if she ever survived the humiliations of the summer, all would be different to her, and she could never be the same girl again.

Rachel, however, had gone ahead with Winthrop. He had seen how her bright spirits were clouded by her sister's gloomy countenance and had made a pretext of some errand to get her with himself. He had in some way found out from Rachel all that her sister had said to her on the street-car the night before, and he was indignant with Maria for being so hard upon the sensitive younger sister. He resolved upon the first opportunity to give her a plain talking-to, and save Rachel from further annoyance of that sort. He managed the seats in the cars so that Rachel should be with him, his father and mother together, and Maria installed with a fresh magazine and a pile of hand-baggage in a third seat. This suited Maria exactly, and as Rachel was in front of all she did not have to think about Maria and her troubles during the journey. Rachel looked a little pale that morning from her unusual vigil of the night before, and Winthrop set himself to make her forget it. He succeeded wonderfully, for soon her face lighted up and her silvery laugh could be heard occasionally, which made Maria look up and frown, to think that any member of the family could make merry on such a journey as this. She felt as if she were attending her own funeral, and the procession would never cease. However the magazine was interesting and she soon forgot herself for a little.

Through pleasant villages of gardens, and then through wastes of sand and scrub they sped, and the time seemed to Rachel short until they wound their way out at last upon the lovely bay and ran for several miles with water on either side and the sea breeze blowing fresh in their faces through the open windows of the car. Rachel and her mother drew in long, life-giving breaths, and even Maria aroused to a sense of relief from the heat and her heart seemed not to be quite so heavy as before, though she did not stop to explain to herself why it was so. Finally they came in sight of Spray View in the distance, its cottages and hotels seeming quite imposing beyond the blue waters of the bay and with the deep green sea as a background; and Maria, when she heard the name of the place, was looking enviously ahead and wishing that that tallest dark green cottage with the trumpet vine in full bloom over its lordly piazza were to be theirs, instead of—when suddenly the train came to a halt and the brakeman called out "Lone Point," and they were all hustled suddenly out upon a bare platform in the sand, and the train sped on toward the towers of fair Spray View a mile ahead.

"What did we get out for?" questioned Maria querulously. "We haven't got there yet. They said that was Spray View ahead there. Isn't the place (scornfully) the other side of it? This isn't any place at all apparently," and she looked about with curling lip on the waste of sand with the cluster of small buildings nearer the beach.

But no one was paying any attention to her, and she was obliged to pick up her umbrella and hand-satchel and follow the rest.

"Here we are, and there it is!" shouted Rachel gleefully, in her excitement clapping her hands and going back to her childhood ways of several years before. "There! that's ours, that green one over there with the white trimmings. And there comes Marvie to meet us, and her brother George. Oh, I'm so glad we're here!" and she flew to meet her friend.

It was all fully as humiliating as Maria expected. To have the "Parker boy," as she designated him—though he was fully as old as young Mr. De Vere—come and meet them, and offer assistance and insist on taking her hand-bag from her; then to be under obligations to the Parkers, whose cottage was next door and who had kindly prepared dinner for the Hammonds and had it served on the table by the time they had their hats off! It was simply unheard-of and dreadful, and Maria had no appetite to choke down the delicate fish and fresh vegetables prepared so nicely. She wished her mother had declined any assistance whatever and would rather have starved until their own servant could prepare some kind of a meal. However, the others of the family did not share her feeling and did ample justice to the dinner.

The afternoon found plenty for even troubled Maria to do and left her no time for thought. The one poor servant whom they had brought down with them and upon whom they depended to make everything move smoothly and bear all the burdens had, it would seem, ideas also about watering places. She went out and took a brief survey of the place, and above all of the terrible ocean, heretofore unseen by her. One swift gaze over the turbulent blue waves, and with a wild look in her eyes she turned and fled. Returning to the cottage where the family had improved her absence to fit up an impromptu partition in the kitchen and so make her a bedroom, she took a hurried invoice of that, exclaimed in dismay over the roughness of things, said "My land!" several times, went out on the porch and took in the narrow stretch of land between ocean and bay, and going in told Mrs. Hammond she must go right back to town by the next train, she "couldn't stand it nohow," that she was "sure that there water would meet and flood the place." Nor could any amount of persuasion on the part of the united and dismayed family change her firm decision. No, indeed, she would not stay over-night! She would never expect to see the morning light. She did not wish to let the sun go down and darkness settle upon her with that awful ocean roaring and surging back and forth so near her. What mattered it to her that the Hammonds had paid her fare down from the city, had indeed bought her a return ticket? What cared she for losing her place? Fear had taken hold upon her, and her frenzied soul cared but to flee; and flee she did on the two-o'clock train.

Then the family sat down in dismay to consider what they should do next. Rachel was cheery. She had been to the beach and it had filled her with exhilaration. She was ready for anything, and to call it fun, even if it meant washing dishes and peeling potatoes. They all looked fearfully at Maria. She had made her gloom felt so severely all day that each one dreaded the effect of this last blow upon her. Then up rose Maria with a martyr-like resignation. She had not been to the beach, she did not wish to go. One spot on this deserted island was just the same to her as another. As she was condemned to stay here, what mattered it where she stayed or how she was employed during that time? If one must have a disagreeable time, why not have it just as disagreeable as possible, and so get greater credit for one's endurance? (This, however, not audibly.) She would do the work. She was perfectly capable of doing as much as that good-for-nothing girl had been. If she wasn't, she would learn. She could at least save a few more cents from the girl's wages to add to the family treasury and so increase the vast sum which they were to make during this summer of humiliation. Their downfall was complete; why not accept it and go to the bottom gracefully? They had to live in a hovel; of course they must do their own work; it was no more than she had expected.

Now Maria did not say all this; instead her sentences were very short, her words were few, but by tone and manner more than by words, she contrived to convey her meaning to the family and made them feel it to the heart's core. The father's face took on a gray look, and the mother's grew old and careworn. Rachel's brightness faded. It seemed as though Maria would manage to dampen the spirits of them all.

But Winthrop was determined that this first day should not be spoiled. Without an instant's hesitation he took Maria's proposal up, not in its spirit, but in its words.

"Why certainly, why shouldn't we? Mother, we can all help. I can't do much all day, but I fancy I can make it up evenings. I'll see that the wood is cut and the coal handy, and make the fire in the morning, and get the ice in the refrigerator, and go errands. There'll be plenty of time for errands before breakfast and train time if I get up a little earlier. And Sundays I'll agree to wash all the dishes three times a day to make up for what I can't do on week days. I can wash dishes beautifully. It will seem like old times when I was a little chap and 'Ri was a baby and mother had no girl, and I helped wipe dishes. Mother, don't you remember? I used to be as proud of the shining white dishes as if I had been a girl, prouder I fancy. Then I can go errands over to Spray View evenings after supper. We don't need to live high, anyway, and there can't be much housework to do in such a small house."

"Of course we can do the work," echoed Rachel eagerly. "I'm sure both Maria and I have had cooking lessons; and besides, here is mother, who knows how to do everything in the world, and can direct us in anything we have forgotten or never learned. I think it will be delightful fun. I'm all ready for it. Come on and let us wash those dinner dishes right away, Winthrop, and then there'll be more room in which to get to rights." And so saying, she ran humming out of the room followed by her brother, and the two had a gay time clattering the dishes.

Maria, with scornful dignity befitting the occasion, followed them, and was soon engaged in stirring up some mysterious concoction for supper and starting some bread for the morrow, as it was found there was no bakery nearer than the neighboring town, and all were too busy to go there for anything.

It was perhaps a half-hour later when all were deep in work; the girls with their sleeves rolled up and hastily improvised kitchen costumes snatched from the open boxes and trunks, Mr. and Mrs. Hammond unpacking and sorting out the most immediate necessities, and Winthrop in his shirt sleeves with a large checked apron tied about his waist and a wiping towel over his arm engaged in mopping dry a thick white-ware soup plate—he was whistling a merry tune and calling out comical sentences to his sisters between times—when a light rig drew up in front of the door and some one got out and came up the steps, but no one in the house heard.

"I say, 'Ri!" called out the diligent brother in a cheery tone, "don't look quite so cross or that bread'll be too sour to eat. It'll be 'rye' bread. See?"

Just then came a distinct knock on the open door, and the irrepressible brother disappeared through the calico portiére which belonged to the house and separated the dining room from the parlor, to answer the knock, supposing the intruder to be a butcher or a baker or a candlestick maker, and caring little as to his appearance. Was he not on a lark and on a desert island where he knew not a soul? Besides, his was a spirit that did not feel degraded by a gingham apron and a dish towel.

He had hardly, however, bargained for the immaculate apparition that stood before the door trying to keep a smile from playing politely round his well-shaped, merry lips.

"I beg your pardon; I hope I'm not intruding," said the young man on the porch, with a graceful touch of his hat, "but is not this Mr. Hammond's—"

"Shanty? Certainly," finished Winthrop with a low bow and mock solemnity. "Walk right in. Things aren't quite ship-shape, yet; but I think we can find you a chair."

Winthrop Hammond was not to be embarrassed by any strange gentleman in fashionable driving costume. He dusted off a chair with a flourish, using the dish towel as a duster. Rachel, with a merry face, appeared in the doorway, one cheek well dabbed with flour and her arms dripping with soapsuds. Her dark hair, a trifle rough and loose about her face, had curled itself into little rings, and her cheeks were flushed with excitement and work. She heard Winthrop's gay talk, and never doubted he was making fun for their benefit with some grocer boy or fish man. The young man at the door with a laugh entered into the occasion and stepped willingly into the room, then catching sight of Rachel in the doorway, he came forward with easy grace.

"Good-afternoon, Miss Rachel," he said. "Welcome to the shore. Have you just arrived? You didn't expect to find me here ahead of you, did you? But you see mother sent me on ahead to attend to some arrangements and make everything ready for them on Monday. Up to your eyes in work, aren't you? Is this your brother? I thought so. Glad to meet you, Mr. Hammond. Having a jolly time, aren't you? I envy you. I'd like nothing better than to pitch in and help. Haven't you something for me to do? Come, now, I've got a horse here and can run all the errands you want. Do put me to work. I've got my own garden all weeded and not a thing to do till the folks come Monday. I'm lonesome, and should enjoy it. Is your sister here?"

"She's in the kitchen making bread," laughed Rachel, entering into the spirit of their guest's speech. "Maria!" she called, and started laughing to find her sister; but Maria had listened to the voice at the door in dismay and had fled.

4

INTO the midst of the turmoil of work and settling came the calm of the Sabbath. There was a little church near by, and at the appointed hour they could see the neighbors in simple dress wending their way thereto. Rachel, having completed her morning work and helped all she could in the preparation of dinner, announced her intention of going to church, but the others were too weary, and even Mrs. Hammond thought it as well to wait until the next week to begin their acquaintance with the place. However, Winthrop took up his hat and followed his sister down the steps, when she came out a few minutes later arrayed in dark serge skirt, clean shirt waist, and sailor hat.

"For pity's sake! Rachel Hammond! You're surely not going to church in a strange place in that rig?" called the horrified Maria as she caught sight of her sister going out the door. "You haven't any gloves, either. I do think you have taken leave of your senses. You might have a little sense of decency left, at least."

But Rachel, happily, was out of hearing and went serenely on her way, drinking in the salt air and the Sabbath quiet as she walked.

Maria, looking after her, wondered how her sister could be so happy, half envied her her sweet, happy nature, and then went by herself to shed some tears of discontent. They had not been able to make her listen to any account of the visitor of the day before. She had kept in hiding during his short stay and disappeared as suddenly again when he returned with some packages which Rachel had laughingly sent him after. Maria did not approve of taking Mr. De Vere into their family at this stage of events and letting him see all the ins and outs of the rude cottage and the makeshifts of the family life. She wanted to receive her guests in the right way or not at all, and so she had left herself severely out of yesterday's affair. Her soul writhed within her at the thought of the laughing account Mr. De Vere would give his stately mother and elegant sisters of his visit to Lone Point. She resolved to keep away from their sight as much as possible, and wondered why it had been considered necessary to add this humiliation to her list of troubles for the summer. After her little cry she went to the kitchen, where her martyr spirit bore her up grimly, while she made the rest of the family uncomfortable with the elaborate dishes she prepared, and of which she tasted but little herself. She did not intend to make them all unhappy, but she was not averse to their knowing how extremely uncomfortable they had succeeded in making her and how well she was bearing herself under the circumstances. She continued this conduct during the week, even carrying it so far as refusing to go to the beach, when she could have gone as well as not. She declared she had no wish to meet the people of the place; they were a common lot, anyway, she could tell that from their appearance on Sabbath, and as for the sea, she never cared much for it. There were none of the usual enjoyments of seaside life here to make this place endurable, and she would rather stay at home and let others who could enjoy things go to the beach. And so she stayed in the cottage and cooked, and arranged the cheap draperies into graceful fashioning, not taking pleasure and pride in her pretty work as she might have done at another time, but urged to it from fierce necessity. If there were danger that the De Veres might call at any time she would at least make things as presentable as possible that they might not see an utterly barren place, though she firmly resolved to always absent herself and be unfindable when they did call. Thus she wrought, and the room grew truly beautiful in spite of the rebellious spirit of its artist. She asked little help from any one, but her brother and sister were both watching to be of assistance and supplied the needful help without being asked. In one corner of the parlor there grew up a cosy-corner or divan of vast dimensions, composed on one side of the woven-wire cot on which Winthrop slept, and on the other of the packing-box in which the curtains and tin dishes had traveled. This was upholstered deftly in dark blue burlap bearing a wreath and crest design, and the whole was united by a deep valance around the sides. In the corner were many cushions, some only filled with straw or excelsior from the packing, others being the pillows used for Winthrop's bed at night and stuffed during the day into calico and chintz covers of gay design. Two or three were genuine eiderdown with embroidered denim covers, and the effect was not only lovely but luxurious. Maria manipulated pretty screens out of cheap torn paper ones, and one corner was curtained off in a most novel way with a heavy bamboo pole Winthrop found on the beach, and curtains of green and brown figured burlap hanging in folds from it. Behind this no one would have suspected Winthrop's washstand and a few hooks on which he hung some of his clothes. It seemed terribly low to Maria that some one had to sleep in the parlor, but as there was no help for it, there being but two other sleeping rooms in the house, she disguised the fact as prettily as possible. *Crêpe* paper lampshades and a quaint little bookcase of odd shape and original workmanship, which knew its origin in a shoe box and an old peach crate, also gave touches to the room, which when done was pronounced to be a perfect gem of beauty, comfort, and coziness by the entire family.

"Isn't this beautiful! What a transformation!" exclaimed Roland De Vere, as he entered the room the next week to announce that his family were coming over to call as soon as the Hammond girls were willing to receive them.

"I declare I never saw such a change. Who is the fairy that has waved her wand so effectually?" he asked, and looked at the sweet-faced Rachel, who immediately disclaimed any part in the work and gave it all to Maria. Meanwhile Maria continued invisible to all callers. Mr. De Vere did not notice this fact so much, however, as he would have done had he been less well pleased with the company of her brother and sister. They began planning numerous excursions and moonlight sails, in which she was always included, but in the preparation of which she did not figure. She felt very much cut at heart at the way things were going and blamed it all on the others, not seeing that it was her own doing. She persisted more than ever in her purpose of isolating herself. She would not even go to the beach, though the others entreated her and invented various ways of trying to get her there. Her headstrong, stubborn will had set itself up against all their pleadings and she would not be coaxed by anything or any one, so at last they gave it up. Maria arranged her hair in the most unbecoming way possible, took on hard, drawn-down lines about her mouth, significant of her martyrdom, and went about in an old work apron most of the time. Rachel grieved over it as much as she had time for amid the merry round of delight that was open to her. She found a great deal of joy in wandering over the beautiful beach in search of shells with her friend Marvie Parker and Marvie's brother George, who proved to be fully as bright and interesting a companion as she had prophesied, though he was a busy student and had little time, even that summer vacation, for a frolic. She enjoyed her brother Winthrop's merry talk in the evenings, and rejoiced in going to the seven-o'clock city train to meet him and their father every evening. She looked upon the delight of a visit from Maria's friend, as she called Roland De Vere, as some great treat which did not belong to her, but by special privilege she was permitted to share with the others. The summer seemed to be unfolding before her with a beautiful promise.

She sat one evening just at sunset in her room. She could look out on the beautiful bay in the distance and see the softly rippling waters calming down for the glassy effect of sunset. The white sails here and there were speeding homeward. In a few minutes the evening train would slip silently along by the water and she would run down to meet her father and brother. Supper was nearly ready. The bisque of clams was perfect. That had been her work and she was proud of it. Maria was busy with some one of her special concoctions and seemed to desire the kitchen to herself, and Rachel had been glad to slip away for this little silent minute to rest and think and pray. Since they had been doing their own work she seemed to find so little uninterrupted time for her Bible and thought that she was glad to find it anywhere. The mornings were now so full of work, and as soon as the work was done Marvie Parker was sure to run in and claim Rachel for some scheme. To be sure it was not yet a week they had been by the sea, and yet it seemed to Rachel that things had settled down into a routine. She thought sadly of it, for Maria, her dear sister, seemed left out of everything. She would not have anything to do with the Parkers, and she seemed fully as loth to have to do with her own friends, the De Veres.

Rachel wondered what it meant and if there was anything she could do, if perhaps she was to blame in some way for having suggested this summer scheme. But no, when she thought of her mother's face taking on a glow of health from the life-giving breezes, and of her father, whose face had dropped its load of anxious care, and who seemed to be really enjoying life once more, she could not feel that she had done wrong; for surely it had turned out to be the best for all of them. No, it was clearly not her fault and she must not mourn over it as such. The next question came: What could she do for Maria? for she was ever one who was looking out to be her brother's keeper. She took up her Bible, from habit perhaps, for her own heart could not answer the questions that multiplied upon her. She felt it fully laid upon her to do something for her sister; but what could it be? Coaxing would not do, sacrifice would avail nothing, and neither would pity; she had tried them all. They merely seemed to irritate the loved one. The Bible opened of itself as it often did, to the sweet old call, "Come unto me, all ye that labor and are heavy laden, and I will give you rest. Take my yoke upon you, and learn of me; for I am meek and lowly in heart: and ye shall find rest unto your souls." Rachel had marked those verses when she was but a little girl with her new pen and some bright red ink. She had turned to them many, many times since, at first because they were familiar words and seemed like old friends on account of the red lines about them, and afterward because they had comforted her and had grown dear for their own sakes.

It was not strange that she opened to them now, and as she read them mechanically, though reverently, she did not linger there, for at first thought their message seemed more for her sister than herself, and she sighed as she half turned the leaf and wished that Maria could find rest, so that her life would be all peace and a joy that she could reflect everywhere. Then suddenly a thought stopped her hand as it slowly turned the leaf. Wait! Was not that message for her after all? She was burdened with the gloom of her sister. Might she not find rest from that as well as from some burden of her own? The dear Lord surely would not have her carry that burden. He would show her if she "came to him" what it was, if aught, she could do, to help lift the cloud that was over Maria, and she could come to Jesus and find rest and strength, so that even the burden of her sister's attitude would not disturb her calm, for it would be his calm. She turned the leaves slowly to another verse also marked and which had been her help many a time before. "Ye have not chosen me, but I have chosen you, and ordained you, that ye should go and bring forth fruit, and that your fruit should remain, that whatsoever ye shall ask of the Father in my name he may give it you." Then it was not her business to look after the fruit. She was to do his work because he had chosen her. She would do whatever he put into her hands to do, and meanwhile she had forgotten that whatsoever she would ask of the Father he would do it for her, and she might trust him to do it in his own good way and time. She would trust him with this dear sister. And so she knelt and poured out all her heart, full of worry, that had been so anxiously filling from day to day with the many little petty irritations that had arisen in kitchen and parlor and all over the house, and which she had tried to bear patiently but which had worn on her sweet spirit till now and then sharp words had escaped her. She told her Heavenly Father all and then asked for her dear sister's happiness as the greatest joy that could come. After that she smoothed her hair and rushed out into the kitchen with her heart full of love for Maria and trust for the answer to her prayer, and putting her arms impetuously around her warm and weary sister's neck gave her a great big hug and whispered softly: "'Ri, dear, forgive me. I've been awfully cross and teased you a great deal to do what you don't want to, and I have not helped you half enough. Will you forgive me? I'm sorry."

Now Maria was frying fish and was just in the act of turning over a large beautiful piece so that its perfections should remain unmarred. Besides, she was very warm and the stove had been acting abominably all the afternoon, and the brownness of the fish was only due to repeated shakings and coaxings on Maria's part with kindlings and bits of paper. Maria's hair was coming down, or was so nearly so that any movement on her part was precarious. Also she had burned her wrist and the pain was quite severe, aggravated as it was by the heat of the stove. Therefore Rachel's eager hug was scarcely pleasant just then, and Rachel's willingness to confess her fault, when she herself, the greater offender, was very unwilling to do so, irritated Maria more than words can tell. Perhaps she was not so much to blame, poor child, for she certainly was having a very uncomfortable time, largely her own fault though it was. She had just received a letter from one of her dear friends describing in detail the delights she was enjoying in a popular hotel in a lovely mountain resort. It was no wonder perhaps that her tone was ungracious.

"For pity's sake, do get out of my way, Rachel!" she said crossly. "Don't you see what you're doing? You'll make me break that lovely piece of fish. I do wish you would ever be considerate. I'd much rather you'd show your sorrow by your actions than your words. Words are cheap."

With that Maria jerked the fish over and pushed the tea kettle and two or three pans around on the stove with such a nervous clatter that there was no chance for any more words even if Rachel had chosen to speak them, and Rachel, with the tears brimming over in her eyes, went her way to the train, full of sorrow that she had made another mistake. "I never seem to know what to do or say to please her," she said to herself. I'm sure if she had spoken crossly to me and had asked me to forgive her I should have been so happy and forgotten it all, but it only seemed to make her feel crosser with me." Then Rachel remembered that it was not her work to look after results, and that she had taken her burden to her Heavenly Father and given it to him to carry. She must not pick it up again and bear it away with her; it was hers no longer. So she cast it all aside and hurried toward the station with a lighter heart.

5

MARIA stood on the piazza later that evening. The sunset glow was fading over the bay. The supper dishes were all washed and put away. There was nothing more to be done in the kitchen that night. She was at liberty to watch the pearl-colored sail that floated lazily on the pink and gray waters. Winthrop and Rachel had gone over to the pavilion directly after supper with Marvie Parker and her brother. They had not thought it worth while to ask Maria to join them to-night. Indeed, Rachel had hinted to her brother that perhaps it would be better to say nothing of their purpose to Maria, as everything of the kind seemed only to make her feel badly, and so for the first time since they had been at the seaside, they had gone off without coaxing her to go with them. Although Maria had declined these invitations quite curtly every time, she nevertheless felt cut by the omission to-night. Tears filled her eyes and blurred the pearl-colored sail as she thought how easily they could get along without her. Heretofore she had been the life of the family, the center of every excursion, the witty talker, the graceful leader in all. Now Rachel, her younger sister, hardly grown up as yet, seemed to have taken her place. She was not then so indispensable as she had thought. Even her father and mother had strolled away, arm in arm, like a pair of lovers, pointing out a bright star overhead or calling one another's attention to a sail in the distance. Maria felt very lonely.

Things had proved a great deal worse even than she had feared. She had supposed that after the family saw how uncomfortable things were going to be they would set about to right them in some way. They would perhaps go over to Spray View and take some sort of a respectable cottage where they could live in some decent style, as she phrased it to herself; there would be some enjoyment in that, and perhaps they would try to get another servant, though she herself would be willing to help in the kitchen and get along with a very poor one, if they might so save enough to be able to live in what seemed a respectable manner and, what was more important to her, would seem so to her friends. Then she would gladly welcome the De Veres and enjoy whatever they could offer her in the way of pleasure. Now, however, all was different. The family seemed entirely indifferent to their surroundings. They were actually happy. As she thought over it she realized that she could not remember to have ever seen her father and mother so thoroughly enjoying themselves before. She wondered that they did not see how unhappy she was. Oh, if she could but go away to that mountain resort where her friend Nellie Mayhew was having such a delightful time! To be sure she couldn't hope to share in everything because she could not buy the clothes in which to go to many of the entertainments and social affairs participated in by her friend, but she told herself that if she could but get there, be in that great hotel, one of its guests, she would trust herself but that with a very few dollars she could construct a wardrobe that would make her look well enough to vie with the others. But what was there here? She cast her eye about. Nothing but views and air! She curled her lip. And a father and mother and sister and brother who were too absorbed in their own pleasures to think of her or know that she was at home moping alone after a long day of hard work in the kitchen.

Now at that very minute father and mother, as they pointed out the stars and the sails, were discussing whether or not they could possibly manage to scrape together money enough to send Maria to the mountains in the style she wished to go. The mother, strange to say, was the one who objected this time.

"No, Richard," said she, "I cannot help feeling, even if we felt it right to afford it, that it would not be best. Maria is young yet, and while I think she is perfectly to be trusted to behave herself and take care of herself in every way, I am not sure but it is much the best thing for her to have the discipline of this summer. Already she has shown traits of character which I did not dream that she possessed. It has grieved me to the heart to see it. She has behaved in an utterly selfish and inconsiderate manner. You do not see it all day long as I do. She works, oh, works like a slave, harder than she ever worked before. I shall put a stop to that overwork pretty soon, for it is utterly unnecessary, a great part of it; but she is unlovely to me and to her sister, and as disagreeable as she knows how to be. I have been meditating how to go about it to have a talk with her, but it seemed best to wait a little while and study her present mood. Sometimes I am afraid she never has understood what it means to be a true Christian, she is so utterly rebellious at her lot."

And then in tender tones the father tried to excuse her

and pity her, and so they talked and walked much farther and longer than they had expected to do, and the evening wore on while Maria sat alone, until from very weariness of herself and her own thoughts she was forced to go to bed.

It was the very next day that Maria was at last driven to the beach. It was Saturday. Winthrop had remained at the shore as his father felt he would not be needed that day at the store. The dinner being out of the way, and Maria's dress being soiled beyond hope of further use until it was washed, she retired to her room to make a severe but crisp toilet. If she could have found anything ugly to put on she would have done so, but fortunately for her nearly everything she possessed was tasteful and pretty, and the ugly things brought along for rainy weather or hard usage she had entirely used up for that week, therefore she was obliged to betake herself to a dainty sheer dimity, clear blue and white. The belt and collar of this dress were light blue ribbons with fluttering bows. Maria tried to fit on a linen collar and go without a belt, but the effect was so incongruous that she finally gave in to her own innate sense of beauty and put on the blue ribbons. Then her hair did not seem to harmonize with the costume, and by this time her sense of fitness had been sufficiently aroused to make her loosen her hair and coil it in the old way which was so becoming. Altogether she was quite like the familiar Maria when she was ready to leave the room. As she passed the window to pick up a novel that she had been reading, her eye caught sight of a double surrey, drawn by handsome horses, just turning the corner by their cottage. There were three ladies and a young man in the carriage and the elder lady was leveling a lorgnette at the unpretentious little dwelling. That lorgnette made up Maria's mind. That carriage contained the De Veres—

mother, daughters, and son. They had come then, at the son's instance, to patronize the Hammonds. Maria, for one, did not intend to be investigated through a lorgnette. Her soul boiled at thought of it. Quick as a flash she caught up her book and a white parasol belonging to Rachel lying on the bed and flew out of the back door, straight across the sand lot to the next street and in line with the house so that she could not be seen from the carriage, which was now standing in front, and then turned and went swiftly to the most unfrequented portion of the broad beach she could find; there she established herself behind her parasol and a fortification of sand, and gave her mind to the reading of her book, assured that no unwelcome visitor could find her here.

Meanwhile Rachel, as she opened the door all smiles and played the gracious lady to the elegant Mrs. De Vere, remembered with satisfaction, not for her own sake but for Maria's, that she had caught a glimpse of Maria's blue dimity on the bed as she had passed the door, and that by this time she must be arrayed in it, for of course Maria would be obliged to come out of her shell now. But lo, when the anxious mother, who felt that Maria would need an extra word from her in order to make her put aside her new and foolish notions, came in search of her elder daughter, she could find her nowhere, and Rachel, being sent in search, though she looked in all Maria's former places of retreat, could find no trace of her. Much puzzled, Rachel returned to enjoy the call and forget all about her sister's disappearance.

Perhaps the DeVeres thought it strange that Maria was absent from the house, especially as they knew from their brother and son that she had always been absent when he had called; but if they did so think they were far too well-bred to let any one know it. They were not nearly so overpowering in grandeur of manner as Maria had anticipated. Mrs. Hammond was quite charmed with the gracious and cordial friendliness of Mrs. De Vere, and a mutual liking seemed at once to draw the two elder ladies together. Meantime the young people planned innumerable pleasures in company, and the time flew by and the call was prolonged far beyond the usual length prescribed by fashion. In a most unceremonious manner, and one that would have shocked poor Maria beyond believing had she been present, the three De Veres followed Rachel through the sand and gayly fell upon George and Marvie Parker with a demand that they join their moonlight sail planned for the coming week. How it had come about Rachel could hardly understand, but they had found out she had friends in the Parkers and had delicately suggested the invitation and then proposed that they go at once and give it. Rachel wondered as they went whether Maria would blame her for it, and if she would make trouble about the Parkers going with them, and finally resolved to say nothing about it to her sister, letting things come about as they would.

Meanwhile Maria, clothed daintily, as was her habit to be, and having attained her purpose of getting away from her visitors unseen and unsuspected, felt much more at peace with the world than she had done for many a day. She settled herself without the usual hard cloud upon her brow to really enjoy her book. So much are clothes of value that the subtle consciousness of being well-dressed has often power to lift one for the time at least above a seeming fret of circumstance or sordidness of surroundings.

Now had Rachel Hammond been consulted as to the answering of her earnest prayers for her sister, she would have said that the most unpromising thing that could happen for Maria was to have her run away from the De

Veres and spend the entire afternoon by herself in a lonely part of the beach, reading a highly-wrought novel wherein the heroine suffered impossible things and was crowned with untold rewards for her pains. Rachel would have said that a pleasant afternoon in the company of pleasant people, planning a delightful excursion, forgetting things that might have been, and learning to be interested in things that are and are to be, would have been the best thing for her sister. But God knew better. He was leading this child of his through a narrow, thorny path, it is true, but through the only straight road that would take her home. She sat there and read, and as she had not visited the beach before and knew little of the peculiarities of wind and tide, she did as most newcomers do, settled herself by the edge of the surf, as near as seemed safe and pleasant, that she might watch the water. Then after a good look she forthwith forgot to watch the water in the tide of the fortunes of her heroine. The ocean's tide at that time was going out, but almost at its turn. It receded a little and a little, and Maria read on, and by and by it did not recede, and then it gained a little and a little, until it crept nearer and nearer to the seat upon the sand and the straying blue ribbon that fluttered out from the white silk parasol. Now a larger wave came and almost stretched its lip of foam to kiss the foam of white lace on the blue dimity ruffles; then it went back again for a while to gather force, and now another came and did just touch the dainty ruffle and dampen it, but still the wearer read on oblivious to recession or approach. She had turned herself sidewise to keep the ocean glare from her page and did not notice. Moreover, the heroine was just on the point of being rescued from a desert island on which she had been cast with a noble hero who loved her, by an ignoble lover who had come in search of her. The situation was a thrilling one and Maria had no eyes for aught but the story. Neither did she see a young man who was sauntering leisurely down the beach toward her from the direction of the lighthouse, a mile or two away.

The Rev. Howard Fairfield, in the most unclerical dress he could find in his very unclerical wardrobe, had been visiting the Point Rock lighthouse, and joking with its keeper, entering with zest into all the stories the old man told of his wild life as a young sailor, himself posing as a young man who understood and enjoyed all such escapades. Now he was walking slowly along the beach and, wholly unconscious of any inconsistency or incongruity, was engaged in weaving the wonders which he had just seen and heard of God's providence and man's skill into a fine illustration that should well set off the conclusion of the address, both eloquent and learned, which he was preparing for the first sermon he should preach after his vacation was ended. He was a very young man for the important charge he occupied, and he had chosen this simple, quiet summer resort as a suitable place for him to spend his vacation, with the idea that the absolute quiet if not loneliness of it would conduce to the rest and study which he meant to alternate so judiciously, and thus send him back to his city church thoroughly fortified in health and with a store of material for sermons for the winter's campaign.

He was not an unspiritual minister, neither was he ashamed of his calling; but in college and seminary he had acquired some "advanced" notions concerning the doffing of clerical clothes and the "clerical manner" which, while they might be good in a degree, had been carried by him to their utmost extremity. He delighted, on going to a place, to keep the people from finding out that he was a minister. Indeed, he carried this so far that he would sometimes allow himself to be taken for almost anything else rather than let others know his true character or profession. He had a fancy that he could do a great deal more good in this way, by entering into other people's lives and sympathies and not letting them feel that the good he did was because it was his business to do so. Perhaps there was truth in this, the great drawback being that he spent so much time in entering into people's sympathies and lives that he frequently forgot or found it awkward to do the good that might have resulted from the influence he had gained thereby. Sometimes too, others felt that he allowed the line between right and wrong to be glossed over a trifle in this "entering-in" business. He called it "being all things to all men." However that may be, he was a student, an eloquent preacher, somewhat conceited because of the extraordinary praise he had received during his short pastorate, and very much opinionated, but nevertheless very much in earnest. He considered himself very spiritual indeed, and in his heart longed to be all that his Lord would have him be. In person he was handsome, with a scholarly air, graceful in manner, a little distant but exceedingly attractive to most people, especially when he chose to be so.

Rachel Hammond, had she known him, would have considered him the most unlikely person to help her sister Maria that could be found, and yet he was coming toward her on the beach and the waves were creeping toward her on the sand, and the Lord was ordering it all. For the winds and the waves obey his will, even in so seemingly slight an affair as this.

The young man had advanced quite near to Maria and without particularly noticing her, except to realize that his favorite combination of light blue and white was lying over there on the sand making a pretty picture against the background of sky and sea. As he drew nearer he saw it was a young woman with a shapely hand that held a book, and he wondered, because he was a student of human nature, what sort of a young woman she was, reading thus alone so close beside the sea, and what was the book which so absorbed her that she did not mark the approach of the hungry waves. He thought he must warn her if she did not look up before the next wave, and lingered a little to see if she stirred. Then, before he could think further, there came one of those unexpectedly large waves which take people, and almost themselves it seems, by surprise, and rush and tumble in mad glee far beyond any predecessor. It not only touched and soaked the crisp ruffles of the dimity, but it merrily dashed into the young lady's lap, wetting her feet and book and sending her flying back from the spot in alarm. And then it calmly seized the white silk parasol which was a treasured present from a rich uncle to Rachel, and boasted a solid gold handle, and hurled it out in its retreating arms, a toy upon the billows. Maria, finding herself on solid ground and seeing her sister's precious parasol tossed on the water, made another dash to catch it on the crest of the next wave, but the water was again too quick for her and it floated out, this time a little farther, where the breakers tossed the delicate thing so rudely that Maria despaired for its frail structure. At this juncture the young man standing by took two strides into the saucy waters and brought the wet and dripping thing to Maria with as much dignity as he could command considering the wet and flapping condition of his white duck trousers.

It was certainly an embarrassing situation for both young people, but the Reverend Howard Fairfield rather enjoyed carrying off trying situations in a graceful manner, and he certainly did himself justice in this instance, to the admiration of the young woman concerned.

"Oh, not at all, let me carry it home for you," he said, as she reached her hand for the sunshade. "Your cottage is near by, is it not? Nothing is very far away from anything else in this place, is it?" Here he stopped to pick up her book, actuated more perhaps by a curiosity to know its name than anything else. "No, no, let me carry it. You will have enough to do to walk in this sand with your wet gown. I am going this way, you know, and it's no trouble whatever."

And so Maria, much against her will, walked the length of the beach to her home with a stranger, a young man, her dress wet and bedraggled, her borrowed parasol and book carried by him, and his own costume rather the worse for water. It was altogether too dramatic for Maria's liking to appear at home in this condition after the lofty way in which she had been acting. She knew her brother would never cease teasing her. She was trying to plan some way of retreat, or getting rid of the stranger who was chatting pleasant nothings to which she need not reply except by monosyllables, when lifting her eyes she saw her sister, accompanied by the Misses De Vere, their brother, and Miss Parker, coming toward them. There was no escape. They were on the point of meeting. It was horrible! Maria caught her breath, and then she heard her sister's exclamation and knew there was no hope but to turn and face the situation.

6

IT turned out that Howard Fairfield was an old college friend of Roland De Vere, and the two young men met with great delight and gayety. Introductions followed all around, and Maria's chagrin was covered by this ceremony, until she had time to recover herself and smile an apologetic retreat, leaving the minister to make explanations. The merry little party, however, followed her. Rachel, who had hurried on with her sister, was kind and eager to help, solicitous lest she might catch cold, and plied her with questions as to how it happened. The others came more slowly to the cottage and chatted a little till Rachel and Maria, who had hastily replaced the dimity skirt by one of black serge, again appeared. Then the De Veres said they really must be going home, and drove away with promises for the next day and many merry words about the moonlight excursion. The minister lingered a little after the departure of the carriage, politely saying he hoped no harm had been done Miss Hammond by her unexpected sea bath; thanked her for his part in the affair which had resulted in so pleasant a meeting with his old friends; and bowed himself away to the hotel, leaving a good impression behind him.

As he walked he reflected:

"Two very pretty girls. I had not bargained for friends this summer. Perhaps it may interfere with my plans for hard study; but, after all, why shouldn't I take a little recreation? I can't enjoy ladies' society at home, because if I look at one young woman more than another, I feel as though all the gossips of both sexes were proclaiming marriage banns from the housetops for us; but I don't believe it is good for a man to be forever with men alone. One forgets how to treat one's sister after a while. It was a pleasant interruption to the monotony of the place to meet De Vere. I always liked him in college. Well, things are turning out better than I had expected. I don't know but that I shall stay the month out, after all. At any rate, I won't give up my room yet until I have time to decide."

Then he went in to prepare for supper.

The afternoon's experience had done this for Maria: she was drawn out of her shell at last and by necessity pledged to go on the moonlight excursion. She reluctantly gave up her *rôle* of martyr little by little, and by Sabbath evening was sufficiently herself to go to church. It really would be more bearable than this continual staying in the house, which was beginning to wear on her patience. Besides, her brief glimpse of young, merry company the day before had made her restless for more.

There was no settled minister at Lone Point. The church itself had been built by the donations of visitors, who had spent their energies one summer in raising the money and making as pretty a little house of worship as could be desired for the chance sojourner by the sea. Some of those who lived for a large part of the year in the place took it upon themselves to keep the services going all the summer. Occasionally there were ministers visiting over Sunday who preached, to the great delight of the little audiences; but during the rest of the time, earnest workers from city churches, who were not taking a vacation from their religion as well as from their other work, took turns in either reading a sermon or making a short talk to the little company gathered there, and the songs of praise swelled forth from worshiping hearts as truly thankful as if they had been feeding on the bread of life dealt out by regularly ordained hands. These services were divided among several men, who were always willing to do with their might what their hands found to do. Rev. Howard Fairfield, in spite of his experiences of the day before in finding old friends, had succeeded in keeping his incognito so thoroughly that no one dreamed of asking him to preach, for which he was in his heart truly thankful, since he really needed the rest. He had perhaps, though, a little of the natural feeling of a man who was fresh from the ecclesiastical atmosphere of the seminary, a slight doubt as to the genuineness of Sabbath services conducted by a man who not only had not been through a seminary course, but who was not even college bred. It amounted almost to a feeling of sacrilege, as though they were "playing church" as children do, to have the laymen handle sacred phrases and forms. Young theologues are apt to feel at first more anxious for the orthodoxy of the worship than for its spirituality, though if you asked them, they might tell you it could not be truly spiritual unless it was thoroughly orthodox. Mr. Fairfield sat through the morning address, given by a white-haired brother who had served his church for full fifty years, and was amply competent, by reason of his wide Christian experience, to have ministered even to the needs of a theological student. His face wore a look of gentle toleration, which scarcely masked the critical impatience he was feeling all the while. He told himself that an hour spent at home with his Bible would have been more profitable. But by reason of the command of his Lord, which he reverenced, not to "forget the assembling of yourselves together," he went again in the evening.

Now in the evening the service was led by a younger man who had spent some time in a training school for Christian workers, and who, though thoroughly versed in the Bible, was yet not so thoroughly trained in the English language. He did not attempt a sermon. The service was largely composed of song. His own part in it was two or three gentle, earnest talks interspersed with illustrations, carrying home to the heart the true meaning of as many Bible verses, whose practical teachings were linked together into a single, fully developed theme. There was singing between each of these talks. They seemed to scarcely belong together, and yet when the hour was passed, the thoughtful soul went forth with something to carry into daily life to help in making ready for heaven.

The service was short. No one need complain that he grew weary. They issued forth into the bright moonlight from the cheery little chapel, some with kindly greetings, some with earnest words or merry ones upon their lips. The minister, quite as a matter of course, walked along beside the two young ladies he had met the day before, and they chatted pleasantly as they walked. He stopped a moment on their piazza to watch the moonlight on the bay, and they began talking, for want of any other topic of common interest, about the place, the people, the church, and the day itself with its services.

"I supposed, of course, we should hear you preach this evening, Mr. Fairfield," said Maria pleasantly. She was regaining her good-humor and quite liked the young man. She had never had a ministerial friend. It was something new and interesting.

"Oh, no indeed," said the minister laughingly. "I took good care no one should know that I was anything other than the most ordinary of idle young men on a pleasure trip. I don't want to preach. It isn't fair when one is off on a vacation. It isn't fair to my people, either, you know. They expect me to rest and not use up my strength on some other church when they are sending me away to recruit it. You don't know how a minister feels when he gets away from his work. I have a clerical friend who said last year, when he started off on his vacation, 'No more preaching, no more praying, no more reading of the Bible, for six whole weeks,' with a sigh of relief. I wouldn't go quite so far as that myself," laughingly; "but at the same time it is a relief to get away from all reminders of work when one goes off to rest."

Maria laughed gayly at the story. She thought the young minister very clever. There was a prospect of something enlivening, after all, in this desolate place. But Rachel glanced up quickly.

"Did he really say that?" she said with a troubled look in her eyes; "a minister of Jesus Christ?"

There was something embarrassing in the anxious expression of those clear eyes that made Mr. Fairfield, for the first time since he had told that story, reflect that it was not altogether the feeling for a minister of Jesus Christ to have, even if the expressing of the thought had been merely in fun. He was a trifle vexed with himself for having told the story and began excusing his friend, and finally mildly condemning him. But there was an uncomfortable consciousness of something, the minister did not exactly know what, which he was certain he would have to face out with his own conscience after he got by himself.

"Well," said Maria, hastening to cover what she considered to be an impoliteness on her sister's part, "I suppose it's all very well for the poor ministers who have to work all the time, but I must say I don't enjoy hearing a man who don't know how to conduct a service. Did you ever see such a hash as that meeting to-night? Upon my word, I began to wonder if they wouldn't ask us all to get up and recite some little verses or stories next." She ended in a bubble of laughter over her own fun. She was in the habit of saying bright, daring things and of having them laughed at. The young minister was no exception. He laughed. He was tired of loneliness and her laugh rested him.

"Well," he said, "that man did very well for a layman. I fancy he got some of his thoughts out of some one of Moody's books, or something like that, but really that first bit of a talk he gave us on what we live for was not so bad. I never heard that story about the old sea captain before. It did sound odd when he kept repeating 'When I'm at the North Pole I live sperm whale, when I'm at the South Pole I live sperm whale.' It was well expressed too, and a good illustration. I suppose some of those old fishermen would say for them to live was fishing. I know a man in the city whose entire life is for money, just like the man he was speaking of to-night. It really was a good thought to bring before those young people."

"But," said Maria laughing again, "did you hear him say 'opportoonity'?" She brought out the broad "oo" in exact imitation of the tone in which it had been uttered so earnestly a few minutes before. But her laugh was interrupted by Rachel.

"Mr. Fairfield," said she, lifting those clear, thoughtful eyes of hers with the moonlight shining into her pure face, "do you suppose that it is possible for any one—

that is, for young people—well, say for—me, to be able to say with perfect truth, 'For me to live is Christ'?"

The minister felt once more that strange embarrassment, mingled this time with a desire to answer the question aright and a feeling of inability to do so. His pastorate had been a short one, his experience was small, and there had not come to him many times in this earnest way an inquirer who seemed to be searching for the light. It is true, in a theological sense, the question was easy enough to answer; but he knew by the look on Rachel's face that she meant more than an ordinary question asked out of curiosity. She really wanted to know in order that she might if possible use the knowledge.

He searched his mind and his catechism for a suitable reply, but none would come. At last with his usual tone of positiveness, which carried weight with so many who questioned him, he replied: "Why, yes, surely; why not? If you are a Christian, you certainly can say that."

"No," said Rachel, shaking her head in a thoughtful, troubled way, "I can't. I have been thinking about it ever since Mr. Brown told that story about the sperm whale. My life isn't 'sperm whale,' but I am afraid I would have to say if I answered truthfully, for me to live is having my own way, having a good time, and having everything go just as I planned it. I'm afraid I put that above Christ. I certainly must, or I would be happy with whatever Christ gives me, if for me to live were Christ."

Maria listening was surprised. She had thought uncomfortably that evening during the meeting that for herself to live was to have her own way, but she would never have laid that charge at her gentle sister Rachel's door. Rachel, who was always willing to give up when others insisted on having their own way! But Maria did not like to have the conversation drift into so solemn a theme, and she hailed the coming of her brother upon the porch with relief.

"Mr. Fairfield," she interrupted just here, "you have not met my brother yet."

During the introduction that followed, Rachel slipped away. She felt that she wanted to be quiet and think. Perhaps sometime she could find that minister alone for a few minutes and he would have some help for her; ministers all knew how to help, and he was young and she would not be afraid to ask him, unless— unless he should be like that other dreadful minister, who had said that awful thing about not wanting to read the Bible or pray for six whole weeks. She shuddered as she thought of it again, and her literal soul was greatly disturbed that a minister should be so like the rest of the world. But just now she wanted her Bible to answer her, and she went softly in and lighting her little shaded lamp went to her Rock for help.

Mr. Fairfield did not remain long that evening. It was Sunday, and he did not as a rule make calls on the Sabbath, unless it were an errand of necessity or mercy. He looked about for Rachel as he left, and was both troubled and relieved to find her gone—troubled, because he felt in some indistinct way that he had not done his duty; relieved, because "what business had duty to follow him around on his vacation?"

After all, the little girl's question had been true enough. How many people were there in the world who really could say that? Could he himself? Was it Christ for him to live, or was it fine sermons, a good name, a large church roll? Did he think most when he preached of whether he was speaking to the hearts of men and leading them to see Jesus, or was he looking after the praise of men? Was he not sometimes looking about to see if there were a committee from that big

Chicago church sitting in some dim corner of the room and wondering what they thought of that rounded sentence? Could it be possible that for him to live was getting to be whether he would in a few years receive a call to a better church with a larger salary and a greater name?

He wandered down by the sea in the deep moonlight where he could be alone with his conscience and his God. As he walked to his retired musing place he said to himself: "How strange it is that that man, who is evidently not a highly educated man, can with his few words so touch a heart that it will ask itself such questions as that girl asked me to-night! Did any one ever go home from one of my sermons and ask himself such searching questions as that, I wonder? There it is again. I am looking out to see what other people think of me and my words. No, not all that either. Perhaps I'm looking out now to see what God thinks of me. I must find that out to-night."

7

DOES Satan also walk sometimes beside the sea? Perhaps he saw the trend of this young man's thoughts, and hoped to turn them aside. Perhaps he feared too much the searching questions that would surely come to this thoughtful heart, which if once awakened to itself and its possibilities would be a dangerous enemy to the powers of darkness and of this world. Or it may be that what happened next was just another link in God's wonderful chain of influence that was to draw this disciple nearer to himself.

"Ho! I say! Stop a minute!" shouted a voice, that at last made itself heard above the roar of the waves, sufficiently at least to attract the attention of the preoccupied man.

The voice proved to belong to a fellow-boarder at the hotel. "Is that you, Mr. Fairfield?" called the man, hurrying along the sand almost out of breath with his efforts; "I wasn't sure in this uncertain moonlight. There's a telegram down at the hotel for you and they've been hunting all over creation for you. They went to church but found it closed. The boy came over from

Spray View with it and he is almost frantic to get back and seems to consider it a part of his duty not to surrender the message till the right man turns up, though a number of us offered to pay the requisite fifty cents, the ridiculous price they charge to bring a message over to this forsaken spot."

The minister thanked his informant, turned hurriedly and retraced his steps along the beach to the hotel, wondering meanwhile if aught had befallen his mother or sister far away on a foreign trip, or if some member of his church was lying very ill, or perhaps dead. Telegrams may mean so much or so little, they always set one's heart beating faster till he has them safely read.

It proved to be only a notice of a special business meeting of importance to himself and his church, to which he was called home early the next day to accommodate a member of the church committee who was himself called suddenly away and wished some matters attended to before he left. The minister stood on the moonlit piazza a moment after he read it, and crushed the yellow paper irritably between his fingers. It did not suit him to rush back to the city in the heat just now. He had expected that meeting to be deferred until the first week in September. It annoyed him too, to have such a message as this sent on Sabbath evening. He did not stop to analyze why, except to think that it might have waited, or have been sent the night before. A feeling came over him of how utterly it lacked harmony with the day's quiet resting and his evening's high thoughts. So much was he disturbed in mind that he did not again go back to his musings by the sea. His line of thought as well as his walk was broken off. The hour was late. He must take a very early train in the morning. He must prepare his mind for the business in town which awaited him, and there were a few preparations he must make for his hurried journey. So he went reluctantly up to his room, wondering vaguely whether he would ever get back to the time and place to have that talk out with himself alone by the ocean and resolving that he would take the first opportunity for it. He remembered the moonlight sail planned for that week, the new friends he had found and the old ones he had discovered to be near by, and resolved to leave his baggage here in this secluded place beside the sea and return on the evening train or by the next day if possible, rather than pack up and move on to some new place as he had half resolved to do three days before. Somehow there seemed to be a new charm to the place now that he had found friends, even though what he had wished to get away from was all social obligations. He was interested in the family who had such a pleasant little cottage around by the bay. He believed he would like to talk further with that bright, intellectual older sister, and perhaps even hear more of the flower-faced younger sister's searching, innocent questions. He felt that they were not bad training for him in many ways.

Mr. Fairfield was scarcely seated in the uptown car the next morning on his arrival in the city when he became aware that two bright eyes were watching an opportunity for their owner to claim his attention, and looking up, he beheld across the car a young lady who was one of his parishioners. She greeted him with gushing frankness. There was always a good-natured openness about Miss Lou Marlow. Everybody called her Miss Lou, except those who went a little further and called her "Lou." She was hail-fellow-well-met with every one, as intimate on the first day of acquaintance as she bade fair to be in ten years from that time, a large, pretty girl, with good spirits to overflowing, and a laugh and joke for every one. The minister always felt as if he had come in contact with a splash of brilliant sunlight unrelieved by any softening shadows when he met her, and yet she affected no one unpleasantly; there was too much true good-nature and native humor about her. Still, one always looked with her to have their faults or virtues hauled out and laughed over with jolly, ruthless hand, and for this reason the minister rather dreaded a *tête-à-tête* with Miss Lou. He particularly shrank from one in a street-car, as Miss Lou's voice, like her taste in dress, was not altogether subdued, but she had moved to one side and made room for him beside her on the seat, and her movement was unmistakable. Besides, she plainly showed that she had something good to tell and would scarcely be deterred from it by so small a circumstance as having to talk across a car aisle. The minister changed his seat, but as he did so put on his most dignified air in order to check as much as possible a too exuberant manner, should such appear.

"Oh, Mr. Fairfield, when did you come back? Why I'm so astonished," began Miss Lou volubly. "Really this is quite a coincidence. I had the strangest dream about you last night, and it was so real and vivid, and now to think I should meet you when I thought you were far away! It really looks as though there must have been something meant by it," and she giggled uncontrollably.

Mr. Fairfield looked nervously about the car to see if there were others of his acquaintance present, and his informant went on between her gurgles of laughter.

"Oh, it was too funny!"

"Yes?" said the minister helplessly. He hoped it was nothing connected with selecting a wife for him or anything of that sort, but he greatly feared from the young lady's tone it might be some silly dream linking him with some one of his congregation. That it would be something embarrassing he felt sure. He waited helplessly, hoping he would be given the grace to keep from looking too red and angry if it were, and prepared a hearty unfelt laugh to bring forth at need to cover her telling.

"Why, I dreamed I was riding in a car down this very street, and it was summer just as it is now, and you were away, at least we all supposed you were away, on your vacation, and suddenly you came into the car and spoke to me, and you told me that you had been called home to attend a funeral." Here Miss Lou uttered another spasmodic giggle. "And I asked you who it was and you said it was that little Lillie Hartley,—don't you know,— the carpenter's little girl who sings in the children's Sunday-school exercises so sweetly. You told me when the funeral was to take place and asked me to come and sing, and I said I would. Well, I went to the house at the hour, and we sat there, and sat there, and you didn't come, and it got awful late and still you hadn't come, and they had to go way out to Mt. Laurel to bury, so they got awfully worried, and finally they sent after you, and the girl where you board said you were in your study,—that is, she hadn't seen you come out,—and they went up to the study and found the door locked on the inside. The girl said that was the way you always had it when you were studying hard, and they called and knocked and got no answer, so at last they burst in the door and found you sitting there dead by your desk with your book of funeral prayers, or whatever you call it, beside you, with the page open to the children's burial service, and everything looking as if you were just ready to go out, and you dead! There was an awful time just beginning, but I woke up and didn't see the end. But wasn't it too funny that you should come in the car just now? Oh! here's my street; I must get off. I hope you haven't come home to any funeral. Good-bye; wasn't it funny?" and the loud-voiced young woman swung herself off the car, having completed her last two or three sentences as she moved hastily toward the door, and ended with a loud giggle in which the minister felt somewhat called upon to join, at least with a sickly smile. Then he sat back with a scowl of annoyance on his face. Of all disagreeable things to happen, this seemed among the most disagreeable just now. Not that he cared about the dream, of course not. He was neither superstitious nor nervous, but it grated on his fine sensibilities to have the solemn and ridiculous mixed in this way. He could scarcely brush it aside and forget his unpleasant entrance into the city. He bought a morning paper and tried to bury his mind in that, but he felt irritated even when he reached the house he called home, and went to his rooms for any letters or papers that might have gathered during his two weeks' absence, which had not been forwarded.

It was almost time for him to go out again to meet the Board of trustees, when the house servant tapped at his door.

"Please, Mr. Fairfield," she said, "there's a man downstairs as has been here yesterday to see you, and when he found you wasn't here he come back again this morning to get your address, and I told him you had come back unexpected, and he's most awful anxious to see you."

"You don't know who it is, Jane? He didn't send up his card?" said the minister, anxiously consulting his watch, "I have an engagement in five minutes. I can't spare much time."

"No, sir," said Jane deprecatingly, "I don't; but he's a plain-lookin' body, and if you're busy I'll just tell him to come back again when you can see him."

"Oh, no, I'll go down," he said, gathering up his hat

and some papers he wished to carry with him to the meeting.

It struck a chill to the minister's heart when he reached the hall to see plain, honest Mr. Hartley standing there, heavy-eyed, his whole figure drooping with unmistakable sorrow.

"Mr. Fairfield," he said, the tears beginning to start to his eyes, "I'm so glad you're here. I made certain you'd come when you heard; but I didn't have the face to trouble you so far; but the wife she did want you and say she couldn't have Lillie buried without her minister she loved so much, and it's to be to-morrow afternoon. And could you get somebody to sing? The wife, she wanted 'Safe in the Arms of Jesus,' same as Lillie sung herself last Children's Day in the church."

There was something very strange about it all. The minister thought of it after the man had gone, tarrying until he had to hasten not to be late to his meeting.* The broken-hearted father had had so much to say about his little girl and how she loved her minister and how ready she had been to go to heaven! He laughed a mirthless laugh as he walked down the street in the hot sunshine and told himself that if he were a superstitious man this would be a good chance for him to run away. He held his head high and rather gloried in the fact that he was not superstitious, but in spite of it all he could not get away from Miss Lou's dream and the strange coincidence of the death of the child. He wiped the perspiration from his brow and longed for the cooling sea breeze he had left behind, half wishing he had told the father he could not stay and suggested a brother minister for the

---

* Lest criticism of the unreality of this incident should be called forth, it may be said that the dream and its accompanying coincidences were taken, exactly as told, from the writer's own experience.

funeral. Then his heart accused him sorely as he remembered how the father's face had lighted up when he saw him coming down the stairs. He knew in his heart he never could have done such a thing, and was glad with his better nature that he was here and able to be at least of so much comfort to the stricken parents.

It was strange too, after the day's business was over and he had time to think about the funeral and remember the father's request for a singer, that the only singer to be found in the city who could possibly be at leisure at the hour of the funeral was Miss Lou Marlow. He knew she would come, and that her voice was rich and sweet, though not so highly cultivated as some others. He knew that her generous nature would be willing to do anything in her power for the sorrowful family, and that she often went to funerals to sing, and people liked her singing then because she sang with so much sympathy in her voice. There were good things about Miss Lou, and her pastor knew it. Nevertheless, he searched far and thoroughly before he made up his mind that there was no one else to ask. He told himself it was not in the least for his own sake he did this, but merely because he shrank from what she might say in her blunt way, and the giggles with which she would intersperse it, whatever it was. He sent a message by Jane at last with the request of the father and mother, leaving himself out entirely. He did not care to have Miss Lou see any more likeness to her dream than was necessary.

Then he shut himself into his study, and as he turned the key, he remembered Miss Lou's words vividly, how they had come and knocked and called with no answer, and how they had burst in the door and found him dead. Nevertheless, he locked the door as usual and sat down in the study chair, as was his custom, beside his desk and tried to think. A strong feeling of destiny laid hold upon his mind. He felt as if he were living out something that had been laid down for him to do. He felt as if he could not help it, but must go on living it out to the end, even to dying. He could not shake it off. He had heard of people dying with less cause than this, just dying because they thought the time had come. He didn't feel afraid that he should, but in spite of him, he began to wonder what he would do, what he would like to do before he died, and to realize if it all should prove to be true, what a short time he had in which to prepare! There were papers to be put in shape, if he knew he was going. There were messages to leave; there was his mother and sister and his church. How could he leave his church? His work was not completed. He had not carried out his plans; he had not won the souls he hoped, intended. There were those young men who sat in the back seat by the door and whispered sometimes and never listened. Something ought to have been done for them. He had in times past thought seriously of applying for a policeman. Now it seemed as if he might have won them some other way. Was it forever too late? There was—why, there were all his people, as they started up one by one! He might have brought comfort to one and a word of warning to another; and what had his preaching been, now that he faced the thought of its being over forever? True he had spent hours of labor and study upon his sermons; but while the sentences were finished and perfect as to grammar and rhetoric, and sometimes even eloquent, would that stand before God? And then he looked upon himself. Was his soul ready to meet his Master? Had he not been living selfishly, serving the Master as second and himself as first, living a self-life, gratifying his desire for the intellectual, filling his soul with ambitions for a high calling on earth rather than one in heaven? Then the souls he had been set to keep!

What of them? While he had supplied them with the flowers of his oratory, or sought to, had they starved for lack of a little of the plain bread of life? He was searching his own heart and accusing himself now as he never had done before. He seemed to realize all that was about him, to know that the time was near for the funeral, that he must prepare, and yet he could not turn his thoughts to anything else. Once he reached out his hand for the book of forms and funeral services, and opened it, finding, as if by necessity, the little child's funeral service, but he could not read the words. He could only think that he must set his own heart right. If some one had stepped to the door just then and asked him the questions, "Are you afraid you are going to die in a few minutes? Are you nervous about this dream and the strange coincidence?" he would have answered almost wonderingly: "No, certainly not. I am not afraid to die. I know that these strange coincidences cannot hasten or delay the day of my death one second. I know that all is just as it was with me before I heard of these things. But in some way I have suddenly realized what it would be to leave this world and my work—my unfinished work—with these few moments' notice. I know that it is not impossible that I may die at any moment. If not now, it may come, *will* come, at some equally unexpected moment, and I feel that I am not ready—not so ready as I *would* be."

That was the undercurrent of his reasoning as he sat in the study chair, his face buried in his hands, and thought. And now he heard footsteps below, and it reminded him again that the time of the funeral was near, perhaps was almost come. In a few minutes, if he did not hasten, some one would actually come to his door to see why he had not come, or to say the carriage had been waiting and the people were wondering where he was.

Down upon his knees he dropped and spent those last few minutes in prayer, such prayer as he had never known before. Out of the far depths of his soul rose a mighty cry for forgiveness for his past, a great longing for the Saviour to come into his heart and cast out the self in him. Yet, as he knelt, the room was still as death. Not one audible syllable did he utter. It was perhaps such preparation as he had never made before for any of his public duties of the ministry. And when a few minutes later Jane did tap at the door to say the carriage had come, he rose from his knees, his face shining with a holy light of something deeper than he understood, and found that he had forgotten the curious dream and had not watched to see if he should die at all, but had been getting ready to live. He took the little book of services and went to the funeral, feeling utterly unprepared, and yet, strangely enough, not worried about it. He knew that preparation was worth all he had felt it to be, but that there were times also when God took that out of his messengers' hands and made them look at him for a while, and then supplied the words. And the words were supplied now. Verse after verse of comfort from God's holy word, with now and then a comment of tender explanation, were all he essayed; but surely the Lord himself guided his selections, made as he rode along in the carriage, for the broken hearts were comforted and the sorely wounded spirits bound up, and many other hearts not so sore wounded, but there from sympathy, were touched, and made to feel how near and sure and grave a thing is death, and the life to come.

As the clear, rich voice of Miss Lou broke the stillness of the room that followed the minister's prayer, in the tender old refrain of "Safe in the Arms of Jesus," the minister, listening, remembered the dream, and bowed his head in thankfulness that he was yet alive with a hope before him of better living and better work, Christ living in him, the hope of glory, and no longer the hope of the glory of his own intellectual powers.

8

IT was night, and along the coast the wind raged wildly. The ocean fairly thundered its waves against the stolid black sands. The sky was of black velvet, slashed here and there with vivid flashes of lightning. Above the roar of the waves and the voice of the wind came the distant roll of the thunder as it muttered its approach.

In the cottages the dwellers nestled closer in their beds at thought of the comfort about them which seemed all the more delicious as they slept, indistinctly aware of a storm without. Mrs. Hammond gave a sigh as she turned over on her pillow, a sigh of relief that now there would be rain water in the cistern again and they would not be obliged to scrimp and save water on account of having to carry it so far, from the hotel well. It was a little thing to give comfort, perhaps, but she felt that lack of water had been one thing which had made Maria's life so hard the last few days, and the mother was troubled on Maria's account. Now it seemed as if things might be a little easier, and Maria was getting in with pleasant young friends, and perhaps their summer would be a happy one after all. It was such a comfort that this pleasant little house had been procurable, so cheap that they need not feel they were extravagant in taking this vacation. Then she slept soundly again, aware that the storm was almost ready to break, and glad of the refreshing sound thereof.

The great raindrops came at last and pattered rapidly down on the high roof, sounding almost like tumblers full, they were so large, and soon the rain fairly poured down. Rachel was awakened by the cold wet touch of a great drop falling plump upon her cheek. It startled her at first and she could not make out what it was, but before she was fully awake it was followed by another, and they fell at regular intervals. Rachel remembered having read somewhere about criminals who were sentenced to be executed by a peculiar method, the falling of a drop of water at regular intervals upon the person from a great height, for a certain set length of time. She had wondered at the time how this method could possibly cause death, as she knew it did, the long-continued strain upon the nervous system of even so little an annoyance as this, being awful to endure. She lay still, trying to see how it would seem, so interested for a few minutes that she hardly realized that her pillow was growing quite wet. Then she heard movements in her mother's room—her father and mother conversing in low tones, a match struck—the pushing of furniture about. She realized that the roof was leaking in there as well. She could hear drops falling out in the room on the floor, and now a new one that sounded on the dressing bureau. Suddenly her sister Maria started up in bed with an angry exclamation that "there was water falling on her head." It all struck Rachel as exceedingly funny. Somehow such things always showed on the humorous side to Rachel, quiet and sober as she usually was. This was one thing which often irritated Maria very greatly, this having Rachel laugh at a trying time. Rachel always said it was better to laugh than to cry or be cross, and she must do something, and Maria replied that she had a "hystericky nature." She should control her feelings. Then Maria would proceed to control hers by being cross. But Rachel always forgot about hysterics and laughed, a pure, mirthful laugh. It gurgled forth now, sweet and amused, as she hurriedly got out of bed and brought her sun umbrella, raising it over their heads as she got in again. It was very funny to camp out in real picnic style and have to go to bed under an umbrella. She enjoyed it.

Maria lay down again angrily.

"Rachel Hammond, I do wish you would grow up and learn not to giggle when anything happens. I'm sure I don't see anything funny in being leaked on when you are fast asleep."

That was the beginning. Before many minutes had elapsed the movements of furniture in the next room together with the conversation back and forth and the various excursions for waterproofs and awning cloths with which to protect the beds from the constantly increasing drops, had thoroughly awakened Maria and roused her temper to a pitch quite beyond endurance. She found fault with the house, and the landlord, and said it was what might have been expected of the cottage at the ridiculous price they paid for it. Then when the family had hushed into silence she began at her sister, in a low whisper:

"Rachel, I think you really ought to try to realize that you are grown up in years if you are not in mind yet. I meant to speak to you about a thing you did Sunday night that made me so ashamed I didn't know what to do; but I haven't had a chance to talk to you about it; you manage to keep yourself so busy away from us except just when you are helping with the work, that I never have any chance to see my sister any more," this in an injured tone. "I'm sure I hope the Parkers appreciate your society. Perhaps you manage to make yourself more agreeable there than here. But at any rate, please confine yourself to being polite when you are with me and my friends, whatever you do when you are with yours."

"What in the world have I done now, Maria?" asked Rachel in a troubled voice. She really wanted to please her sister, though she found it much harder work than usual these days.

"Done!" said Maria growing irritated at the remembrance of her discomfiture two days before. "Why, you've acted like a perfect little prig, and almost insulted a minister. What in the world did you think Mr. Fairfield would think of you, Sunday night, turning around and as much as contradicting what he said? It didn't make it the least bit more polite that you put it in the form of a question. He is bright enough to see through that. Who are you to set up to rebuke a minister, anyway? You might as well try to find fault with the Bible."

"Why, 'Ri, I didn't rebuke him. I only asked him a question that honestly puzzled me. What do you mean? I never intended—"

"Nonsense!" said Maria sharply. "You were rude and you know it. If a man doesn't seem to come up to your standard you immediately set about telling him so. You will simply get yourself set down as an insufferable little prig for your trouble if you keep on in that way. I was surprised that Mr. Fairfield didn't tell you that you were a child who didn't know what you were talking about. For my part, I hope I shall not be called upon to endure another such insult to a caller of mine; if I am, you may be sure I shall call mother to come and take you in. It is the only fit rebuke for such actions. You talk religion too much, anyway. It isn't ladylike to stick it in every one's face. A minister hears enough of it in his profession without being called upon to talk about it in his social life. Religion is much better acted than talked, I think. I should hope you would take that to heart. If you attempt any of that sort of talk with the De Veres you will find you won't be tolerated in their society very long. I'm sure I'm ashamed of you. Now do go to sleep if you can. I don't want to talk any more," and Maria turned over with a twitch and pretended to go to sleep herself.

But for Rachel sleep was effectually routed. She lay there thinking. The tears chased each other down her cheeks. It hurt her so to have her sister talk to her in this way. She felt as if she ought to make some protest, but what could she say that would help matters? Her protests always seemed to anger her sister more. Was Maria right after all, and did the minister feel in the way she had said he would about the questions she had asked? If so, was she all wrong in her way of feeling about things? Of course a minister must be right, for he had spent his life in getting ready to preach Christ's gospel, and had given up all to that work. He ought to be consecrated if any one was. But surely he ought also to be one to whom any one could go with a question about Christian living.

Then she remembered Roland De Vere and how differently he had talked about religion, just the few words he had happened to speak on the subject. Somehow she felt that Maria was mistaken about Mr. De Vere at least, and she wished that he would talk to Maria and perhaps he would be able to influence her. Perhaps this minister would know how to help Maria by and by. Ministers' lives ought to be an influence on those around them, without any words, as Maria had said. She would pray for that. Meantime, was there not some little thing she could do for her Master? She felt that her life was so full of pleasure this summer, that without some definite, special work to do, she would be apt to grow selfish. She had tried to help Maria, but all help seemed only to irritate her. Perhaps it was wrong in her to set up to help an older sister. She would just pray and try to keep her tongue from doing aught to make her sister trouble. Her tongue did seem to be a very unruly member. So she closed her eyes and prayed to be shown what to do, and then, like a tired child, threw off her burden and went to sleep.

In justice to Maria be it said that she had been feeling deeply chagrined that Mr. Fairfield had neither called nor come upon the beach when they were there, nor in any way appeared since to claim his acquaintance with them, which he had seemed eager to do on Sabbath evening. It puzzled Maria greatly, for while she cared nothing about the man in particular, still she was deeply sensitive to the opinion of any one, either stranger or friend, whose manner and appearance seemed to make his judgment of value in her eyes. She feared that he had set them down as a family of fanatics, and that the whole fault lay with Rachel's babyish way of talking religion, as if it were an every-day matter.

Having nothing else to do, she brooded over the matter until it appeared very large to her. She felt that the minister was intentionally slighting them, and that now as he had found his friends at Spray View, he wished to show them that he had only been polite to Maria on account of the very awkward accident which had thrown them together on Saturday. Maria's imagination was so vivid, that as the days went by—which, by the way, continued to be rainy, the clouds pouring down water in a very deluge at times—she began to think that the end of all pleasant times had come even as they had just begun. Of course there was no moonlight excursion.

Maria stood on the piazza one afternoon, toward the end of the dreary week, gazing discontentedly at the desolate landscape. The mist of fine rain was still falling, when it was not varied by terrific showers. A stiff breeze was blowing, first from one direction and then from another, as if in fitful mood, uncertain what to do. Off at her right Maria could see the banks of sand piled high, looking almost like cliffs in places, with their low undergrowth of huckleberry and wild sage and laurel, the only growth which the island seemed to afford, for there was not a tree in sight. Now and again the waves of the ocean would dash so high that the spray would be carried up in clouds above these sand banks. There was one break in the banks, just at the end of what was supposed to be their street or "avenue," in the parlance of the place, where one could gaze far out over the wild, turbulent ocean in its dull gray and brown tones, with a seething touch of vivid green here and there and froth of maddened yellow-white. It all looked so cold and wild and awful.

Maria turned from it, shuddering; on her left there stretched the steel-colored bay, once so bright and gay, reflecting tints like an opal, now an almost interminable stretch of mist and desolation. The long reaches of waste sand, and heavy, wet-headed, salt marsh grass, bending with the wind, only added to the dismal character of the scene. The girl walked back and forth on the green piazza, which was wet with the mist, and looked with horror, almost with hatred, at the whole view. Yes, for one can hate even sky and grass and water when one is in the right mood for it. The scene embodied to her the desolation that seemed to have come into her life. It was like that waste of water and sand and dark-leaden sky. There seemed in it no hope of brightness for the future, just as it seemed impossible now, after these days and days of rain, that the sky could ever be bright again or the waves would ever grow soft and lovely and the bay take on its gemlike look. God seemed nowhere to her. She felt a kind of desperation, as if she could not endure another hour of this hateful existence.

It almost frightened her to realize that she felt so. She knew it was wrong. She had been too well brought up not to have been conscious during the days that had passed just how wrong and hateful she had been in her feelings and actions. She began to wonder if she ever had really loved God, or been a Christian, and whether there was anything in it. Wild ideas ran through her brain. Where was God, anyway? Why did he want her to be so unhappy? Had he forgotten her? Over and over in her mind kept going a verse of an old hymn learned in childhood, or rather one line of the verse, she could remember no more. It ran like this, "Has God forgotten to be kind?" She tried to shake it off, but it came again and again. She brushed back the hair that clung wet with the mist to her hot temples and went into the cottage.

Anything was better than being in this vast desolation alone. She went to the kitchen and in desperation took out her recipe book, to find the most difficult thing she could make for supper. It would at least occupy her hands and her mind. There were books, to be sure, but she felt dissatisfied with them all. She could not interest herself in one of them. A book was all very nice and cozy on a rainy day, when all was cheery indoors and there were visions of bright days in the hopeful future after the rain should be passed, but Maria felt that for her there were no such visions.

The trouble was deeper than these few days at the

seashore. It went back to the time when her father lost his money. She was rebellious. She was not willing to give up that money and the position which it carried. Now that it was gone, she felt there was nothing else in the world worth living for. She had been a pretty good Christian, according to her own way of thinking, in those days when things had been prosperous. Why had not God seen that? She could have done much more in the world for him if he had left her life as it was. Now she was no Christian at all, and he must see how he had made a failure of her Christian work by taking away her father's money and her social position. She did not say these things, even to herself, in so many words. She would not have dared, because she had been taught to be reverent in her speech, and in a degree this teaching had reached to her thoughts, but she felt them strongly, deeply, fiercely.

And Rachel sat in the other room and apparently read her book, while all the time she had been uneasily watching her sister and quietly praying for her. Oh, why was it that this her great, longing prayer for the beloved sister could not be answered? Had she not prayed earnestly enough? Or must she be willing to pray longer? What was the matter? God had promised to give what the believing heart should ask for. She laid down her book and went into the bedroom, carefully fastening the curtain behind her against interruptions. She would kneel down now and pray again for Maria. But though she knelt and prayed fervently, she felt no sudden sense of answer such as she had heard other people talk about, and when she listened, she could hear Maria rattle the pans and kettles as fiercely as ever in the kitchen. There was no sign as yet in her of any spiritual change. Rachel's was a sweet nature, struggling for light, and she was not being guided by human help perhaps as much as would have been good for her. She believed everything intensely and at once, and wanted to see a vindication of her belief, like many another eager, impatient one, but she was willing to be led. She took her little Bible. It had aided her many times in perplexity. She turned to it now from habit and read one of her favorite psalms. "Delight thyself also in the Lord, and he shall give thee the desires of thine heart."

She had read that verse over without thinking about it, when a thought seemed to arrest her attention. Was it possible that God had sent her that very promise now? Did he want her to delight herself in him first before he gave her what she had been asking? Perhaps that was true and she had not made him her chief delight. She slowly closed the book and went out again to the sitting room and her story, but though she held the book before her eyes, she was not reading. She was going over her life and thinking how she might make the Lord her chief delight, and how she had not done it. It was a revelation to her of herself, for had she been asked a little time before reading that verse, she would have said that Christ and his life-work were her chief delights; but now she saw that she had made other things chief and Christ's work only a part—a very small part—of the pleasures of her life. She saw that there was something which needed a radical change in her whole soul, so that Christ would be in *all* her pleasures, the source and center of everything, instead of a mere outside pleased observer, as she felt she had been wont to regard him heretofore.

Meantime, she remembered that there were peaches to be peeled for supper. She disliked this work intensely, and was not always prompt to remember that it belonged to her; but to-night she arose with alacrity, saying to herself, "He wants me to peel those peaches; I will try to remember I am doing it for Him and then perhaps I can take delight in it." And she succeeded so well in what so few succeed at all that presently she was singing a happy little song:

> *"There is sunshine in my soul to-day,*
> *More glorious and more bright,*
> *For Jesus—"*

"For pity's sake," snapped Maria, "do select something more appropriate, if you *must* sing. It doesn't look as if there would ever be any sunshine any more anywhere."

And for once Rachel was enabled to laugh and make a pleasant reply and then go on with her singing, instead of closing her mouth and letting the tears steal up to her eyes at the sharp words, as she usually did. And so supper was prepared in much more peace than usual.

9

THE sun shone out at last bright and clear as though he had never thought of anything else. The bay, blue in the distance, sparkled in the sunrays like a wondrous sapphire set in emeralds. White-winged sailboats, like great birds, floated lazily across the glassy surface, carried hither and thither by the light winds, in the very joy of life and motion. As one gazed westward toward the bay, not a sign could be seen of the gloom that had shrouded the landscape for days. Turning toward the sea, radiant with brilliant coloring, bordered by a shining garment of newly washed sand, the late rage of the elements was more apparent, for the sea, slower in rousing to terrible wrath, is more reluctant to cease from its anger, and long after nature smiles, pours thunderous billows upon the unresisting shore.

Had Howard Fairfield been there, his whole day would have been passed at the very edge of the surge, gazing far out to sea over the majestic spectacle, still more striking by reason of the contrast it presented to the calm sky overhead, until his soul had been filled with the wonder of the scene. But much to his own disappointment, a series of unimportant details still held him in the city. It was Saturday. Rachel sat on the piazza peeling peaches. Her father had brought from the city the night before a quantity of fine fruit, for in their island home all such luxuries had to be imported. In the salt-laden atmosphere they decayed rapidly, and to Rachel therefore had been assigned the task of preparing them for preserving and canning. Although this was a task always especially distasteful to her, yet the morning was so bright and beautiful that she caught the spirit of its gladness and sang blithely as she worked.

Moreover, was not her life henceforth to have a new motive, to be filled with a joy not of this world? Jesus was now to be to her a delight, and to her surprise, perhaps, she discovered that that delight shone up at her through the most commonplace tasks. It seemed wonderful. She rejoiced in the brightness of the morning because he had made it bright. Thus she sat thinking her happy thoughts, working with deft fingers at her task, and as she worked, caroled forth a little song.

Maria felt very differently about the change in the weather. Of what good was the sunshine when one did not care to go out into it? She had no place to which to go if she did go out; no one for whose companionship she cared, who was likely, as she said to herself, to care enough about hers to seek it. To be sure, there was the beach to visit, mother and sister for company, books and embroidery for occupation, to say nothing of the kaleidoscopic scenery of sea and sky; but these went for nothing with her, having no place in the catalogue of her desires.

A fierce resentment filled her at the mockery of the day's brightness contrasted with the gloom of her own mood. It was plain now, even to her own mind, that she had been taking a sort of grim, self-pitying satisfaction in the melancholy of the weather. It had stood for a distinct grievance, and now she was almost angry that it was taken from her. As her mother passed through the room, she sighed at sight of the discontent that sat now so often on her elder daughter's face. Rachel's song floated in through the open doorway and made her wonder why one daughter should seem to find all the sweetness while the other persisted in drinking only the bitter. It was the more difficult to understand because it had not always been so, for in her younger days Maria had been as sunny as her sister. It was unlike her to cling to her self-conceived wrongs for so long a time, to show to others only the thorny side of her nature.

Could it be that Maria was on the verge of illness, and that here was the hidden reason for her discontent? With this idea stirring in her heart, the mother passed again into the kitchen and urgently begged Maria to resign her place at the stove to her and Rachel for the day and to lie down in her own room. Her advances were met with scorn, and Maria prepared to cook a more elaborate meal than usual, as a proof that there was nothing the matter with her health. The mother, repulsed, went sadly away again to her sewing, on which more than one tear dropped, as she anxiously asked herself what *could* be the matter with Maria. She found herself wishing that that handsome young Mr. De Vere would pay a little less attention to Rachel, who seemed to care nothing about him, and a little more to Maria, who, with the keen intuition of a mother, she feared did; or else that that intellectual-looking minister, who had brought her home that day she got the drenching, would come again—anything to take her child out of herself and infuse a new interest into her life, that she should not brood over her misfortunes so much, and perhaps thus give a permanent bent to her character in the unfortunate direction of melancholy. She had hoped that even the sunshine would cheer her, but it seemed to have rather the opposite effect.

Across a strip of neatly mowed marsh grass, not many rods distant, stood a small unpainted cottage surrounded by a well-kept vegetable garden. The wide piazza, peculiar to the place, ran across its front, and around this, in attempting to cope with the mosquitoes, some one had at one time tacked a blue mosquito bar which now hung tattered, waving in the breeze. This was the home of the Higginses, little and large.

The family was one of many and varied occupations. The father fished a little, and gardened a little, and drove parties of three in his rickety old green spring wagon over to Spray View on errands, at the rate of ten cents per head, or three for a quarter. Rachel, when she heard this, had rejoiced that they might often take the beach drive, it was so cheap; but Maria had curled her lip in such scorn at the idea of driving past the elegant De Vere villa in the old green wagon that Rachel had not mentioned it again. Mrs. Higgins washed for a living, besides sewing and cooking for her large family, carried tomatoes, which she called "tomats," delicious beets, fresh eggs, and chickens, to the few people who lived near enough to purchase them; went into the bay when requested to dig clams, which she sold at a ridiculously low price, and was the delight of all 'curio loving' people who came in contact with her, by reason of her quaint dialect, a mixture of Irish, German, and Jersey.

There were four grown sons with their wives and children, who lived, some in the same house, some near by, and others came often to visit, on which occasions the eggs, "tomats," and fresh fish were scarce for the time being. There were two young women, daughters, who plodded through the sand every morning at five to reach the Spray View Hotel in time to perform their daily duties there of chamber-maid and nurse-girl, respectively. There was a son who worked on the railroad when the trains ran (which was only during the summer) and fished between times, and last but not least were Katy and John, the two youngest children. They solemnly and silently appeared at the door from time to time, bringing milk or eggs or other things which had been ordered, but fled in dismay if any questions were asked them.

Rachel had found out all this about their neighbors during the first few days of their stay at the shore. She was always interested in every human being that was within her sight. The rest of the family knew of them only as a convenience for the performance of odd jobs and for the supplying of cheap vegetables, fish, and clams. Maria knew them but to despise, because they never by any means happened to have the thing she wanted at the time she ordered it. But Rachel was really and truly interested in watching their movements and realizing that they were human beings, with emotions like herself, in spite of the fact that they were such queer people and seemed to exist and be happy under such very different circumstances from her own, which in contrast with her father's former condition in life she had unconsciously come to regard as none of the best.

In one of Rachel's intervals of song, when she had been on a trip to the kitchen in search of more peaches and another dish, which latter was of course not to be had in this cottage of few conveniences, Rachel heard a burst of song from over the way. I will not say it was music, though it was evidently meant for that. The singer was one of the young women members of the Higgins family. Rachel could see that she was sitting in the wide porch behind a tattered remnant of the blue mosquito netting swinging a much-used hammock, which evidently contained a baby, probably one of the many Higgins grandchildren. Her voice was loud and sharp and clear, with a decided nasal twang. The song was a lullaby improvised for the occasion, but sung in such a tremendously high key as to seem to be intended for the benefit of some baby up in the clouds, or away beyond Spray View.

Rachel broke into a low soft gurgle of laughter and called her mother and Maria to listen, as the loud twang of "Sleep, sleep, sleep, baby, sleep, Hush-a-bye, sleep, hush-a-bye, sleep," rang out above the voice of the majestic waves. The song continued for some time, and Rachel hushed her own singing, partly to listen and partly because the metallic tones grated on her delicate musical susceptibilities. By and by the singer changed her song, while the hammock still rocked violently. The baby was evidently being brought up to be a sailor, for certainly no other vocation would be more suitable after spending one's infant days in such a turbulent cradle.

There's a land that is fair-rer than da-ay,

rang out the words distinctly,

An' by faith we c'n see it a-fa-ar.

All through the verses sang the girl, her lungs apparently as unwearied as when she began, and the energy with which she brought out each word distinctly, making a listener sure that she enjoyed her own music, whatever might be said of others.

She finished one song and went on to another, a gospel song, of date so many years back that Rachel could remember it only as having been familiar with it in her very early girlhood. Her eyes grew dreamy as she thought of various occasions when she had sung these very words which now seemed a little out of date because of the many new jingles which had superseded them in a way. She wondered where this girl had become acquainted with all these songs, that she could sing them from beginning to end. The family, she had heard, had been on the island both summer and winter for several years. She had heard that they never went to church or Sunday-school. Indeed, Sunday seemed to be a sort of merry-making time with them, for there were sure to be several sons with their wives there to spend the day, and Rachel had noticed a case of beer bottles outside the porch once when she went to get some clams to make clam bisque for supper.

Where, then, had this girl gotten her knowledge of religious song? She had words enough of the way of salvation at her tongue's end, to save a whole family, if words could save. It must have been acquired before the family moved to this deserted place. It would be interesting to know where and how. Perhaps she had sometime been an attendant at Sunday-school, or perhaps she had gone to a series of Moody meetings and the songs had grown familiar there. Rachel was a bit given to letting her imagination have free rein, and when she had thought out the possibilities thus far she began to grow intensely interested in the family over the way and to wish to know more. She would talk with that girl the next time she came over with the milk and perhaps find out something.

Meantime, how grand a thing it would be if through those very songs some day the whole family should become Christians. What a nice story that would make. Rachel dropped her peach and looked dreamily off over the bay. She liked to scribble little stories herself, just for her own amusement sometimes. She never showed them to any one. This would be a splendid start for a plot. But how would this marvelous change be brought about? The Spirit of God could do it, of course, but he would be likely to use some earthly instrument. Some one must come who would speak words, or do some helpful thing, or get an influence over them, perhaps some young minister on his vacation, like Mr. Fairfield, or even some young lady, or—

Here Rachel's thoughts came suddenly back to the practical from the imaginary and a soft pink color stole up into her cheek. Why sit and plan a story when, perhaps, there was really an opening for work? She had been asking God for some work for him, maybe he was showing it to her through that loud-voiced singing over there. It was not, at first thought, as attractive work as some she might think of, not nearly so interesting in reality as it would be in a story; but perhaps it was work she could do, at least she could try a little of it. She picked up her peach and began to peel it rapidly again, revolving in her mind whether there really was anything she could do after all. She felt herself shrinking from the undertaking when it was presented to her and she wished she had not thought of it at all, nor listened to the horrible grating singing. How could she do anything, anyway? It would only be another trial for Maria if she should associate herself with any of those despised Higginses. They would be less to her sister's liking than even the Parkers. Then she had never been introduced, and perhaps the girl would resent anything she might do or say as patronizing. Rachel had a horror of seeming to patronize any human being. There was not the least danger that her gentle, loving smile and winning way would ever be mistaken for that, but in her true modesty she did not know this.

Finally she cast aside the thought with this feeling: "If God wishes me to do anything in that way he will show me. Perhaps I am as mistaken about this as I was about trying to help Maria." With an upward turning of her heart she cast the thought at her Saviour's feet. He knew best. If he wished her to do anything he would show her.

By this time the peaches were finished and so was the song from over the way. The baby probably had succumbed at last to the boisterousness of hammock and song. Rachel carried her peaches into the house, washed her hands and came out again with her little work-basket of dainty lace which she was making for the border to a center piece, and two little books, still in the paper wrappings as they had arrived that morning, by messenger, for her from Spray View. The handwriting of her own name in bold, manly characters had told her who was the sender, and Rachel postponed the opening of the package until her work was done that she might the better enjoy what was to be found therein. Perhaps too, there was a shy, sweet pleasure in opening the package by herself, and was it to keep up a show of work that she also carried her basket and lace work out with her, or did she really intend to make lace and not read? Anyway, the morning was charming and it was so nice to have a package to open and her pretty work lying beside her, and nothing to do but enjoy it all. Slowly she untied the knots of the string, tracing meanwhile the graceful, strong letters of her fair name, "Rachel Weldon Hammond."

And then she undid the wrapping and brought the two books to view. She had known they were books, for Roland De Vere had told her he had two books which he wanted her to read, as he felt sure she would enjoy them, and they would perhaps lead her into lines of reading which were new to her. Now she looked curiously to see what they were. One was of a dark red paper cover, but attractive in print, short of paragraph and brief of chapters. It was called "A Castaway." A glance through it told her it was the one he had told her would be of special use to help spend the long Sabbath afternoon, and aid her in her Christian life. She smiled with pleasure in her eyes as she turned the leaves a few minutes, snatching a sentence here and there that seemed to have been written just for her, so perfectly did it fit her circumstances and thoughts, and then she laid it aside. Sabbath reading like this, aside from the Bible, did not often come in her way. She must treasure it for the Sabbath. She would just take a few peeps into it and leave the rest of it for a Sunday treat.

Then she turned to the other book, a daintily bound volume all in pale green and gold. The paper was thick and creamy, the print clear, and the whole appearance of the book exquisite. Rachel loved the feeling and the look of such a book. It was poetry. She opened at random. One poem was styled "Day's Parlor." She read, and it seemed to her that that day had been fashioned in just the way described.

> *The day came slow till five o'clock,*
> *Then sprang before the hills*
> *Like hindered rubies, or the light*
> *A sudden musket spills.*
>
> *The purple could not keep the east,*
> *The sunrise shook the fold,*
> *Like breadths of topaz, packed a night,*
> *The lady just unrolled.*
>
> *The happy winds their timbrels took;*
> *The birds, in docile rows*

> *Arranged themselves around their prince*
> *(The wind is prince of those).*

> *The orchard sparkled like a Jew,*
> *How mighty 'twas, to stay*
> *A guest in this stupendous place,*
> *The parlor of the day!*

Rachel caught her breath and looked up at the bay and the blue, blue sky, drinking in all their loveliness. How those jeweled words had brought out the beauties! She turned a few pages and read again:

> *She sweeps with many colored brooms,*
> *And leaves the shreds behind;*
> *Oh, housewife in the evening west,*
> *Come back and dust the pond!*

> *You've dropped a purple raveling in,*
> *You dropped an amber thread;*
> *And now you've littered all the east*
> *With dust of emerald!*

> *And still she plies her spotted brooms,*
> *And still the aprons fly,*
> *Till brooms fade softly into stars—*
> *And then I come away.*

Ah! Rachel drew her breath again as if she had caught some delicate perfume that was new to her, and she feared to lose a single atom of the delightful sensation. This poetry suited her dreamy imagination, which was always personifying nature. She felt that she would enjoy this book to the full. This last poem was just a description of that exquisite sunset last week. She was grateful for the gift of the book, and dimly felt the high, fine perceptions of the young man who had selected it for her. The music of these words and their coloring gave her pleasure clear to her finger tips.

And then in the midst of these thoughts appeared her answer from Heaven and her work ready laid out for her. It was a contrast, perhaps, but a well-tuned nature should always be ready to turn from the high to the low and feel none the worse for it, and sometimes even recognize that what is rated the low is in reality the highest of the high, while the high is merely a picture of what pleasure may be after all.

"Did your ma want any clams to-night?" It was the clear metallic voice of the singer from over the way who asked the question, and the voice was so sharp, and her coming had been so silent that Rachel, lost in her beautiful dreams, started. But the girl seemed not to notice this. Her eyes were intent upon Rachel's work-basket and the beautiful lace work on its pretty blue cambric background pattern.

"Oh, what a pretty thing that is!" exclaimed the girl. "Did you do that?" and as Rachel took up her basket to bring the work nearer for her inspection, "Ain't it awful hard work? You must be just dreadful clever. Does it take a long time? Now I'll just guess that stuff costs an awful lot. I see a woman over to the hotel the other day workin' at a thing like that. You don't say! That's the way you do it. Just sew that braid onto them lines! Why that looks easy! My, but I suppose it's all in knowin' how!" and the girl sighed wistfully. "My! but I would like to know how to do some of them pretty things! I never have no time in summer; but land! in winter, time just drags and drags. Seems like I was fifty years old every winter I go through in this place. I wish I could do something to shorten it."

And thus it was that Rachel's work came to her, and of all things! that it should come through a bit of renaissance lace work! She looked at the gray old cottage with its flapping, faded mosquito bar, after the girl had gone, and then down at her delicate blue and white work, and thought how incongruous the two were, and how little she would have dreamed of beginning to get an influence over a girl from that house through anything as fine as that. God knew best. It was really wonderful, when you left it all to him, how he made that to appear. Why had she never tried that before? It might not be that she would accomplish so very much, for after all she had only promised to teach an ignorant girl how to make lace and that might not lead to anything else, but she felt that she had been given a chance to try, and she thanked her Father for it.

HOWARD FAIRFIELD had not lingered in the heat of the city because it was his wish to do so. He had found an aged member of his church very ill and wishing to see him; and the man who was to have supplied his prayer meeting sent word that he could not come, so he stayed for that; then afterward he lingered by the old saint's bedside till he had gone where spiritual help was needed no more. Thus had come another funeral in that one short week, which yet had seemed to stretch itself out to such a length.

Saturday afternoon saw him free at last, for the pulpit was supplied for the morrow and the man on the ground. There was no need for him to linger longer. There was just time to catch the last train back to the quiet shore. He laid his head wearily against the cushion of the seat while the train whirled him on, and thought over all the experiences of the week. How he had been led! That girl with her dream, and the little girl's funeral, and his own experience in waiting for the hour to arrive! And then those hours by the bedside of the dying saint, where he had gained, more than given, spiritual help.

He had a new feeling toward the old man who had just entered heaven, which he had never felt for any person who had died before. It was as if he had been given to know one of the apostles for a few short hours, and to talk with him, and have his eyes opened by him, and to grow to love him, and then the heavens had opened and he had seen the man carried up to Jesus.

Heaven had a new interest for him now. He felt nearer to it. He loved it more than he had ever before realized he could. He could not help wondering what sights and scenes that dear servant of God was passing through at that moment, while his friends were mourning his absence from the earth. To him the coffin which he had seen lowered into the earth but two hours before contained no thought of the grand sweet soul, who was not buried there, but was high in heaven with the angels. How he wished that he had known the old man better during the time he had been on earth. Oh, those wasted months, when such companionship and help might have been his. It reminded him of the days when the disciples had Jesus with them and had not half known how to value his daily companionship. To know intimately one who was like Jesus was, in a limited sense, like having known and walked with Jesus when he was in the body on the earth.

Perhaps there were others in his congregation who were like this man. Now that he could think over the list, there were several families whose simple, trustful Christian life had evidently strong faith behind it, and rich experience from which he might learn much. There were the Clarks! He had looked upon them as good souls, but had thought them ignorant. Ignorant, perhaps they were in some things, but they read their Bibles and they lived their Bibles, and now that he thought of it there were many ways in which he felt sure they could help him. How foolish he had been! How wise in his own conceit! He had felt that because he was fresh from the seminary he knew more than they all. Now he saw that he had not half learned the true heart-knowledge, which should have gone hand in hand with his head-knowledge.

Had he then wasted his preparations so far this summer? There was that series of sermons he had planned out and half developed on the mystery of the Trinity, and there was the other series which he had worked carefully over and had almost ready for use on "The Life and Works of the Prophets." They seemed empty and useless to him now. There were doubtless many good things in them. It might be that at some time they might even be useful to him for the especial purpose of helping certain minds over perplexing places, but in the light of his new experiences they seemed so wide of the mark, so almost unnecessary when one thought of the tremendous truths which needed to be presented, yes urged, yea, thundered from the pulpit day and night.

He had thought that a quiet summer by God's sea, with his own intellect and God's good teacher, nature, would be of vast assistance to him as a preacher: but perhaps he might have gone somewhere else, to one of those wonderful spiritual gatherings of which there were so many far and near, beginning with Northfield and Mr. Moody. He had always thought he might like to go to Northfield, but it had been in a lofty, condescending way, more out of curiosity than anything else. Now he longed for something of which he had heard, and which he knew by instinct might be found there. Perhaps he ought to give up his present plans and go there at once. It might be the best thing he could do. He closed his eyes restfully, and wondered what his Heavenly Father would have him do about it, and he prayed to be guided; for while he wanted to go, and felt it would be good, he yet had a longing for the quiet and rest of the still seashore place and the chance to talk with God alone. He would wait there at least till he was sure what God would have him do, or whither he would have him go in his great school, for he felt like a new pupil just entering a higher grade to be taught things he had not dreamed there were for him yet to learn.

As the train rushed on and drew nearer to his destination he began to open his eyes and look for landmarks. He had not realized how tired he was, nor how eager for a sight of the mighty ocean. He thought of the few friends he had met and wondered if they would be there; and if they would be helpful; and then, with a strange new feeling, if he could be helpful to them. There was that girl, there were those two girls in fact, whom he had met under such peculiar circumstances. He hardly knew where to place them, he had seen so little of them. The younger girl had asked some strange questions. And now there came back to him vividly his last walk and reverie by the sea. He would go back there and walk and think, but he felt with a grateful thrill in his heart that there would be answers to his questions now which he had not been able to give them. Now his eyes were open and he was beginning to see things differently. He thanked God for this. Meanwhile, if there was aught of good that he could get or do, he wanted to be ready for it. He watched eagerly in the deepening twilight, as the train drew near the station, for the few little cottages, bathed in the sunset glow of the bay, and sprang out on the platform, breathing in the salt air, glad that he was back again. After supper he took his way out beside the sea in the darkness of the starry night alone to think and be with God, and he came back from that walk to deep, dreamless sleep and awoke to the restfulness of the Sabbath.

Now the Saturday which had brought such brightness to the shore, and had blown such a life-giving breeze from across the bay had also brought the little mosquito. On the wings of that delicious breeze he came—not alone. He brought his entire family and all his relatives with him. They were small and sharp mosquitoes. They were harmless and unmusical mosquitoes, but they were wise. They knew those cottages of old with their wide cracks and roomy ceilings for daily hidings. They had been blown across the bay on just such breezes for years, at least if not they, then their ancestors, and they went as straight to their several stopping-places as if they had telegraphed ahead and had rooms reserved for them and meals ready. They arrived all at once and took possession. They swarmed through the piazzas and drove the helpless sitters there inside the screen doors; but they did not stop outside, they rushed in also, and those who failed of the door were not long in finding the other vulnerable points in the cottages. By night, when the lights had begun to appear, they had managed to make their presence almost unbearable.

Maria, like many other people of fair skin and highly strung nervous organization, was particularly susceptible to stings of any kind, whether of insects or tongue. She became irritable at once. Perhaps no one would have wondered who saw the enormous red and white swellings which immediately responded to the attack of the little insect. Mosquito bites poisoned Maria, and she really suffered intensely. Therefore it need not be wondered at that her temper was strung to its highest pitch. She actually sat down in the sitting room before the whole family and cried in vexation and despair over the torment of the little pests. She declared she could endure it no longer, that she would rather die, and a dozen other extravagant things which she did not mean, and then went to bed, sick and sore, to fight them there, and find little sleep to restore her calmness.

Sabbath morning found her aching in body and mind. The mosquitoes still continued. Maria refused to go to church, though the entire family condescended to urge her to do so, hoping that it would in some way soothe her troubled spirit. They had reason to be glad, however, that she had refused, when they arrived at the church door and entered, attended by thousands of the little insects, and found that they were thick on the white plastered walls, and that the assembled congregation looked more like a lot of dancing dervishes than a company of quiet and respectable church-goers, bent on the worship of God. Indeed, the mosquitoes kept up their part of the performance until people were nearly distracted, some going home in desperation. The speaker of the morning drew his remarks to a speedy close and the people hastened home remarking on the unusualness of the visitation of mosquitoes, and the wind, weather, and state of temperature as causes for the plague. Those who had plastered houses hastened indoors and those who had not took refuge in pennyroyal oil and the smoke of various herbs, and then in despair betook themselves to the beach. There at least was a place of refuge. Even Maria was driven thither very soon after the noonday meal. She would not have gone if it had been tolerably comfortable at home, for she felt in that perverse mood in which she dreaded seeing any one or speaking pleasantly. She even felt a strong distaste to making herself look neat and pretty for the day.

Nevertheless, she finally consented to change her dress and smooth her hair and go to the sand with Rachel. Rachel, in her sisterly solicitude that the afternoon should be a time of comfort to Maria, loaded herself down with cushions, parasols, fans, and a beach chair. Then with her own little Bible and the new book, which had come to her the day before and which she had kept for this precious Sabbath afternoon's reading, she walked cheerfully through the sand and swarms of mosquitoes to find just the right spot on the beach where the breeze and the view were most pleasant, while Maria scolded with every step and declared she would go back, but nevertheless went on.

Rachel pitched her tent, as it were, arranged the beach chair comfortably, fixing cushions and sand for herself, declaring she preferred them, and pressed the chair upon her sister. Rachel opened her Bible first. Maria sat gloomily looking out on the smooth water which had calmed itself into one of those transparent blue-green sheens which look innocent of any possible boisterous to-morrow. Certainly the coloring of the ocean was worth watching to-day, and the sky and air seemed perfect. But Maria was in no mood to enjoy it. Presently she closed her eyes drearily on it all. She felt so weary, poor child. Her life seemed so empty. She was impatient of the day and of the summer, and even of the outlook of her whole life as she seemed to see it stretching before her.

Rachel felt her sister's gloom. It could not but be apparent, and Rachel was so impressionable that it made her quite unhappy. She knew there was nothing she could do to lighten her sister's heart, and yet she could not enjoy her own reading nor her own pleasure in the day. She read one of the short chapters in her new book, wondering over the helpfulness of every word, charmed with the plain, everyday language and tender sympathy expressed by the writer, but in spite of her interest in the book, her mind kept wandering to Maria and she was conscious of every movement her sister made. At last she thought she was asleep and instantly she gave thanks. Sleep would be the best thing for her in her present state of mind. Unconsciously Rachel relaxed her tension of muscles and resting back among her pillows enjoyed the day and her own happy thoughts for a little. She let her mind wander to the Higginses and the promised lesson in lace-making, and wondered how she could get in a lesson on something else besides lace. By and by two little figures, which she had been watching for some time when they were but mere specks away down toward the lighthouse, came nearer, hand in hand, and now were near enough to be distinguished as the two younger members of the Higgins household, Katy and John, wandering along, bareheaded and barefooted, picking up a shell now and then and trotting on again.

Rachel watched them interestedly. How different the sea must seem to them, who lived there all the year and knew it at its wildest! It was evidently their friend and they loved it. Rachel could tell that from the way they looked out upon it, pointing now and then to a distant sail, or cloud of smoke from some steamer far-off against the horizon.

The girl watching, wondered if the sea ever spoke to them of God, and what idea they had of its majesty and its Maker. Did they associate the two? Had they been taught enough for that, she would like to know; or did they perhaps have some natural instinct which would lead them to feel this without the teaching? She began to frame questions which she would like to ask them, and grew eager to know how they would answer.

And then her second opportunity came, as the children sat down on a great broken spar which had been washed ashore some time ago and been half buried in the sand. Katy dug her bare feet in the sand, making a soft cool hole for them, and the boy John sat quite still, looking out, perhaps the sailor instinct of his family stirring within him. They evidently meant to sit there some time. Rachel might go over and talk with them. They looked lonely too, perhaps they would like her to tell them a story. She missed her class of little girls at home in Sunday-school which met at about this hour. It would be a real pleasure to her to teach the lesson of the day, which for the sake of keeping in touch with her class during her absence she had been studying all the week. What if she should go over and talk to those two children and God should open a way for her to tell that beautiful Bible story to them? Might she? Would Maria miss her? She glanced at her sister, who seemed to be fast asleep, and then moving gently she laid her books by Maria's side and rose and slipped away. She would go for a few minutes, anyway, and see how she was received. And so with beating heart, for she was young and this seemed a grave and responsible mission to her, Rachel went to see what her first opportunity had for her of possibility in the way of soul winning.

Katy and John were startled when they found the pretty young lady sitting down beside them on their spar, and actually speaking to them, and they picked up their shells and prepared to flee, but Rachel's winning smile and her eagerness over the pretty shells they had gathered soon made them forget this intention, and before they knew what they were about they were sitting on the sand at her feet, listening with large, wondering eyes and wide-open mouths to a story she was telling them. She had found that the questions she wanted to ask would have to be deferred until she had won a place in their hearts and had been able to loosen their tongues, for they were shy of speaking any words at all but yes and no, and blushed deeply even at these.

They evidently were not used to being talked with much by any one except their own family, and perhaps not much by them. And so Rachel's art of story-telling stood her in good stead. She made a shell lead up to the story, and she soon had them interested in it.

Then from that story she went on to tell of Jesus making a fire by the seaside and cooking the fishes for his disciples' supper. As they grew interested she forgot everything in her joy of teaching. She drew a bit of a diagram in the sand, using a razor fish's shell for a crayon, and the children, who had never seen anything of the kind before, bent eager heads over the picture and drank in her words as if they had been listening to music. Perhaps it was not the best lesson she might have selected for a first in religious instruction, but she presently succeeded in making those two young hearts beat with longing to have been of that weary boat load coming in to the supper and the dear and gracious Master.

And then, wonder of wonders! they heard from this beautiful young lady's lips that they also might be his children! his, cared for by him. That great, good Jesus, who was no more associated with their idea of God than they would have associated him with some of their own family, and whose name they never heard but in profanity, he might be theirs. If the young teacher could have looked into those darkened little hearts and known what they really did think and feel about God, and how very little they knew about him, her heart would have sunk at the impossibility of her task, and her words might have grown less eloquent in her hopelessness; but mercifully she did not know, as mercifully none of us know just what is before or about us, and the Father in heaven knew that they were filled with a great longing for the first time in their little lives to know Jesus Christ.

So Rachel talked on and on, and the children did not

grow weary, and the sun was setting in the west before she realized how long she had kept her Sabbath-school, and how long she had been away from her sister, who would doubtless blame her for the neglect.

That night when Rachel opened her Bible in her own room she read these words, "Therefore, my beloved brethren, be ye steadfast, unmovable, always abounding in the work of the Lord, forasmuch as ye know that your labour is not in vain in the Lord." And she wondered wistfully just what those words meant, and if it were wrong for her to claim them and think her Father in heaven sent them as a message to cheer her heart in this new work.

II

BUT Maria was not really asleep. She had closed her eyes because she did not wish to talk. She did not wish to see her sister bending over her Bible. It made her uncomfortable to think Rachel could enjoy the Bible. *She* could not. She told herself plainly that she never had; that she only read it from a sense of duty, as of course all church-members would do. It irritated her to think that Rachel pretended to enjoy it. In her heart she knew that there was no pretense about Rachel, and that she really did enjoy it, but it pleased her to say this to herself. It made her own unhappy, rebellious life seem less black in contrast. When Rachel laid down her books and slipped softly away Maria felt relieved. She wanted to be alone. She felt too utterly ugly in her heart to be near any one. Presently she wondered where her sister could have gone, and why she did not return, and raising herself and peeping under the parasol, she looked up and down the beach and saw Rachel with her young class gathered about her. Maria understood what it meant. She curled her lip a little. Rachel was always doing such queer things. What would the De Veres or some of the hotel people think if they came along now and saw her sitting in the sand with those two barefooted little heathen beside her. She half made up her mind to call her back and reprove her, and then sat back again, asking herself what was the use, and feeling a little relieved that she was likely to be by herself for some time, albeit there was growing in her heart a determination to charge her sister with neglecting her for two little vagrants when she did return.

She settled herself a little more comfortably with the help of some of Rachel's pillows, and seeing the red paper-covered book that had been left lying closed on the Bible beside her, she took it up. It surprised her a little that Rachel should bring a paper-covered novel out on Sunday along with her Bible, for Rachel was apt to be a little puritanical about such things; but she knew that Roland De Vere had sent some books over to Rachel yesterday; doubtless this was one of them. She reached for it, reflecting that Rachel's scruples would be easily overcome by that handsome young man, who seemed to have made up his mind to devote himself to her, even if she were nothing but a little girl.

She read the title, "A Castaway." It looked exciting—that is, the title seemed so. It was probably a story of the sea. She turned the pages and opened at the beginning, a look of satisfaction on her face that here was something to make her forget herself for a little while. But the look rapidly changed to disappointment as she read. A Bible verse at the beginning! It was nothing but a sermon after all, or worse still, one of those devotional books. She flung it carelessly down in her lap and leaned back again. How exasperating! Just when she thought she was going to have a little relief from the monotony and enjoy herself. She picked up the book once more and read halfway down the first page, but it was as if she were reading Hebrew. She knew not what manner of speech this was, and she did not take in the sense of the words. They meant nothing to her, and she closed it again and went on with her own thoughts, her fingers carelessly between the pages, but the look of settled discontent upon her face. It was well for her that the parasol was placed at such an angle as to thoroughly hide that expression on her face else she might have missed what had been sent her that afternoon.

Howard Fairfield had come out on the beach to walk and be alone. He had gone out at once after dinner, feeling that he wanted to get away from the gay chatter of the hotel guests, for the few guests that there were made much of themselves and of each other and chattered indiscriminately. He had walked up by the lonely lighthouse, and now had turned and was retracing his steps, thinking to go to his room to rest or read a little, perhaps. He had gained an uplifting in his walk by the sea. His thoughts had been with God, and there was a softened, sweet expression upon his face, an expression which in a man's face, seldom as it is seen, makes it the more noble and manly, as if he were growing more like the man God meant him to be.

He walked on slowly as he neared the part of the beach in front of the hotel and began to meet one and another of the guests there strolling and chatting in lazy fashion. He guided his own steps farther away, that he might not be drawn into conversation with any of them and break the solemn quiet which had stolen over him. Thus he passed just back of Rachel and her little group of listeners, and catching a word or two of her earnest lesson, walked more slowly and listened too. He recognized the tact and skill with which this mere girl was talking to these two ignorant little children, and wondered thereat. There were things he might learn from even a young girl's teaching, he said to himself, as he passed wistfully on, wishing he dared linger and hear more without danger of spoiling the lesson for the other two.

Then he turned his steps straight down to the sea and stood as close to the waves as might be, looking out and thinking. It seemed to him that his past life was rolling out there before him, wave after wave of it, too far away for him to ever come at and change it, rolling carelessly but certainly on to eternity to meet him again on the other shore. He numbered each wave with a year or period of his life, and saw its glaring mistakes, and wished he might ride over the waters and bring those farther ones back and live them again that they might be better lived. At last he turned with a sigh. It was no use looking back. He must go forward and see that the waves which followed these should be stronger and more resistless with endeavor for Christ. And so walking deep in thought up the sandy bank he came face to face with Maria Hammond, who had of course seen him, in fact, had been watching him for some minutes, and who while she was too proud to arrange her dress or alter her position as if she expected him to greet and talk with her, had nevertheless risen more to a sitting posture, and changed her expression from one of scornful discontent to one of quiet, dignified Sabbath thoughtfulness.

The young man, realizing suddenly that he was in danger of walking over a lady and sun umbrella, raised his head and recognized Maria. Of course there was nothing to do but pause a moment and speak to her, though in his present mood he would have avoided any one—especially a gay young girl, as he had imagined her to be—if he had had the choice beforehand.

But while pausing and exchanging the word of greeting, his eyes fell on the Bible and the little paper book.

He looked up quickly, almost surprised, and yet glad, at the young girl's face. He had not somehow thought of her as one who would be likely to bring her Bible to the shore where others were. He must have been mistaken. She was after all a Christian, an earnest one, perhaps, like her sister over there who was doing her best to work for Jesus. He felt glad in his heart instantly that he had stopped, said to himself that perhaps he had been led to her for help, for he recognized in himself just then a great need for help. His face lighted up.

"May I sit down?" he asked, "or are you expecting some one else to occupy this luxurious chair in the sand? I'm a little tired from my long walk."

And Maria, all smiles and graciousness, though with not a shade too much earnestness for maidenly decorum, told him that he was welcome, and that the seat was Rachel's, but that Rachel had gone on a missionary trip to some little heathen, and there was no telling how late it would be before her return. If Maria had not seen a certain something which seemed new to her in this new acquaintance of hers, she might have put a shade of scorn for Rachel and her menial service into this sentence, but there had been that in the young man's face which had reminded her that he was a minister and that ministers were wont to respect and praise such acts as Rachel's present one, therefore her tone told nothing of the scorn she felt, and she spoke of Rachel's work as a natural, perfectly praiseworthy occurrence. She wondered afterward why she had done this and how she had been kept from saying several things which had been on the tip of her tongue and yet had not seemed quite to be what Mr. Fairfield would expect of her, as they would have seemed two weeks before, during their first few days of acquaintance.

"She is doing her work over there well," said the

minister, his face growing grave again. "I could not help hearing a little of her lesson as I passed, and wishing I were a barefoot heathen too, for what I heard helped me. She must have remarkable talent as a teacher of little ones."

Maria was somewhat astonished, it is true, but accepted her sister's compliment with sisterly pride. Mr. Fairfield stretched out his hand while they were talking and took up the little paper volume. Maria's face flushed slightly, and she was about to disclaim any connection with the book, and to tell how miserably disappointed she had been a few minutes before over the contents, when again something held her back and she sat still while Mr. Fairfield turned the leaves.

"Ah! Mr. Meyer!" he said, as he opened the title-page. "You have been reading this?" He flashed his bright dark eyes up into hers again with that sudden pleasure and surprise that had confused her a moment before. "I never read it myself, and I was foolish enough to lose my opportunity of hearing the man when he was in this country, through listening to some adverse criticisms upon him, which I have since come to believe were utterly false and unfounded. I wish I could undo that loss and hear this address as it was delivered in my own city. A saint who has just gone to heaven told me of it."

Maria listened in respectful, surprised silence, glad that some intuition had kept her mouth closed a moment before. This certainly was not the same young man whom she had known, or thought she had known, two weeks before, and she prided herself on being a quick judge of character, and on being able to read faces readily. What had made the difference? She watched him while he turned the pages slowly.

"Have you been reading this?" he asked again suddenly. "Have you read it all? Perhaps you would not mind reading it aloud to me, if you have not. I never have any one to read aloud to me now that my sister is abroad. Are you fond of exercising yourself in that direction for other people's pleasure?"

"No, I have not read it all," Maria admitted, her face flushing slightly, and she wondered whether, if he knew the fact he would call that the strict truth to answer so, "but I am very fond of reading aloud and shall be delighted to read it if it will be any pleasure to you."

Now it happened that Maria was gifted in the art of reading aloud. It is true her family very seldom had the benefit of this gift, for there were few occasions when she thought it worth while to exercise it, and they seldom asked favors at her hand. But on occasions, when her audience was appreciative and worth while, she could charm a friend, or a whole room full of friends, as she read from story or poem, and bring their tears and their laughter at her will. Her voice was low and sweet and clear, and her expressive face helped to interpret whatever she read, by flashes of fun or earnestness. Everybody liked to hear Maria Hammond read, and in her younger days when she was a little child, guided by the wishes of her family, the father and mother and brother and sister had been exceedingly proud of her powers.

There was something exceedingly interesting, not to say romantic, to a girl who had been moping at a dull seaside with nothing to do but cook and be cross, in the situation of sitting by the lovely sea with a very handsome, evidently cultured, young man and being asked to read aloud something in which he was deeply interested, and which had to do with his own especial, personal lines of thought, all for his benefit. Even though the book was one which she had just now scorned, and the theme chosen was to her uninteresting, what mattered it? Religious writing was always easy to read and capable of much good expression in an elocutionary way. She took the book with alacrity, much pleased over the turn the afternoon had taken, and wondering why the sea looked so much more beautiful than it had done a half-hour before.

She read impressively the wonderful Bible text with which the address began, and then went on as naturally as if the writer of the simple, earnest sentences had himself been present delivering them. She was aware constantly of the pair of earnest eyes which watched her, listened intently to what she read, taking in every slightest turn brought out by her good rendering, appreciating to the full the homely, apt illustrations with which the short sermon was sprinkled, and unconsciously to herself, she was thinking most about what he thought of her reading, though as the reading went on, she could not fail to be interested too, for a good reader, like a good singer or a perfect actor, for the time being throws his whole soul into what he is voicing, and lives it and believes it with all his heart.

On to the end she read without interruption save an occasional half-articulate emphasis from the listener as some peculiarly good point was noted by him, and as she finished the impressive prayer with which the address closed, she raised her eyes to his and they were full of tears.

There seemed to be something almost dreadful about those tears to Maria, as she thought upon them afterward, as if she had given an impression she had no right to give, and she dropped her eyes quickly. There had been a strange, a kind of exalted, look upon his face too, as if he were pleading for forgiveness with his eyes from one unseen, and realizing something in his life which hurt him. He had hardly seemed conscious of the young girl by his side. But then he spoke slowly, quietly; he was very grave, with a strange light in his eyes, she saw, as she glanced shyly up again.

"Miss Hammond, I cannot thank you enough for the help you have been to me in reading that. It seems somehow to fit my life better than anything I ever heard. Do you know, it touches me in a vital spot. I have been fearing within the last few days that I myself have been a castaway, even before I have ever been of any real use. I did not think an hour ago I could have spoken of this matter to any one, but perhaps it will do me good to tell it to some one, and you have been so kind and helpful. In fact I can see that you know just how to help some one in trouble." Here he looked up with a pleasant smile, not in the least the smile of the ordinary young man of society who is giving a young woman a compliment, but more a sweet, grave acknowledgment of her womanhood and its natural province of helper, comforter, sympathizer.

"I have had a strange experience since I left the beach so suddenly. I never thought to tell it to any one, but I believe I will tell you if you do not mind."

And then he went on and gave the astonished Maria an account of his hasty summons to the city, of his meeting with the dreamer, and of the strange fulfillment of the dream. He even told her of his own feelings as he waited for that summons to the funeral, and of his full surrender to God, and the following experiences by the bedside of the dying saint.

And when he had finished and they rose by tacit consent to walk slowly toward home, he gathering up the cushions and parasol and silently assisting her in getting her things together, she walked subdued and wondering beside him. Not that she was utterly silent.

Oh, no; she was naturally too tactful for that. She knew how to sympathize with people in other things than religion, she knew how to put in the quiet, helpful word and to listen with rapt attention. Moreover, she was wonderfully interested in this young man and his story. She had never listened to a real heart history like this before. No one had ever before given her his confidence to such an extent. She could not help but be sympathetic and to feel that there was something in all he said that was true for her as well as for him. She murmured, "It is all very wonderful," as they neared her home, and Mrs. Hammond, awakened by approaching voices from an uncomfortable nap in the mosquito-netted hammock on the piazza, looked up to see a strange new light on her elder daughter's face and to wonder over Maria once more.

They paused at the steps and the minister said earnestly, "You have helped me this afternoon. I should like to talk with you more about this matter. May I hope to have some more of that wonderful reading soon?" And then something was said about attending the evening service in the church. The mother, behind the porch screen did not hear nor heed. She was wondering how it was that Maria, the Maria whom they had known since their stay at the seashore, could possibly be of any help to anybody in her present state of mind.

12

"THAT is a remarkable girl," said Mr. Fairfield to himself as he walked slowly back toward his hotel. "Her acquaintance will indeed be a help to me, I can see that at once. And what a fine reader she is! She seems utterly unconscious of the fact. She is as sweet and natural as a flower. She must be an unusual Christian!"

It is a good thing that people are blind sometimes, else much of the good of this world might be left undone because the workers would think it was hardly worth while. God in his mysterious kindness makes us see each other, now worse, now better than we really are, in order that we may help and be helped. It is doubtful whether the Hammond family, had they been permitted to know the young minister's conclusions about Maria, would not have thought it their duty to warn him how mistaken he was. And yet nothing that could have come to Maria would have been likely to do her so much good as this afternoon of being happily misunderstood and the consequent impression she made upon the minister. How, if this had not been, could she have ever spent those days which followed in reading and talk such as she had never dreamed of taking part in before, and of pleasant companionship of a higher character than any which had been permitted to fall to her lot before? God had just as surely sent Mr. Fairfield to be a missionary to Maria Hammond as he intended Maria Hammond to awaken and help the young man. And yet a weak human judgment would have kept these two utterly apart for the spiritual growth of each.

For the first time since her coming to the shore Maria entered the low door of the despised green cottage without a thought of the cottage or its shabbiness, or her own hatred of the surroundings. She went thoughtfully to her own room and laid down the two books she had been carrying on Rachel's little table, making a few slight changes in her toilet preparatory to getting supper, but her face did not wear its now usual expression of distaste and weariness. Instead, she really looked bright and happy.

It is true she was not thinking of the deep spiritual things she had read from the little book, nor yet entirely of the young minister's experiences which he had given her, though they had impressed her strongly. She was instead pleasing her own starved love for admiration with thinking that the young man had cared to confide in her, had thought her worthy of such confidences. She recognized that they were unusual confidences, and her own conscience, which was a well-educated one, soon began to trouble her that she had let him suppose her to be better than she was. She went back over the afternoon talk, and while she realized that she had not told any falsehoods, nor indeed done anything or said anything out of keeping with actual truth, still she acknowledged to her own soul with crimsoning cheeks that she had remained silent several times, when, in order to have been perfectly honest, she ought to have spoken out and told him that she was not at all what he thought, that he must go to her sister, or others, whom she had half despised for their very eagerness about such things, if he wanted any help.

And yet, if she had done this, she would have lost the privilege of that talk, and she began to realize that it had been a privilege to her. Nor was it wholly on account of her desire for companionship and pleasure. There was something deeper in her heart, which had been so restless, which said to her, "Here, here is something you have been longing for. This man may show you a way to get it. He is different from what you thought him at first, and perhaps you are a little disappointed that he is, for you fear you cannot have quite so much of what you call 'fun' with him if that is the case; but underneath it all you know you like him better that he is of a higher type than you at first thought him."

What queer conversations people carry on with themselves, and how they analyze their own feelings and think they know themselves, and yet can only read a little piece of their own hearts and know not its follies, nor its goodness either, and then straightway forget what manner of men and women they are and go on committing the very same follies again.

But Maria's cheerfulness lasted while she prepared the evening meal. Rachel coming in and expecting a storm on account of her desertion, was astonished, almost uneasy, and finally felt called upon to explain to her sister how it was she had not come back sooner. But Maria answered pleasantly that she had been listening to an account of the delightful little lesson she had been teaching, and she hoped it was not all thrown away on those poor ignorant children. It was a pity Rachel had not some better material to work upon down here, but it was good of her to be willing to help those poor children, she supposed. Then Maria went out to the refrigerator actually humming a little tune under her breath while she took out the butter for supper.

And Rachel went to the piazza where sat her mother, and said: "Mamma, is Maria sick, do you think? She doesn't seem to act like herself. I wish I had not left her alone this afternoon, but I thought she was asleep."

The mother glanced up anxiously, always full of foreboding for her children, and then remembering, smiled and answered: "No, dear, I fancy she has been having a little glimpse of pleasure, and perhaps it is doing her good. She has had a hard time, poor child, though of course we could not help it."

"Well, mamma," said Rachel, a little careworn wrinkle coming in her smooth brow, "I think she is working too hard, and I wish you and papa would make her stop and go out on the beach and let me take my turn awhile. I know I can't do so well as she, but I will try my best. I don't feel happy having Maria work so hard."

"You dear child!" said the mother, drawing Rachel toward her and smoothing her hand. "I know just how much that means for you to say. You do not like kitchen work one bit, and you have been brave and good at it too, thus far. But it is not necessary for you to do any more than you have been doing. Your father and I have talked over the same thing, and have been worried about your sister's health. We decided last night to have that Higgins girl come over every day. She is not skilled, and will need help and watching, but she will learn; and she is willing to come for very little if I will teach her our ways, she says; so you need not think the expense will be too great. That will set both you and Maria free for most of the time, and I am much relieved."

Maria called her mother just then to ask some question about the supper, and Rachel was left standing in the dying twilight pondering. How wonderful was everything! God was actually going to send the girl whom she had planned to help a little, right into their daily life, and she would have endless opportunity. She closed her eyes and lifted her heart in prayer that she might be shown how to live so that her life would show forth God's glory, and that she might be given power to lead that ignorant girl to Jesus. It was sweet to her to remember the eager little faces that had listened to her lesson that afternoon, and now that she could not think of them without reproaching herself for having left her sister alone, she could not drive them from her mind, but went over and over again their questions and her answers and the way they had been received, her heart leaping within her at the thought of really telling the story of Jesus for the first time to two little human waifs for whom he had died.

Maria saw the minister only a few minutes more that night. The mosquitoes were too merciless for them to linger outside the house or to dare light up the cottage and invite people in, and the minister was not one who would propose a walk. He felt that both their hearts had received a benediction, and that the young woman would sympathize with him in wanting to be alone with God a little while after the Sabbath blessing.

But Maria's conscience had grown decidedly prickly. He had thanked her again as he bade her good-night for the help she had given him, and she felt guilty as she let him go away thinking of her in this way. She felt that her natural honesty would not long allow her to accept quietly this homage to her supposed goodness. She must explain soon, and then good-bye to all friendship with him, for he was evidently much in earnest. He would hardly waste time on such as she had been. Well, what did she care? She could go on as she had done and endure the summer to the end. The man was but a stranger, anyway, and not of her kind. Her restless spirit was returning. She knew nothing of the proposed domestic help. She remembered the morrow and all the petty miserable cares which she had of her own free will taken upon herself. The mosquitoes again began to be a terrible thorn in the flesh, and she saw in imagination the piles of greasy dishes which would have to be washed in the morning, and the struggle with the grocery boy to get him to send the yeast in time for the morrow's baking, with probably the necessity for buying some of the miserable baker's stuff offered under the name of bread which all the family cordially detested.

And then the brother came in with his never-ending flow of fun and capacity for teasing, and choosing the wrong time, proceeded to poke questions at her about Mr. Fairfield. Maria's replies were short and sharp; she said with freezing dignity that she cared nothing whatever for Mr. Fairfield and wished he would keep away; that she supposed he was some nobody, anyway, as no one else would come to such a place for the summer unless he had to. Then she went to her room with tears of vexation in her eyes and thought of the same man's earnest "thank you" spoken a few moments before, remembered her own gentle, subdued good-night, her assent to his words of Christian friendliness, how she had so evidently deceived him as to her character, and felt herself a very hypocrite indeed.

It is no wonder then that the morning found her unrested and unhappy as in the days that had passed. She was even disposed to resent the new arrival in the kitchen instead of being glad and relieved, and after repeated attempts to monopolize the entire work and so show that a girl was a superfluous addition to the family expense, she went grandly to her own room with a sweep of her head, declaring that if they would not let her work she supposed she could sit down and endure life in some way with folded hands. No, she would not go to the beach, and she would not go bathing, and she would not fix up her muslin dress to wear to Spray View that afternoon for she was not going to Spray View to call on those two stuck-up girls. She did not care to be patronized if Rachel did, and as for Roland De Vere, she thought she had been greatly mistaken in him. He did not seem nearly so intellectual as she had at first supposed. Then when Rachel in despair had left her, she had barred the door and burying her face in the pillow had cried as hard as her overwrought nerves demanded.

Fortunately for her, she had not cried long when Rachel's voice called to her again that there was some one in the parlor to see her. This stopped the tears suddenly, but not the stubbornness. She would not go into the parlor to see any one. Rachel might make any excuse she pleased, that she was too busy or sick, but she would not come out, and she would not unfasten the improvised door which the father and brother had contrived for more privacy than the cottage afforded. Nevertheless, she rose from beside the bed and went to the small disfiguring looking-glass. She knew by former experience that the few moments crying in which she had indulged must have left its marks already on her face. Yes, her eyes and nose were red and swollen. She could not go out if she wished to do so, without disgracing herself. She began to wonder who it could be who wished to see her; perhaps some of those De Veres, now become hateful, because she fancied they were looking down upon her and hers; perhaps, the minister. Well, if it was the minister, what did she care? she asked herself fiercely and she went nervously to the wash bowl and began to dash the cold water on her swollen eyes.

Then at the other door came the mother's voice, always low and sweet, but very low now lest the caller in the parlor of this very "open" house should hear. There was also a note of command in the voice which Mrs. Hammond seldom used toward her children, but which Maria did not dare disregard.

"My daughter, let me in at once. I have something to tell you."

Maria with the wet towel in her hand answered her mother's summons then, and quickly let her in, mopping her face violently the while:

"Are you ill, daughter?" asked the anxious mother as she saw the traces of excited tears on her elder daughter's face.

"No," answered Maria, choking suddenly at the tenderness in her mother's voice; she almost wished she were really ill and lying in bed to be petted and taken care of. It made the tears start again to her eyes.

The mother wound her arm about the daughter's waist.

"Well, then, dear, is there any reason why you do not care to see Mr. Fairfield? Tell me all about it. I must know the reason, you know, before I can excuse you."

"Is it Mr. Fairfield?" asked Maria, a little gleam of satisfaction showing in her voice in spite of herself. "But you see, mother, I can't go out. Look at my eyes. I am a perfect sight. It will be hours before I get over being a fright. You will have to tell him something." There was disappointment in Maria's voice, very evident to the mother, and she determined that she would make a strenuous effort to get Maria out of herself, and into the fresh air, where her overwrought nerves might have a little chance for rest.

"Nonsense! Your eyes will be all right in a few minutes, dear!" she answered quickly. "Bathe them and brush your hair. Here, slip on your pretty beach dress. You have not worn it since you came and the air is quite fresh this morning. I want you to get out and have the air and sunshine. You will be ill if you do not, and that we are not going to allow. Now hurry, dear, Mr. Fairfield is quite anxious to see you. I will excuse you for a few minutes, and Rachel shall take him down to the new clam beds while you are getting ready. Now hurry," and the mother hastened out to do what she had promised with more confidence in her manner than she felt in her heart that Maria would do her bidding.

But something seemed to have come over Maria. She desired suddenly above all things to go out with her pretty beach dress, walk beside Mr. Fairfield, have him think her good for a little while, and say she helped him. It would not do any harm just for once and she was tired of the hateful way things had been going. She washed her face feverishly and furiously and hastened her toilet as much as possible and between times took hurried trips to the disfiguring little glass to see if there was any hope of her eyes and nose soon assuming their proper color and shape, and the mother, coming back, was relieved to find that Maria was ready.

And so it came about that Maria and the young minister started out on a tramp to the life-saving station, two miles away, on that lovely summer morning, with a fresh breeze blowing in their faces, and Maria looking her very prettiest in her dark blue and white yachting suit, her cheeks becomingly pink from the recent tears, and her whole face as expressive of sudden happiness as could well be, for when Maria gave way after a fit of stubbornness she was often really lovely and subdued and humble, and somehow her mother's tones and wistfulness had conquered her that morning.

Moreover, she felt humiliated in her heart and the

humility sat well upon her face, where there had been so much haughty pride of late. The minister, looking at her in this Monday morning light decided that she was very fair as well as good, and he was glad to walk with her and talk beside the sea, and before the morning was over they had found many points of interest in common. Maria coming back did not feel half so much a hypocrite that she had not confessed to him how unworthy she was of his praise, because the talk had not been on things in which she felt she was lacking. The Lord in his wisdom saw that this child of his needed a little of the brightness and joy of life and he had given it to her, weaving, as he gave it, about her the cords of his own love which were to draw her to himself. Let no skeptical one fancy all this beneath him. We barter away the whole comfort of life if we so think. For these things, and things like them, are among the "all these" the Master promised should be added to those seeking first the Father's kingdom.

13

THE afternoon was warm and lovely. It was several days since Maria and Mr. Fairfield had walked to the life-saving station together, and since then there had been several like expeditions. Maria lay in the screened and netted hammock on the porch with a book before her, but she was not reading. Instead, she was thinking. Her troubled conscience had pursued her day after day through all the pleasant walks and sails and rides and talks. She felt herself to be more and more a hypocrite. She had tried feebly, two or three times, to explain to the minister that she was not "good" as he seemed to think, in fact that she was very wicked and worldly and unlovely in her character; but her efforts had failed, for it had been so pleasant to have some one think well of her, and make her a part of his pleasure as this man had done.

This afternoon her conscience had arraigned her most strongly. Something ought to be done. She must not go on reading religious books and pretending to be devoted to them, though the fact was growing plain to her that the books themselves were not so wholly without interest as they had seemed to her last Sabbath. She had learned that there was much that was intensely interesting in them, and she liked to hear the minister talk of these things. Her own part in these conversations had been a meek assent to what he said, but still she had managed to assent in such a manner as to keep unchanged his first impression that she was heart and soul with him in what he said. She had even added a word or two now and then when he had seemed to expect her to say something, and when something quite original had occurred to her which seemed to fit into the discussion. He thought her an exceedingly bright young woman, and so she was; those little additions of hers to the religious conversation had been apt and striking ones. She knew that her bringing-up had been largely the cause of her ability to say such things well, and to know when to say them.

But she also knew that her life for some time had run counter to her words and she hated hypocrisy above all things. She had planned conversation after conversation in which she should tell her new friend exactly the truth about herself. In some of these imaginings she was humble and begged him to teach her to think as he did. But for that she was too proud. In others she withdrew from his acquaintance entirely, told him she was not of his kind and that he had been mistaken in her. And then it occurred to her, "Why not turn about and try to be what he thought she was?" She had reached that point this afternoon for the seventeenth time, and she had asked herself over and over again whether she could do it and how she should begin, and whether if she did, it would be exactly honest in her to do so? And then, why, after all, should she do it? Mr. Fairfield was a pleasant acquaintance, but in all probability he would go away in a few days and she might never see him again. Why did she care to try to appear well before him, and not only to appear well, but to really be what she appeared? She could not understand why he seemed to bring out the best and highest longings her soul contained.

Well, supposing she should set herself the task of being good, what should she do first? She might refrain from being cross, it is true, and saying sarcastic things; but that seemed rather a hopeless task, for her tongue was so used to bitter words that she scarcely knew when she spoke them. Then too, there was nothing interesting in that. Still of course that would come in as a necessary part of any such change in her life. She might take up some philanthropic work. But what could it be? Rachel seemed to always be able to find some work to do for others, but now that there was help in the kitchen Maria felt that her life had been made too easy for her to show forth her good works by any great sacrifices such as she was seeking.

It was just at this point in her conversation with herself that her sister came upon the porch with low rocking-chair, work-basket, scissors, and thimble, and in the distance across the sandy dunes could be seen the lank, awkward form—arrayed in a neat blue calico and white apron—of their new serving-maid, bearing in her arms a bundle of old hats, apparently. Her work was done for the afternoon and Rachel's first lesson, instead of being in lace work, was to be in millinery, for it appeared that Annie Higgins' greatest desire in the line of worldly possessions was a nice hat to wear to an entertainment that evening over on the mainland, to which her cousin's wife's brother had asked her to accompany him in his sailing vessel, along with some other members of the family. Rachel, through tact and kindness, had discovered this need and desire of Annie's and had readily offered her assistance, sighing as she thought how much better hat Annie might have if only Maria were to make it instead of herself; but she quietly kept the matter to herself, as she supposed, dreading Maria's scornful looks and words which would be sure to come if she knew.

She had reckoned, however, without remembering the cracks in the kitchen wall. Maria had heard the entire arrangement that morning as she sat in her room mending a rent in her blue dress, and had thought to herself, how easy it seemed to be to Rachel to find out and do such things for other people. Had Rachel been there and known that she heard it, Maria would have felt called upon to show her scorn of such a proceeding, but away from sight Maria was able to appreciate something of her sister's kindness, although she wholly disapproved, and wished she would not do such queer things. Now as she saw Rachel come out and Annie also issue forth from the little unpainted house across the marsh she remembered, and half wished she were gifted with doing things for other people so that she might not feel so utterly unworthy of the friendship of a good and earnest Christian minister. She languidly watched Rachel as she put on her little white work apron and selected the needle with which she expected to work. She knew that to Rachel the task of making a hat was a great one. Rachel would much rather write a description of the hat, or draw a picture of it, than go through the necessary manipulations in order to produce one. It was not likely to be an artistic affair when done, either, as both the sisters well knew from former experience. However, Rachel would do her best, hoping for the best results.

Just at that moment around the corner by the little church came two beautiful horses drawing an elegant carriage in which sat Roland De Vere and his two sisters. The two sisters were on the back seat and the front seat beside the young man who was driving was evidently left vacant for some one they expected to pick up. The carriage drew up at the little green cottage doorsteps and its occupants greeted Rachel effusively. Maria was glad that she was well screened from their view, for somehow she felt as utterly out of sympathy with them as she did with herself or anybody else, though several months before her heart would have jumped with joy at their appearance and she would have done anything to be the fourth member of that riding party. Now she knew that they had come for Rachel, and she saw by the sudden rush of glad color to her little sister's cheek that Rachel knew and was glad, gladder perhaps than they had any idea of, for Rachel was always so quiet about her likes and dislikes that sometimes she was in danger of being allowed to lose much that she cared for in life through other people supposing that she did not care. Maria's eyes were opened a little by the look on her sister's face as she quietly laid aside her basket and went down the steps to greet her callers and ask them to come in. Maria was glad that they immediately declined, for she could not get away unobserved and she did not wish to be seen; but she could not well help listening to the conversation.

Roland De Vere, in his gallant and courtly way, invited Rachel to put on her hat and get into the carriage at once, as they were off for a long drive up the beach and must have her company else their pleasure would be spoiled. Maria saw, through the cracks in the porch screen, how the soft color stole again into Rachel's cheeks and then how her bright face clouded over with disappointment.

"Oh, I'm so sorry I can't go," she answered instantly; "I would love it so, and it is such a perfect day for a drive on the beach. I have often thought how delightful it would be to fly along on the edge of the waves with horses like those. But I can't, I really can't."

"Now we won't have any 'can't' at all. What is it in the way?" asked the young man earnestly; "because whatever stumbling-block there is, I shall remove it. Have you been a naughty girl and won't they let you get up out of your chair till you're good, or are you mending and can't leave your task till it's finished? If that's it, give me a needle, and I'll help and we'll have the work done in less than no time."

Amid the laugh which followed Rachel's perplexed face grew firm.

"No, it isn't anything like that," she answered, laughing, and yet sorry and troubled. "It's the Higgins girl."

"The Higgins girl! What has she to do with it, and who is she? Bring her along, that'll be all right; we can stow her in somewhere and make her comfortable, I guess. Fannie, can't you and Evelyn make room back there?"

But Rachel hastened to explain, with an irrepressible smile at the idea.

"No, no, it's her hat. I promised to help her make a hat to wear to an entertainment to-night. She is the fisherman's daughter who lives over in that little house, and she wants to go to an entertainment with a friend to-night. I have promised her and she seems very happy over it, so I must not disappoint her."

Mr. De Vere emitted a prolonged whistle and the Misses Fannie and Evelyn looked curiously at Rachel, making Maria's blood boil within her.

"Dear me!" said Evelyn, shrugging her shoulders, "can't you put her off?"

"Yes," put in Fannie seeing her brother's evident disappointment and Rachel's firmly-set red lips, "tell her it is a great deal more smart to go bareheaded to entertainments this time of year and wear a flower in her hair."

These girls were well-bred and liked Rachel very much, and moreover desired to please their brother, but they were not quite equal to giving up an afternoon's pleasure for the sake of making a hat for a fisherman's daughter, it was evident. Rachel felt this more than saw it. Meanwhile she also felt that she had the brother's sympathy in her perplexity.

Maria, listening, saw it all and suddenly resolved. This was her opportunity. Without her usual calm deliberation, she acted impulsively, almost as Rachel might have done. She called her sister's name.

"Rachel!"

Poor Rachel! No small part of her perplexity, embarrassment, and trouble had arisen from the fact that Maria was listening on the porch, unable to get away, and that she would let fall all sorts of sneering comments upon her, ruthlessly, as soon as the visitors should be out of sight. But she had not supposed that Maria would dare speak at the moment bringing out the fact of her presence, for she knew Maria's hair was tumbled with lying in the hammock, and Maria's gown was not the one in which she would array herself to appear before the De Veres. With cheeks crimsoning and eyes burning with tears she was too proud to let be seen, she excused herself a moment and went to her sister, trembling as if she had been a little child lest Maria was about to reprimand her severely in the hearing of these friends, as she had once or twice threatened she would do if Rachel persisted in her puritanical notions.

But to her utter amazement, instead of the proud, scornful look she expected to see upon Maria's face there was one of interest, and Maria's tone was low and sisterly as she said: "Rachel, go! I will trim Annie's hat. Yes, go on at once; it's all right. You know I can do it as well as you. Get ready right away."

Rachel could hardly believe her ears. Maria offering to trim a servant girl's hat! Maria giving up her ease, without being urged, to do a work of kindliness for one she despised!

But the friends in the carriage were waiting and Maria was hastening her. She must go and explain. She hesitated but a moment. She saw her sister meant it, and would be displeased if she did not accept it, so she went back to the carriage with a happy face and explained that Maria would see to the hat and then ran in to make her hasty, simple preparations and soon drove away with a bright face. Roland De Vere as he touched his whip to his gay horses said to himself: "I must have been mistaken in Maria after all. I would not have expected her to do so kind a deed."

It seemed that Maria was fated to give false impressions of her goodness nowadays, in spite of herself and of her honest endeavor to right matters with her conscience. As soon as the carriage was out of sight she went in to the kitchen to the solemn-faced girl, who had slipped around to the back door with her pile of old hats and soiled ribbons and funny bright artificial flowers, watching the expected helper drive away in the beautiful carriage with growing dismay gripping her heart, the thought of her own expected pleasure dimmed by the shade of the old worn-out hat.

She was only a poor girl after all, and of course Miss Rachel wouldn't stop for her when she had pleasure of her own on hand! Then she sighed and told herself Miss Rachel was no better than other folks after all, if she did teach the children a whole lot of religion last Sunday. Christian folks were all alike. She had been almost tempted to believe Miss Rachel was different, but now she would never believe in anybody again who had pretty clothes and lots of friends and pleasures. Then she had sat down disconsolately in the back door and looked off at the sea, and felt gloomy, and thought of the long dull winter which would come so soon.

Maria explained how it was that Rachel had gone, and said pleasantly that she would do the work, inviting Annie at once to bring her materials that they might look them over; but Annie had not formed so charming an idea of Maria's character as yet that she did not feel a trifle afraid of her, so she only sat still and said she needn't bother, it didn't matter, anyhow. Maria found that her services, which she knew were so much better than her sister's in this particular line, and which she had expected would be accepted with overwhelming joy, had actually to be urged upon this poor fisherman's daughter. It made her indignant and she told herself that she wouldn't touch the hat if she had not promised Rachel, that the girl deserved no hat at all.

However a promise was a promise, and so she set herself to win Annie out of her glumness and soon had her interested in the hat. And while Annie heated irons, according to her direction, for steaming velvet, she hunted among her own ribbons and flowers for something suitable to help out the meagre array of trimming, and she pondered within herself why she had done this. Was it for Rachel, or for the minister, or for her own conscience' sake?

14

THE PORCH was the only comfortable place in which to work that warm afternoon, so after a brief struggle with her pride, Maria transported Annie and her trimmings to a place behind the screen. It was true there was a possibility of some neighbors passing, or of the return of the driving party, or that the minister might come by before she had completed her task. But for the neighbors she cared little, and her feeling toward those De Vere sisters was such that she would rather enjoy shocking them, and, as for the minister, well, she was not sure but she had done this for him, and if he did not understand, her work would have been in vain.

She settled down determined to make a pretty hat and be friendly with this uninteresting girl if she could. She was determined for once to try her hand at philanthropy. On the whole, after the first half-hour she found it not so uninteresting. Trimming hats was always pleasant work to her. She enjoyed thoroughly making "a whistle out of a pig's tail," figuratively speaking, and to make this old hat into something respectable, nay even into a work of art, was as good as playing a new game. She really liked it when once she got into it.

Annie was kept so busy steaming velvet for the first few minutes that she had no time to talk, for which she was thankful, for she felt half resentful at Maria for touching her hat. She had had no reason as yet to like Maria, and would almost rather have done without a hat than take a favor from her. She felt as though she were being patronized. But when she at last emerged from the kitchen with the carefully brushed and steamed velvet and saw the hat which had looked such a hopeless, shapeless mass to her but a few moments before, assuming under the skillful hands of the manipulator the shape of hats she had seen in the stores and on the heads of the ladies of fashion in the hotels, her heart gave a great bound of joy and her allegiance forthwith went out to Maria even more warmly than it had done to Rachel. Such is the vanity of all flesh. Shall we say feminine flesh? To watch those white fingers tastefully twist the renewed velvet folds about the now gracefully shaped straw, was a wonder. Annie sat and gazed in speechless delight, proving herself a sharp and foreseeing helper, because of the quick, alert way in which she always seemed to anticipate the needs of the milliner, handing her a pin or the spool of thread at just the right moment, and restoring the scissors when they slipped to the floor, as scissors have a habit of doing. Maria could but notice and appreciate this, and felt an impulse to speak a kind word, but could think of nothing except about the hat.

"I think it will look very well when it is done," she said at last, holding the hat off to survey it, and feeling that this admiring silence was becoming oppressive.

"It's jes' perfec'ly lovely!" exclaimed Annie effusively, her eyes shining with the delight of possessing anything so altogether satisfying. "I jes' don't see how you can do it so good! Don't you feel awful proud to be able to? How did you learn how? Did you ever work at a milliner's store?"

Maria's cheek flushed. She did not like this question. She felt inclined to be indignant and take the girl's words for an insult. The idea of her working in a milliner's shop! This came of their hiring such a ridiculously cheap cottage and making even the poor fisher folk think they were from the common walks of life. Then she glanced up and seeing the evident admiration in Annie's face, reflected that the girl had lived on the island much of her life and knew little of the different strata in society. Of course she had no intention of insulting her. Indeed, she perceived from the girl's face when she answered no, that she would have stood a trifle higher in her estimation as a skilled artisan if she could have boasted that advantage. So she let the little discomfiture pass, a fact which almost surprised herself and would have astounded her family beyond measure; she even smiled at the queer questions which followed, getting a little quiet amusement out of them.

"Your sister Rachel says you know how to do most everything," went on Annie, clasping her hands about one knee and rocking back and forth on the broad low step on which she was seated. "She said you could paint pictures. Say, did you ever do any of them crayon pictures of live folks? What they hang in best parlors, I mean, that look just like the folks, only all dressed up better than they gen'ally are when they're alive? They have two of them over to my friend's on the mainland. They've got red plush and gold frames, awful pretty, and they hang over the organ and the sofa. It's of her ma and pa when they was first married. I'd like awful well to get one of my oldest brother, that died when he was ten, for ma. She hasn't never forgot to mourn about him. Jes' seems if none o' us could take his place. Do you s'pose you could do one if I was to tell you how he looked? You see he never had no photograph taken, cause they didn't even have a tin-type place here when we come here to live, nor in Spray View either. Could you do one o' them kind o' pictures, do you think? If you could I'd work all summer jes' fer nothin' to get that picture, fer it would please ma and pa so; and I know where I could get a real pretty frame made cheap; a friend of mine is in a store where they make 'em."

Annie's eagerness quite overcame the milliner. She tried to repress the smile that would keep coming and to explain that no one would be able to make a likeness of a person who was dead, without some kind of a photograph to go by, especially one who had not known the person in life. Annie looked disappointed. She had gone from one extreme to the other and felt that a person capable of transforming her old hat could do anything. She was silent a few minutes watching the deft fingers at work, and then she began again.

"Your sister says you made them couches and pretty stuffings and curtains in your parlor. I think you must be awfully smart. You're sort of a 'Jack at all trades' as the sayin' is, aren't you?" She laughed heartily over this intended joke, and Maria could not refrain from joining in. Maria coupled with her powers of elocution a rare ability as a mimic of the tones and manners. She began to think she would have rich material in this girl for quite an amusing entertainment of her friends if she should choose to give it to them.

Annie, in a wistful sort of way, finally asked: "Say! if I was to get some caliker, would you kind o' pin it up fer me like that there green stuff hangin' in your dinin'-room door? I'd like awful well to fix up our front room a little. I hate it the way 'tis. I never knew how to do them kind of things, but I always knew it looked horrid. I tried once or twice. I sent all the way to New York for a motto I saw advertised in a paper I had. It was "Little Church around the Corner." That was just the year they built the chapel there and I thought it would look kind of nice to have that motto in the parlor. It said it had the directions how to make it, and the stuff an' all fer twenty-five cents, so I got it an' it took me a good part of the winter workin' evenin's to finish it. I done it in blue with green trimmin's and a brown steeple, them was the colors they sent, and it looked real pretty and I stuck some shells on pasteboard and made a frame for it, but I ain't never had anything else to go with it. I would jes' give anything if we had a organ. It would look so nice under where it hangs, an' Jim and the girls would all like the music so much. I guess they could play it too after tryin' a little, for Jim can play the accordion real good. He plays 'Swanee River,' and 'Home Sweet Home,' and 'Sweet By an' By' every Sunday night when he don't have to go down the bay. Say! How did you get them cushions in that corner to stand out so pretty with them ruffles all around? Do you s'pose I could fix up our house a little like this if I tried real hard?"

Maria could not help being interested in the poor, forlorn little house and this girl's helpless, hopeless attempt to "fix it up." She began to suggest some simple things which seemed to Annie quite too simple to make any effect, but as Maria went on and grew interested herself in describing the changes she should make in a bare room if she had but limited means, Annie's eyes began to sparkle and her cheeks to grow red with eagerness. She really saw ahead of her some chance that their home might have a few bright, cheerful things some day as well as others.

"Why, I could do that," she said, as Maria paused with

a pin in her mouth to try the effect of the ribbon she was arranging on the hat. "Jim, he could saw the boards. I know he wouldn't mind helping. He has lots o' time Sundays."

Maria's strict training as to the Sabbath as a day of rest made her feel a little doubtful of the good she might be doing if she were but starting a family to work on the Lord's Day, but Annie's eager tongue went on, leaving her little time for reflection.

"Say! would you mind coming over some day soon and jes' lookin' at that room an' tellin' me where you thought that shelf you said how to make, would look pretty, and how far down the side of the wall the seat had ought to reach? It ain't very far over there, you know, an' I could show you some cunnin' little chickens and ducks if you'd come."

Maria began to see that her philanthropy was expected to last beyond this one afternoon, and she was doubtful whether she relished the idea. She had been willing enough to make a hat, but as for enduring much of this cross-questioning, and being taken on such a friendly social level, she did not have any such intentions. She already felt herself swelling in her own estimation until she almost came up to the minister's ideal. Surely she must be pretty good, after all, to smilingly undergo such a storm of talk as she had been sitting under for the last hour.

But worse was to follow. She did not like to refuse the girl's eager request, so she said perhaps she would come some time, in what she meant to be an indefinite time, but the eager Annie accepted it all in good faith and began to thank her in most intense terms. Suddenly she turned full upon her. "Say!" said she earnestly. "You're one of them church folks too, ain't you? I didn't think you was at first, because you didn't go so much to the chapel, nor seem to run around talking Bible like your sister, but I knew quick as I saw you at that hat so nice an' good that you was. I never thought much of them church folks till lately. Pa he thinks they're all frauds, 'cause some of 'em have treated him mean; but then folks ain't all alike, an' I always used to say that folks that is mean will be mean even if they are church folks, an' the church can't make 'em any worse, only it looks worse, them pretendin' so much; but when that there minister come along and was so awful nice about our boat an' all,—I s'pose he told you how it was,—why I jus' made up my mind it wasn't the church that made 'em all so mean, 'cause he bein' a minister an' a kind o' head of it all, he would be meaner than the hull lot of 'em if 'twas the church made 'em so, an' I began to tell pa that he must uv made some mistake. Well, he did allow that if that young feller should run the chapel awhile he would go an' hear him preach himself. He's awful nice, ain't he? Say! ain't you an' he goin' to marry? Folks says you are. I heard it over to Spray View. It's awful nice you like the church an' are so good if you're a-goin' to marry a minister!"

Before Maria could lift her flaming face, or steady her voice to reply to this remarkable series of questions and remarks, she heard a step on the single board which formed a walk over the sand in front of their cottage, and looking up, annoyed beyond measure, to see who was coming and perhaps overheard the last remarks, she saw Mr. Fairfield standing before her. His face was a study, to say the least, perhaps a trifle too grave; but it was evident that the gravity was put on to hide a twinkle which Maria felt must be in his eye. It was impossible to tell how much he had overheard. He betrayed no sign whatever of anything having been overheard at all, but the irrepressible Annie arose from her step in confusion, adding to Maria's consternation.

"Goodness gracious me! If here he ain't now! 'Talk of angels an' you hears their wings,' as the sayin' is." And she disappeared most unceremoniously into the cottage and began rattling the cook stove to hide her embarrassment.

15

THE minister sat down on the step vacated by Annie. His acquaintance in the Hammond cottage had progressed so far that he felt sufficiently at home to be seated without an invitation from the young hostess, who was evidently too perturbed to think of offering him any seat less lowly. He looked her over with a new and curious expression upon his face. She was appearing to him in a light in which he had not as yet considered her. Her blushes were certainly becoming. He rather enjoyed her embarrassment. He was quiet for a moment, not caring to interrupt his study of her face. She meanwhile was earnestly engaged in struggling with her thread, which had snarled in the most unaccountable way just as she was taking the final stitch in the completed hat. Her cheeks instead of cooling down grew fairly purple, and her horror and indignation over what that impertinent girl had dared to say to her grew with every minute, as she realized how much the man before her might, yes, must, have heard.

"What are you supposed to be doing?" at last questioned Mr. Fairfield, with an amused expression upon his face.

At the first sound of his voice the spell which had been cast upon Maria's tongue seemed to be broken. She ignored his question. Indeed, she did not know a word he had said:

"Mr. Fairfield," she burst out impetuously, "I do hope you will not believe from the last words that impertinent girl said that *I* have been discussing *you* and your affairs with *her!*" She emphasized each pronoun a little more till the final one was intense and well expressed the scorn she felt.

"And if you had, am I to understand that my humble self would have been a subject so far beneath your notice that you should speak of me in that tone?"

Howard Fairfield's tone was light and cheerful. It was more the tone in which he used to speak to his young associates ten years before when he was just entering college, and before the grave things of life had as yet reached him. Something in this afternoon's occurrence had seemed to put him back again for a little and make him feel young and full of mischief. Besides, he was one of those rare beings who possess wonderful tact, and he saw that Maria was extremely embarrassed and could only hope to regain her composure through being able to laugh it off. He proved himself correct in this conclusion, for his tone, so different from the grave, earnest one he had been accustomed to use in their intercourse, roused Maria from her painfully overwrought feelings to look up and wonder, and even laugh. She essayed to make him understand once more that she had not been discussing him, but had been treated to a catalogue of his virtues,—something connected with a boat,—and she suddenly remembered to her relief that Annie had suggested that he might have told her the story, therefore she at once asked an explanation. Although the young man was evidently annoyed that a mere act of kindness on his part should have been so brought out that he was obliged to tell of it himself, he saw that it would help Maria to regain her composure if he did, and so in a few words he told her how he had helped the father with a bit of advice and a trifle of a loan of money when their fishing boat, their largest source of revenue, had been in danger of being confiscated for a small debt. Had Maria been less upset in her mind she might have read much between the lines which was to the young man's credit, for she must have seen how little he made of the affair and how lightly he told of it. And then he launched into an account of a walk he had taken that afternoon and a most beautiful spot he had discovered, and made Maria forget her discomfiture entirely in the charming powers of description which he exerted for her benefit.

Suddenly he asked, "And what have you been doing all the afternoon? What is that creation you are holding? It looks as if it might be pretty, and certainly is marvelous in its construction. Are you preparing to leave this desert island, and fly back to civilization, and is that a part of your plumage?"

Maria had to laugh again, although the color mounted in her cheeks as she looked at the hat, now grown contemptible in her eyes, and wished she had never seen it nor ever might again—realizing that it had been the cause of her discomfort. It came to her at the same time that she had made an utter failure of trying to do good, and she made a resolve to be honest with herself and him and everybody else and not let people think her better than she was. She would show everybody just how mean and contemptible she was. Then at least she would be no longer tormented by her conscience, whatever other unpleasantnesses she might have to endure.

"No," she answered half laughing, half troubled, "it represents a vain attempt on my part to right myself in the eyes of the world and be honest. I have been trying to be 'good' and do unto others—well—as they would have me do to them, at least, if I did not do as I would have them do to me. But I think I will give it up. I am not constructed on those lines, I see, and seem to have made a failure in every way. And, indeed, Mr. Fairfield, I have been rarely punished for my attempt to deceive others and myself."

"I don't understand," said the minister comically, puzzled and reaching out his hand for the hat. "It seems to be all right as far as I can judge, though I own I'm not a judge of millinery; but I was told that a hat to be all right must have so much straw, so much ribbon, so much velvet, and so many flowers or feathers, put together in the right proportions. You seem to have all those things. Isn't it becoming? Is that the matter?"

Now Mr. Fairfield had seen at once that there was behind Maria's half-laughing, troubled face something deeper, something which he felt he would like to know. Their intercourse together had been of the sort which draws human hearts to sympathize with one another. He saw she needed help, or thought she did, and as he felt she had helped him, he wished to help her. But he would find out what she meant from her own lips, he would not ask her questions, for he judged from his own nature that that method might only serve to shut the truth from him forever, so he continued his bantering tone.

But although Maria laughed, her face sobered suddenly.

"The hat isn't mine," she answered him quickly. "I am supposed to be doing it for the love of doing good to others. It is for Annie Higgins. It is some of my sister's philanthropy. I never originated any, not to carry it out, in my whole life. Ray had promised to trim this hat so that girl could go to some sort of a picnic to-night, and then her friends came for her to take a drive, and I acted on a sudden impulse and offered to do it for her. I think the real reason I offered to do it was to see if I could just for once be as good as you have persisted in telling me I am. But I'm not. I want to tell you the truth. I can't be miserable any longer at being thought to be good, and helpful, and all that, when I don't know nor care the first thing about it. I let you misunderstand me in the first place and then it went on, and I began to see it was all just as bad as if I had started out to act a lie. I have not had the usual experience of the rich reward of doing good that you find in the Sunday-school books. I may have succeeded in making a respectable looking hat, but I have had a most uncomfortable afternoon, in addition to having been almost insulted by questions and an intimacy which is exceedingly disagreeable thrust upon me, and which I can foresee will cause me endless embarrassments. Now you can see just how much of a fraud I have been. Of course it does not matter to you, for there are other people in the world who are really what you thought I was and can talk with you on these subjects you enjoy and be honest, but I cannot rest comfortably to have any one think me what I am not."

Maria had tumbled these words out one on top of another, scarcely realizing what she was saying, only being anxious to get the horrid explanation over and have the visitor go, so that she might escape to her room and cry as she had never cried before. The tears were already coming to her eyes and as she raised her face to make her meaning more impressive Mr. Fairfield saw them. He became aware also at that moment of what neither of them had noticed before, that the carriage containing the De Veres and her sister Rachel was just driving up to the door. His heart went out to the overwrought girl before him with sympathy and something deeper—a longing to help which he could not understand. His ready tact stood him in good stead now. He arose with a graceful bow and came forward to the carriage and shaking hands with the young ladies and saying a bright word to his friend Mr. De Vere, thus gave Maria time for recovery before she came forward. He spoke of the charming day and how delightful the drive must have been, and said in a loud cheery tone that he had just dropped in to see if Miss Hammond would not like to walk to the pavilion and watch the double sunset on bay and ocean for a few minutes, that there was to be something rare that evening. Then he half turned toward Maria, and said in an aside:

"Are you nearly ready to go, Miss Hammond? I am afraid that we shall miss the best of it unless we hurry. Just get your hat and let us go without waiting longer, can't you?" and he turned again to the carriage to help Rachel out.

It was a venture almost doubtful in his mind, for he felt one could scarcely tell what Maria in such a mood might or might not do, but he was relieved to see that she took his words as a cover for a hasty retreat into the cottage, ostensibly to get her hat, and he hoped she would there get her equilibrium as well, at least enough to come out and meet and pass the De Veres and go with him to some secluded spot where they two could understand each other and where he might if possible help this young woman who had seemed before so strong in faith and without need of help.

When Maria reached her room and the tears came tumbling down with more prepared to follow, she was tempted, nay she was almost determined, not to go out of that room that night, but to give herself utterly over to misery. And yet, so queer a thing is human nature, she wanted to go out and walk with the minister to the beach and see what he would say to her—for she knew that he had some intention in his kind and strangely given invitation—more than she wanted anything in life. And so without the least delay she dashed the refreshing cold water over her flushed face, smoothed her hair, and seizing her hat made haste out to the piazza, relieved to find that the ordeal of speaking to the visitors was made a short one by the evident haste of her companion to get away and see the sunset.

And the walk to the beach was a brisk one in which the minister talked incessantly, letting Maria have no chance for even a word, pointing out a cloud over the bay, or the etching of a lonely deserted fisher's hut in the distance, against a sea of pink and gold off at the right. He even joked about the shape of some of the cottages, and indulged in a humorous remark or two on some of the inhabitants of the small town, not in any malicious way, only a little laugh, just to keep Maria from thinking of herself or what she had said, or what she meant to say. He was scarcely aware of what he was saying as he strode along. His one aim was to talk. And so he guided her to a quiet knoll a little way up the beach, too far to be disturbed by loiterers at this late hour. He even talked on while he arranged a seat for her in the sand, with two pillows and a shawl which he had not forgotten to take from the hammock on the porch, and he made her sit down in the purple and golden light which hung between the glittering bay and the opal-tinted sea. Then he stopped a moment and turning to her with a quiet smile, as a reminder that their friendship was deeper than the talk of the afternoon had been, said:

"And now, will you explain just what you wanted me to understand by what you said a few minutes ago? I think you are troubled in some way, and I couldn't get quite at it. You surely did not mind my hearing those foolish things that poor girl said. It was something deeper. May I understand?" His tone was gentleness itself, a tone Maria had never heard him use before except once; and that to a little frightened child they had passed one day running in terror from the incoming waves. She felt as if she were a little child adrift and now that he had found her, somehow she would be brought ashore. She dropped her eyes to the sand and tried to tell just what was in her heart.

"I mean that I am not 'good.' I am not like Rachel, or like you, or anybody that *loves* good things. When I first knew you, I did not feel that I was so different. You seemed to enjoy fun and I did not think you cared very much for grave, solemn things. But when you came back and were in some way changed, I was quite surprised. I understood the difference after you honored me by telling me of your strange experience. You were good before, I think, only I had not seen that side of your nature brought out yet. You took me for better than I was because, when we first met, I had my sister's Bible and a religious book which Mr. De Vere had sent her, lying beside me on the sand. I saw you thought more highly of me because they were there, and it pleases me always to please those with whom I am thrown. You asked me to read, and I like to read. I am afraid I am proud of my reading too, and it was mere selfish pride that made me read that book well, for I had scoffed at it a few minutes before, having taken it for a novel at first and thinking I would enjoy reading it. I let you think that I had been reading and enjoying it before you came. Then you told me all those wonderful things about yourself, and I felt ashamed to think I had let you do so, for I knew I was not worthy of so grave a confidence. Well, there isn't any more to say only that I have let you go on from day to day supposing that I was interested in religious things more than in anything else, just because I was lonely and it was pleasant to have an intellectual person to talk with who could make anything, even religion, interesting. I have been ashamed of it every day, but I did not know how to get out of it, and there seemed to be a sort of a spell upon me when I was with you which prevented my showing you my real character. I have tried once or twice to see how it would seem to really act out what you thought I was, but I don't succeed. I'm nothing but a frivolous creature who loves a good time and her own way. I feel very much relieved that at last I have mustered up courage to tell you the truth; but I would like to thank you for the very pleasant hours we have had together before we part, for I feel sure that they *have* helped me, and you have been very good to spend so much time in making it pleasant for me." All this in a torrent of words as though it had been one long sentence.

She started to rise, as if she were ready now to bid him farewell and go, but he detained her.

"Please sit still," he said quietly. "I want to ask you just a few things. In the first place, you surely do not suppose that because of what you have said that you and I are going to be any the less friends than before? Friendship cannot be cut in two by a few words and a farewell. You have come into my life, and have helped me, in spite of all you say, and if you have felt as you say you have there is all the more reason that I should try to help you if I can. Will you tell me one thing, Miss Hammond? Do you mean by all this that you do not love the Master?"

It is very strange how hard a simple little question is to answer sometimes. Maria had heard and read that question so many times, and in her childhood had answered it glibly and carelessly, taking it as a matter of course that she did. Now her eyelids and voice trembled and she hesitated long before the earnest question. At last she said:

"I'm afraid I don't," in a very low voice, almost inaudible above the sound of the waves.

"And do you mean you do not *want* to love him?" went on the quiet voice.

This time the hesitation was longer than before. Maria was questioning her own heart carefully, and shuddering at the thought of answering it in the affirmative. Very slowly came the words, by and by:

"No, I do not mean that."

"Thank God for that!" said the listener under his breath, and Maria looked up to see a light in the minister's face which awed her into silence and made her drop her eyes again and wait for him to speak.

One step further the minister dared to go as he breathed a prayer for guidance, so much concerned was he about this young friend, who suddenly seemed in his sight one very precious to his Master.

"Wouldn't you *like* to belong to him, to rest in him, just as we have talked about so many times? I cannot think that all we have said together has been utterly without interest to you. Do you not care in the very slightest to be his dear child?"

And Maria answered in an unsteady voice and humbly, "Yes, I *care*. I believe I care about that more than anything else on earth. I didn't know quite what it was before, but that is what I want. But, oh, I cannot get it. It doesn't belong to me," and the cry of her soul reached out to her Father in heaven, as she seemed to be groping in the darkness for his hand.

16

THE sunset flashed and faded unnoticed. The twilight crept softly over the ocean and stole up the sands; the young moon looked out and began to climb the sky; and still they sat and talked.

What they said is recorded above, and it meant much for both lives. The minister was going through his first real experience of leading an immortal soul to Christ, and the girl was face to face with the Master. Out of the gathering shadows on the waters it seemed to her that he came, as of old, and spoke peace to her troubled heart. Many days after, she found a poem among others in a book sent to her sister, which seemed so to fit into her memory of that evening and her experiences that she copied it on the margin of her Bible. These were the words:

> *Out in the night on the wide, wild sea,*
> *When the wind was beating drearily*
> *And the waters were moaning wearily,*
> *I met with him who had died for me.*

And there was a sense in which for a little space the existence of each to the other was blotted out as these two held converse concerning the things of the kingdom. The man felt that he was conveying a message of vital import from his Master, the first of the sort ever entrusted to him, perhaps, or at least the first whose importance had ever so impressed him. He must not think of himself, he must choose only the words the Spirit spoke, he must not let his faith waver, he must pray as he breathed every instant, for he felt that Satan might step in at any moment and thwart the work. It was wonderful beyond any experience of his, this overpowering anxiety, this trembling joy, as she seemed to yield hers to her Saviour's will.

To the young woman who sat thus reviewing her life and her motives, the man beside her but carried a heavenly message. She forgot that he and she stood in mutual relations in the world which made it natural that she should desire to appear well in his eyes, and that she should admire his earnest, well-spoken words and be pleased that he cared to spend his effort upon her. Her heart-hunger for something better in her life than had ever been there before had at last spoken and she was recognizing its eternal right to be heard. She heard Jesus pleading through those words spoken without any excitement, and yet with such tremendous earnestness.

And yet each knew that there was a sense in which Maria was already a Christian, that is, before the world. She had taken Christ's vows upon her. She had been brought up to keep the commandments outwardly at least. She had even not been inactive in Christian work, to the extent of being zealous at certain times, when the work was particularly pleasant to her. And yet she sat and waited and hesitated, and knew that if she once gave over her will the decision would mean that her whole life hereafter must be changed.

They sat so long upon the sand that their figures, etched against the fading sky, became blurred by the mist of the evening, and when the great decision was finally made and the minister sealed it with a prayer whose few low-spoken words were from the deep new joy of his heart that God had blessed his message, the quiet night shut out their bowed heads from view.

Supper in the hotel was long over when they walked back along the sand and passed the gay piazza, filled with the merry talk of guests who watched the new moon travel its silver pathway over the waves, and laughed and made commonplace remarks, as though it were a common night and a common sight.

Supper in the green cottage was long over also, although it had been delayed for Maria's coming for some time. Rachel had gone over to the Parkers' with her brother, the father and mother had taken a stroll to the bay, and could be seen in the distance slowly walking up and down the little platform by the water, the sky, lit by the last memory of the dead sunset, making a clear background for their dark figures. The Higgins girl was seated on the front steps impatiently waiting to tell Maria, when she should come, that the hot biscuits were in the oven covered with a tin plate and the butter was in the top of the refrigerator, and the rest of the things were on the table for her supper, before going home to join in the merry evening attendant upon the arrival of several brothers-in-law and other relatives. Boisterous laughter issued across the marsh from the little house. Her errand accomplished, the Higgins girl hastened away. She felt embarrassed before the minister and Maria after what had happened in the afternoon.

Maria was relieved to find the house empty. She

wanted to understand herself before she met any of the others. She paused at the top step to say good-night, and then bethought herself that the minister had missed his supper. She asked him to come in and have something to eat, and to her surprise instead of declining he hesitated and said: "May I?"

Maria scarcely knew whether she was glad or sorry he had accepted her invitation. It was rather an embarrassing position, this eating supper together, after foraging in the refrigerator and the oven, exposing the crudeness of their dwelling to this young man evidently used to luxury, and yet it was pleasant too. He entered into it like a boy and held the lamp for her while she got the butter, and stirred the fire to make the kettle boil for a cup of tea which he declared he should enjoy if she did not mind making it. It covered her shyness too, for after their long, serious talk, and the solemn words she had spoken, it had seemed to her she would scarcely dare to attempt common every-day living again at once lest she should do something to mar the wonder of the great peace which filled her soul. She did not take her change of heart as Rachel would have done, with a bubble of joy that entered into everything that touched her life. It was too new, and her nature did not so quickly accept and appropriate new situations. She felt that her experience was too sacred even to think about yet awhile. Indeed, it could hardly be called an experience. She felt no joy though she did feel at peace; she did not think that life was now to be all rose-colored. She was not perfectly sure but to-morrow she might fall from her high resolves. The only difference in her feelings from two hours ago was this deep peace, a peace which comes of decision, and a fixed purpose to surrender her will and to trust. Henceforth her life was to be different. Not because she could make it so, but because she had chosen another motive for its center. Now she only knew that her life was to be ordered for different ends, and whatever of joy or sorrow came, they were alike to be brought to Christ, the end to be his glory.

It was a novel experience to Maria, this free and easy getting supper together with the minister. Heretofore her intimate friends had not been of the sort who were admitted to the kitchen, and indeed the kitchen in their home had always until lately been under the rule of a regiment of good servants. There was a homelikeness, a comradeship, in their sitting down together. Maria felt embarrassed at first at the idea of it, fearing lest Rachel should come in, or her brother, and find what was going on and be surprised at her, for she had always looked down upon such proceedings as plebeian in the extreme and not to be encouraged—more like what the Parkers might be expected to do. And yet here she was actually enjoying it. She wondered why it was, and then forgot to wonder. Mr. Fairfield seemed boyishly happy, and Maria could but catch the infection of his spirits and be happy too. Each realized that there was deep feeling in the heart of the other, and the minister fully intended to go away at once as soon as they should have put away the remains of their impromptu repast, thinking that Maria needed the rest and quiet and a time alone with God after the long strain of the struggle of decision. They were just going to the piazza, the minister to say good-night and leave Maria with her own thoughts, when they heard steps and merry voices. Maria hastily set the lamp, now turned low, on the little shelf back in the kitchen, where its light would but dimly reach the front door, and so tell no tales of the *tête-à-tête* supper, and quietly, with all possible speed, followed her guest to the piazza. She did not wish her brother and sister to find room for teasing in anything that went on to-night, for it seemed to her she could not bear it. It was Rachel and Winthrop, with the Parkers and some others, come to sit on the veranda and sing.

In the little change that took place while the quartette grouped themselves on the steps and Rachel brought the lamp for them to see the penciled words of a recently written song, Mr. Fairfield drew nearer to Maria and said in a low tone: "You are tired."

He did not put it with the rising inflection of a question that demanded an answer, nor was there time for an answer before the singing began, but Maria felt that he was reading her thoughts and feelings with a fine sympathy, anxious to aid her. She smiled gratefully. Then the singing began. All at once Maria realized that these were the people to whom she had most clearly showed her dislike and disdain. With a sudden resolve, which seemed to her to be in response to a hidden, bidding voice, she determined to take the first step in a new direction at once. Throwing aside the distant manner which she had worn ever since coming to the shore, except when in the company of the minister or the De Veres, she forthwith joined in the talk and laughter, when the song was ended.

The Parkers were delighted with her bright words and ready assent to any plans they might propose. She was indeed a charming girl, and why had they been so deceived in her at first? Rachel and Winthrop sat silent through sheer amazement, and the minister wondered and divined the reason. It was strange how well he was beginning to understand this young girl who had been to him a stranger a few short weeks before. He sat looking at her in the dim lights and shadow thrown by the flickering lamp, as she talked, and he saw a gentle, softened look which was not wholly stirred by the pleasant things she was saying. He remembered now her face at different times as she had been pondering his questions down by the shore that evening, and the grave sweetness in her eyes, when she at last decided. To him she seemed all sweetness. He had not yet realized that she had indeed been hateful, as she told him. Isn't it blessed, sometimes, that there are people who cannot and who will not see our faults, even though we tell them they are there?

Maria was glad when they all rose to leave; not that she was not enjoying the talk. It was pleasant, and she was surprised to find herself interested in those Parkers; but she longed for the quiet of her own room.

Mr. Fairfield had been watching her during the last few minutes and now, as they rose to go, he took her hand for good-night and said in an undertone: "Are you any happier, Miss Hammond, than you were this afternoon?"

"I think so," she answered softly. "And oh, I want to thank you. I never should have found the right way if it had not been for you."

The young man bowed his head humbly. Said he:

"I think that is the most welcome thanks I ever received, for I never before to my knowledge was the means of leading any one to Christ. That seems a terrible admission for me, a minister of the gospel, to make, and perhaps, oh, I hope, it may not be true! But I never knew it at least and I have not been the sort of minister I should have been, you remember. You have helped me, you know, in spite of all you have said to the contrary, and so I am grateful beyond expression to be allowed to bring a little of the same blessed comfort to you."

Then Maria went in to the quiet moonlit window of her room and sat there in wonder, thinking of all that had passed since she left that room so hastily a few hours before; of the kindness of the minister, his earnest face and tender words, of the quiet lovely night about them, then of the walk home, and the pleasant little supper together. Somehow the fact of their eating alone together had made them better friends. There was something about the thought of that supper which she did not like to put into words yet, a strange, pleasant something, into which she dared not look for explanation. Perhaps sometime she would think it all out and see if there was any foundation for real pleasure in it, but now it was to be allowed to hover on the horizon of her mind, a pleasant memory connected with this wonderful night. Then she thought of the coming of the young people, and their songs. And there had been a new duty for her in their very fun. She must learn to join in it. She realized that perhaps this might be one of the hardest things for her to do, this letting down of her prejudices and being agreeable when her heart was not in what was going on. Would she be able to do it? She trembled at the mountain of difficulties which rose before her untried feet.

Of the great central event of that day, the decision that she had made to make Christ the center of her life, she almost feared to try to think as yet, it seemed so new and sacred. She could not begin to get used to it. She must wait till all the others were asleep before she could let her thoughts dwell much upon that.

Rachel came in soon and softly stealing up behind her, put her arms around her neck and kissed her, and she returned the caress lovingly and rose to prepare for rest. She felt she could not sleep soon, there was so much to think about, and when she knelt to pray, as was her habit, the act and the words meant so much more than they had ever meant before. Then, contrary to her expectations, she fell into a deep dreamless sleep, for her Father knew she was wearied and needed rest, more than to think of high resolves and to plan difficult paths. Now that she was willing to walk as he would have her, he would choose her paths and carry her over the hard places without the resolves which are sometimes merely signposts for Satan to read which way we are intending to go, that he may lie in wait for us there and intercept our progress. If she would but put her hand in Christ's all would be well.

> Trusting the one great Pilot of the deep
> To be for aye my tender, low-voiced Guide,
> I look aloft and say—
> Though tossed upon life's ocean wide—
> "All's well! All's well! By day or night, all's well!"

17

"SHE is a great friend of Maria Hammond's" said Fanny De Vere, as she skillfully opened an egg at the breakfast table. "I suppose that is the reason she chooses that place for the remainder of the summer."

"Well, I should imagine she would be just about Maria Hammond's stamp," said Evelyn; "they must have a good many interests in common. Nannette Davenport cares for nothing whatever but her own pretty self. She is the most self-centered person I know of. I suppose it's very unkind in me to say so, but positively, I don't believe her grief over her mother's death is more than skin deep. She never seemed to care for her in the least when she was alive."

"I am sorry she is coming," said Fanny. "Of course we shall not necessarily have much to do with her, but at the same time there will be a certain amount of civility which must be exchanged for decency's sake. It is a great pity she could not have gone somewhere else, but truly I suppose the real reason of her selecting Lone Point this summer is because she is in deep mourning and the society in which she moves would be scandalized if she were to appear anywhere else. Here she can do as she pleases. She is supposed to have retired from the vain world. If she chooses to indulge herself in a little amusement no one is a whit the wiser. I suppose Maria Hammond could not stand it any longer without some of her friends about her. Roland, I wonder why it is that girl is so different from her sister. You never would dream they were of the same family, would you?"

Thus appealed to the young man hesitated a minute before answering.

"I'm not sure," he said. "I've seen several things lately that led me to think she might be other than we at first thought. There must be something about her that's interesting or Fairfield would never waste his time on her. He isn't a lady's man, by any means. In college he would never have anything to do with shallow, insipid girls. There had to be some intellect before he would look at them, much less talk with them, unless he was absolutely compelled to do so."

"Oh, I suppose she is bright enough, as far as that goes," said Evelyn; "but for my part I think she is decidedly disagreeable, and I can imagine that she will be twice as much so when backed up by Nannette Davenport. I can't think how Nannette will endure the simplicity at the Lone Point Hotel. She never washed out her own bathing suit in her life, nor waded through deep sand to get to the beach. As for the rude cottages there, she will probably take the next train back home when she has seen them. Are you sure, Roland, that Miss Hastings said she was going to Lone Point?"

"Perfectly sure," answered the young man. "Miss Hastings had been up there yesterday afternoon to engage her room for her at her aunt's request. The young lady in question is coming unchaperoned, as her aunt considers that in so quiet a spot, so near Miss Davenport's intimate friends, a chaperon is hardly necessary."

Evelyn laughed.

"If she is the same Nannette who went to Boston a year ago, she will need a chaperon more in Lone Point than she does in a crowded city. She is kept somewhat in check there by custom and her position, but Lone Point she will consider good game. If you have the least friendliness in the world for your friend, the intellectual minister, you would better warn him to flee, for in spite of his intellect and his devotion at present to Miss Hammond, he will shortly be in the wiles of Miss Nannette. Why, consider, my dear brother. He is about the only eligible young man in the whole of that lonely Lone Point, unless perhaps Mr. Hammond and Mr. Parker might be counted in. But she counts it nothing to have three or four on hand at once."

"Well, if Fairfield can't take care of himself, I'm sure he deserves to suffer, that's all I have to say," said the young man with a laugh as he arose from the table and took up the morning paper.

It was by the morning mail Maria received a letter from her quondam friend, Miss Nannette Davenport. It was gushingly characteristic of her. She was always gushing when she had a point to gain. Just at present it suited her purpose to spend a few weeks in a quiet place, and Maria would be very useful to her in helping to pass the time. The letter expressed great delight over the thought of a quiet summer in which to hide the deep grief she professed. She said she wanted to get away from the world and had decided to come near to her friend. She had delayed to send Maria word until the day before her arrival that her coming might be a pleasant surprise, but her room was already engaged at the hotel and Maria might meet her at the Lone Point Station at three the next afternoon.

That this was a surprise to Maria need not be doubted; but it was anything but a pleasant surprise. Nannette Davenport had never been a deeply loved friend. She had a certain prestige because of her mother's wealth and standing in society which Maria had thought she could not well afford to ignore. Through Nannette she had gained entrance to several homes in a high social circle where she feared she would not have been able otherwise to go since her father's failure. Indeed it was through Nannette she had met the De Veres. The two girls had been thrown together not a little at the beginning of their friendship, if it could rightly be called a friendship where there was no real love nor even very strong liking, when they were both away at school. Maria knew just how much real friendship Nannette held for her. She knew what a shallow, heartless girl she was. And she did not rejoice at the thought of her coming to Lone Point.

Had the letter come three or four days before it did, she would have worried greatly that Nannette should come and see her in such humble surroundings, but somehow the events of the past few days had made surroundings seem of less importance; so that now, as she read the letter and pondered over it with a distressed little pucker between her eyes, it was not because of the little green cottage nor yet of their straitened circumstances that her first objection was raised. Her first thought was for her new life. How hard it would be to mix thoughts and feelings so utterly at variance! Her utter distaste for Nannette's pleasures was a sort of revelation even to herself as she read. She had not known how much her own likings and longings were wrapt up in her desire to carry out her new aim in life.

She sat down and began to ponder what she should do. It would not do to be rude to Nannette. Christ would not wish that. Was her trouble that she was afraid to stand out against her and say decidedly that her motives in life were changed? Or was it that she feared her own self and dreaded lest she might lose this wonderful calm that had come into her life three nights ago? Did she think that it might be she would be tempted back to old ways, old thoughts, old bondages? There came to her suddenly with this thought a remembrance of a verse she had read that morning from Rachel's Bible. Rachel's Bible was always lying open somewhere about, and Rachel's Bible always had marked verses to catch her eye when she was in a hurry. She used to say she kept her Bible near at hand that she might snatch a thought now and then as she was going by, as it helped to keep her from temptation. Maria had not yet gained the courage to bring forth her Bible openly as Rachel did. She wanted to read it by herself first and get used to the thought of her new way of living, and so she had chosen a verse from her sister's Bible as she dressed. It was:

"God is faithful, who will not suffer you to be tempted above that ye are able; but will with the temptation also make a way to escape that ye may be able to bear it."

How strange that that verse should have come in her way that morning! How wonderful to think God was actually answering her thoughts in his own words! Surely, this girl's arrival was nothing she was responsible for, and therefore she was not to blame. He had allowed the temptation; could not she trust him to make a way of escape for her? She arose and fastened the door, and then knelt down to ask for faith. She knew it would seem very strange to Rachel to come in in the daytime and find her praying. She was still in bondage. Her fetters had been forged tight, and it was hard for her to drop them even now that they were broken.

She did not feel that she knew how to pray very well, but she knew that God would understand; and as she rose she began to wonder if perchance he would in some way turn the decision of Miss Davenport and send her somewhere else even at the last minute. Or had he other ways of working? Of course he might mean that this was a discipline through which she was to pass before she was fit to be his child. If so she would try to do what was right, but it seemed much harder even than to take in the Parkers. They had grown quite tolerable, even to pleasantness, and it was only three days since she had decided to become acquainted with them. With the remembrance of the Parkers came the question, "What would Nannette think of the Parkers? Would she make it very unpleasant?" Maria knew that Nannette possessed, among other uncomfortable qualities, that of sneering at people and things, and making one feel that one would rather do anything than confess to a friendship for the person or a liking for the thing which she had scorned. What was she to do with Nannette?

It must not be supposed that Maria had grown good all in a night. By no means. To all outward appearance she was the same Maria grown a little sweeter tempered, a little more willing to give up her wishes for those of others, and in one respect rather surprising, in that she freely mingled with the young people and notably with the Parkers, making them feel perfectly at their ease and happy in her company. She had lost her temper once or twice. She had forgotten to refrain from a scornful remark about the pump on one occasion, which, while she felt no peculiar animus at the time, had still grown to be such a habit with her that she scolded without realizing it. She had noticed the weary look about her mother's eyes at the time the words were spoken and she instantly knew the mother was sighing over her. There had come an impulse then to throw her arms around her mother and tell her how different she meant things should be, but something within restrained her and the next instant her mother had passed out to talk with the grocer's boy and her opportunity was gone. She reasoned also that it would be better for her first to show some "works meet for repentance" before announcing to the others what she was going to do. Moreover, she felt that her recent experience, if it could rightly be called an experience, was too sacred yet to be talked about, and that it was no question of witnessing for Christ in this case, as they already knew she was his professed follower. It would be much wiser for her to let them see that she was different. She forgot that to the mother and sister there would have been great relief in the fact that she was willing to try to be different: that they would have overlooked many things in her and helped her in numberless ways, if she had once taken them into her confidence. If people only understood each other in this world there would be much less of friction, less sighing, and less worry about one another. And so the mother was praying daily for her daughter, and wondering why it was her prayers were of no avail—whether because she was unworthy to be answered, or because of her lack of faith; while all the time the dear Lord had prepared a loving answer and put it down beside her and she was too taken up with worry to notice it. It would be well, in our praying, to sometimes lift the head and see whether the answer to our payers is not shining in the heavens or standing joy-clothed beside us, or even lying at our feet waiting to be recognized.

Maria pondered deeply over what to tell her new friend the minister about her old friend Nannette, and finally decided to let him judge for himself. However, she had no opportunity to tell him anything, as it turned out, for Mr. Fairfield was all that day and the next away attending to some business on the mainland, and only arrived at Lone Point on the very train which carried Nannette in her black robes.

The three days which lay between Maria and her decision had been bright ones to her. Her friendship with the minister was growing to be an exceedingly pleasant thing to think about, not that the intimacy had as yet grown into its larger possibilities as personal; but there was growing in each of their hearts something warmer than a mere interest for the other, and occasionally little glimpses of alluring perhaps would flit across the mental horizon of each.

It is just possible that underneath Maria's distaste for the arrival of Miss Davenport there was an undertone of uneasiness lest the pleasant friendship between herself and the minister might be broken in upon, but if this was so she did not even confess it to herself. She was never a girl who was quick to think a man wished to pay her special attention, nor to seem to appropriate one to herself. She rather erred in the other direction; and he on his part, while he admired her for this, was, in a certain sense, kept at a distance by her, even though they talked more intimately than most young people are apt to do about that most sacred emotion of life, one's personal love for his Saviour.

18

MARIA waited on the little platform the next afternoon for the incoming train. Her emotions were not pleasant. She seemed to see Nannette's curling lips as she first took in the situation and observed the rude cottage life. She seemed to hear her sarcastic comments, and strange to say they were, in her mind, much what her own had been on arriving here. Suddenly there flashed over her the thought that she had changed, in this respect at least, for she seemed to have in her heart some real love for the place, some desire to protect it from what scornful strangers might say. Why was it? Was it because she had found Christ here? Or was it, perhaps, on account of her new friendship with the strong true man who was becoming her friend? She looked up at the blue sky and smiled in answer to its heavenly look. She gazed over the yellow-green waves of the marsh grass, so bare to her once, and lo! they had taken on beauty, and she felt a sense of gladness in their smooth stretches of level green, and discovered that in a night they seemed to have burst into a million stars of meadow pinks dotted all over among the grass as far as eye could reach. She stooped and gathered a handful of them and placed them in her belt, adding a very pretty touch to her toilet. Nannette's influence had already begun to be felt in her careful arrangement of that afternoon's toilet. She had worried more about her dress and taken more time for it that day than she had done altogether since she had come to the island. Even now she looked down at herself doubtfully. She hardly cared to come in for sarcasm herself just at the outset. She had chosen, after much indecision of mind and careful scrutiny of her wardrobe, to wear for that a day a white duck costume. It was plain, of course, and in a sense inexpensive. Its great beauty in her eyes was its exquisite cut and fit. She had committed her greatest extravagance of the summer by taking that duck dress to a notable tailor to be cut, and in her eyes and in the eyes of Nannette as well, she knew that fact would cover a multitude of sins in other directions. She half intended Nannette should soon discover that Melton had cut her dress. Nannette would then be sure to admire it. And yet, do her the credit to observe that she was annoyed over finding herself so deeply concerned about her dress, and descending so low as to actually think how she could tell where it had been cut. She sighed and wondered if this were a sign that Nannette was going to win her forever back to worldly things. Then before she went out she knelt and prayed. She had seen Rachel kneel often before going out, when she thought she was by herself, and she felt that now perhaps such a habit might be a good thing for her. Certainly she needed much help.

She did look fresh and pretty and thoroughly in keeping with her surroundings, all in white with black velvet belt and collar and band about her sailor hat. Even the most exacting taste could have found no fault with her. The fresh ocean breeze had blown loose a few soft strands of a waving lock about her forehead and flushed her cheeks, and the touch of pink blossoms in her belt made her look exquisitely pure and sweet. At least so thought Mr. Fairfield as he alighted, hot and dusty from his ride in the train, and his face lighted with a sudden joy that was pleasant to see. In spite of her, the color would come into Maria's cheeks as she bowed to him. She was a trifle embarrassed too, for just a moment, since it must look to him, until Nannette appeared, as though she had come to the train to meet him.

But now the porter handed Nannette, with her bag, and her dress-suit case, and her bundle of golf sticks, and her tennis racquet, and several other accessories of the fashionable girl at a summer resort, down upon the platform, and the train moved on toward Spray View, and Maria found her hands full.

Nannette's greeting was effusive, a mingling of kisses and adjectives, and a few stylish tears which necessitated the pushing up of the very becoming black veil in which her head was swathed in spite of the heat. This over, Miss Davenport turned her dark eyes upon the minister who stood by Maria as if he belonged there, and an introduction of necessity followed.

Maria felt annoyed beyond measure that she had not ere this told the minister of Nannette's expected arrival. Just why she should feel so much annoyance she did not then look into her heart to see. As a matter of course the minister rode with them in the surrey which had been sent down from the hotel to convey the new guest from the station, and though Maria also went with them and sat in the back seat with her friend, Nannette monopolized the conversation entirely and addressed it all to Mr. Fairfield. She spoke gushingly of her friendship with Maria, dating its origin much farther back than Maria had supposed it could be, showing reasons why Maria was her warmest friend, and therefore had been the one to whom she turned in her deep trouble. Here she punctuated her remarks with a few tears wiped carefully away with a correct handkerchief, deeply bordered with black.

She was a dashingly handsome girl; tall, slender, with black eyes and reddish brown hair. She wore her hair loose over her ears and coiled low at the nape of the neck which gave her an innocent, childlike appearance. She was an excellent actress when she chose to be. Mr. Fairfield was nonplussed and disappointed. He felt instinctively that this girl would have little sympathy for the quiet walks and talks in which he and Maria had been indulging of late. He feared that her presence at the shore would be anything but a good influence for the girl in whom he was becoming so deeply interested.

Maria, on her part, was greatly distressed. What would Mr. Fairfield think of her friends? What would he think of her past life? She must hasten to explain, at the first opportunity, how little of real friendship there ever had existed between them; and yet how could she, without deliberately making the other girl out a liar? It was all very unpleasant. She was glad when the surrey drew up to the hotel and they could get out. She was more glad than she dared say, even to herself, that no conversation concerning the place, and the various cottages they had passed during the short ride, had come up, for at least she was spared having the truth dawn upon Nannette while the minister was with them. She went upstairs with Nannette at her request, though she would have preferred going straight home to have a good cry, or wandering off on the sand and telling Mr. Fairfield all about it. She felt a childish desire to tell him her troubles and ask him what she should do, but she shut her lips tightly and walked up the stairs like a soldier, so that he thought she was only too happy to have one of her own sort with her again and he would have no more opportunities to see her.

Nannette's several trunks were at last deposited and unstrapped and she was at leisure to take off her hat and talk with her friend. She laid her hat on the bed and settled herself in a rocker by the window: "Now, 'Ri, tell me all about this hole," she said familiarly. "Is there anything going on to keep one alive? Isn't it dreadfully dull? But you see Aunt Mortimer is old-fashioned and terribly rigid, and she wouldn't at all consent to my appearing at any interesting place. She wanted me to stay at home with her all summer! Just fancy! She said I ought not to want to go anywhere when my mother was dead, but dear me!"—with a shrug of her shoulders—"what good would it do mother for me to mope? I told aunt I should die of grief among those associations of mother, and that seemed to touch the right spot, and she consented to my going away. She would have come with me if she could, but Cousin George is worse this summer and not able to be moved and she couldn't leave him. I think she would have liked me to stay and devote myself to him, read to him and make messes for him; but Cousin George is altogether too devoted to the memory of his dead wife to make it interesting to waste one's time on him. Besides I hate sick people and he isn't likely to get well, anyway. So I'm here. First of all, who is that very handsome Mr. Fairfield? A minister? Dear me! Is he very good? Because that would be dreadfully tiresome."

"I'm sure I don't know," said Maria; "you'll have to find that out for yourself." Her voice showed her disgust plainly, but Nannette was too much interested to notice. She went rattling on.

"Say, 'Ri, is he very devoted? I thought he looked at you as if he was. Are you engaged?"

"No, *indeed,*" answered Maria freezingly. It flashed over her then that there was something about Nannette's face that reminded her of Annie Higgins and she thought if the two were compared there would be a balance in favor of the Higgins girl.

"Not engaged? Then I give you fair warning, 'Ri dear, I shall do my best to have a good time. You don't mind, do you, dear?"

"Certainly not," said Maria again, in a voice which the minister never would have recognized.

Nannette seemed to feel that it would be just as well to change the subject. She leaned out of the open window nearest her, looking toward the cottages.

"And now do tell me where the town is, what there is of it. Of course I know it's small, but I've seen nothing but cow-sheds so far. What in the world do they need so many of them for? Or are they bath-houses? No, they are too far from the ocean."

The Maria of a few weeks ago would have blushed crimson and hesitated, tried to apologize and explain, or even have invented some way out of the truth, perhaps; but the Maria of to-day was too deeply stung and disgusted. She was shown herself and just how low she had fallen in being ready to bow down to a girl whose thoughts and feeling were as low as this one's. It was so great a contrast with the high and holy thoughts in which she had been dwelling with the minister lately that she was in great danger of going to the other extreme and despising this girl for motives really lower than belonged to her. For Nannette Davenport was only selfish, that was all. But that is perhaps enough.

Maria arose and with grave dignity walked to the window and pointed out.

"Those are cottages," she said, trying to control her voice steadily. "That white one nearest to you is where our friends the Parkers live. The green one trimmed with white next to it is ours. The others belong to very nice people. You will meet them all soon. There is no reason why one should not have a pleasant time here if one chooses."

Maria remembered her own actions of two weeks ago, and was amazed at herself. Nannette looked curiously at her, and then without further remark turned toward her trunks, saying with a sigh:

"You don't say so! Well, I suppose I've no choice but to make the best of it this year, with these horrid black things on, but I shall make up for it next year, you may be sure. And I warn you I'm going to be just as wicked as I please, so look out for your own interests. By the way, 'Ri, haven't you a brother? Is he nice looking? How old is he? One must have friends, you know, in such a desert as this. They say Roland De Vere is over at Spray View. He and I had a terrible quarrel a year ago, but I may be able to patch that up. He is so old-granny particular! Now what shall I put on for dinner, and what hour do they have that meal in this out-of-the-way place?"

"They have dinner at one o'clock. It is over four hours ago. Supper is at six," answered Maria severely. She somehow took a fierce pleasure in shocking this girl. She felt glad that this feeling possessed her instead of the fear which she had been afraid would tempt her to do things out of accord with her new views. She felt so little trust in her own self, poor child, and her trust was so recently given to her Saviour, that she did not realize that he would hold her and she would not need to worry lest she should not hold to him. She was anxious to get away now, and the many elaborate dresses which Nannette began to take out and spread upon bed and chairs for her admiration, wearied her. She felt as if she had always given an undue amount of time and thought to clothes. No doubt these things were pretty, yes, they certainly were. She could not help letting her eye dwell in pleased delight upon an elaborate waist of black taffeta. Nannette certainly had good taste, there was no denying that, and plenty of money with which to exercise it. It was hard, of course, this gay season when everybody was flaunting bright colors, to get up a beautiful and varied outfit with only black and white, with strict severity and much crêpe a necessity, but Nannette had succeeded, and Maria, in spite of dislikes and resolves, began to grow interested in the pretty clothes. Nannette insisted upon her remaining until she had arrayed herself in a severely plain white gown with black ribbons, and Maria was obliged to say, at the demand of the new-comer, that she was bewitchingly pretty even in the trying dead black and white.

"Now, you may go, dear, for I suppose you are awfully tired of me. But please tell me first,"—holding Maria off at arm's length,—"do you think I shall captivate him? I mean that young minister, of course. I must have something to amuse me, and I should hate to fail at the very beginning."

"I'm sure I don't know" answered Maria in her most sober tone. She drew back, stung deeper than she realized.

"Ha, ha!" laughed Nannette, "he must be good and have infected you. Never mind. I sha'n't hurt him much, you know, and I'll let him go in the end. Don't blame me much, dear. It's all I have to live for now, you know." And she put her mourning handkerchief to her laughing eyes in the smart little pat which she affected.

Maria coldly promised to come back that evening and walked away. She could stand no more.

All she had to live for! Flirting! How boldly she had

confessed it. Was it possible she had ever admired a girl like that? She bowed her head and was ashamed.

The minister, standing at the window of his room in the hotel, saw her, watched her down the street, wondered and sighed and turned away thoughtfully.

19

WHEN Maria reached the cottage her mother looked at her searchingly, expecting to find her face wreathed in smiles on account of the arrival of Nannette. Instead she saw a gray, weary look about her eyes, and felt the anxious tugging at her mother-heart again which had been there so often the last few weeks. Was Maria plunged again in gloom because of the talk and dress of her gay friend? Was she contrasting her own life with that of Miss Davenport?

When at supper her brother Winthrop asked some laughing question about Nannette, Maria looked up at him anxiously and answered him more shortly than she had spoken to him for at least three days. The family could not understand it. They had expected her to be pleased at the accession of a friend in this lonely place. She ate very little supper, and when Winthrop proposed going with her to the hotel to call upon the young lady, she promptly declined his escort, saying Nannette must be tired and would not want to see any one that evening. Her conscience gave her a sharp twinge as she said that, but she looked after her brother with a sigh as he whistled and left the table. Then she went quickly out to the piazza and stood alone in the purple and pink twilight with tears blurring her vision. There had suddenly stirred in her heart a new feeling of love for her brother. She saw a possible danger to him lurking in the future and she felt herself inadequate to ward it off. Oh, if she had but always been such a sister to him that a word from her would have been as a shield to him. But now she felt that if she should point out to him her fear he would walk straight up to it laughing, more perhaps to tease her than anything else. Things were becoming complicated. There was her brother, and there was the minister, and there was Nannette, and there was she, and where was the Lord? She thought it reverently. She stood looking up into the clear opal tints above and wished she might see him, if only for one little second of time, that her poor weak faith might have something to bind itself to forever. She felt a great longing for Christ to come and touch her. She wanted him more than anything else just then.

Her mother came softly out behind her and putting her arms about her daughter drew her head down to her shoulder.

"What is it, little 'Ri, tell mother" she said tenderly, just as she used to speak when Maria was but a baby and came in with bumped head or bruised knee from a fall.

Then Maria hid her face in her mother's neck and cried, and tried to tell her all her troubles, and of how she wanted to live a changed life.

The mother's heart grew glad and light suddenly. It seemed too good to be true. She drew her down to a chair beside her on the porch, stroking her hair, talking low and tenderly with her as they had not talked together for many a long day. Yet even as the mother talked and comforted and was glad, there came and stood beside her the shadow of a possibility of happenings for the future which held in them both sorrow and joy, and she put away what she heard to think of by and by. She was not a mother who often talked with her children about personal religion, therefore it would have been hard for Maria to tell her mother of her changed feelings on the subject if it had not been for this sudden letting down the bars of her nature and her mother's opportune coming. It was hard too for the mother to talk on religious subjects and therefore her words of comfort were not many, but to Maria who well knew her mother's nature, they meant much, and carried true solace with them. When she said, "Maria, I am glad," Maria knew that she meant more than if she had used a whole dictionary full of adjectives, and when she advised her daughter to "give over worrying and take her trouble to her Heavenly Father," then Maria felt that her mother spoke whereof she knew.

One load the mother carried on her heart when her daughter finally kissed her and went to the hotel, which she had not had before. Maria had dropped a hint as to possible danger for Winthrop in the coming of Miss Davenport, and the mother-heart grew anxious at once as soon as she had time to think, and she had need to take to herself the advice she had given her daughter.

Winthrop, her only boy, was very dear to her, and she knew him to be fond of bright company and very susceptible to its influence.

When Maria reached the hotel, she began to frame an excuse for being so late, but on ascending the steps of the long wide piazza which ran all around the building she saw in the distant corner, standing out against the background of moonlit ocean, the figures of Miss Davenport and Mr. Fairfield. The sudden chill which crept over her made her pause and draw about her shoulders the light shawl she had carried on her arm. She half turned to go away again, thinking Nannette was in no need of her presence and she would come again in the morning, but Nannette had seen her, and waved her handkerchief and called, so there was nothing for it but to go over and sit down in another large rocking-chair beside them.

"You dear naughty thing, you deserted me!" said Nannette in her most gushing voice. "Why in the world were you so long coming? If it had not been for Mr. Fairfield I should have been so lonely that I should have wished to take the morning train back to the city. But he has been so exceedingly kind that I actually forgot this place was called Lone Point."

It had been no part of Mr. Fairfield's intention to have any more to do with Miss Davenport than was absolutely necessary. The feeling of dislike he had experienced for her at first sight only deepened as they rode along to the hotel. But a gentleman cannot be actually rude to a lady, especially if that lady is a professed friend of one who has his deep friendship and respect. Therefore, when, by some skillful maneuver, the old lady who usually occupied the place at the right of Mr. Fairfield in the dining room, was placed across the room, and Miss Davenport was found seated beside him, he was obliged, in ordinary courtesy, to talk with her. It could not be said that he exerted himself to any great degree to make the conversation pleasant for her. Indeed, this was not necessary. Nannette was vivacity itself. She was an adept in small talk and almost made the studious young man feel ill at ease. His replies grew short. But the young woman perceiving her mistake at once subsided, grew meek and inquiring, and presently discovering that books were a delight amounting almost to a passion with the gentleman, molded her conversation accordingly. Before the meal was over she had professed an overpowering desire to read and have explained to her a certain book about which there was a great deal of talk in the literary world. To Mr. Fairfield's exceeding disgust he found that he had not only promised to lend her the book, but to give her at no late date an exhaustive explanation of the discussion in current magazines over certain passages in the book. How they had come to get quite so far as this he was not able to explain, but he awoke to the fact as Nannette was thanking him most sweetly for being so kind as to be willing to help her.

As they rose from the table she said innocently enough, "What in the world do you do here in the evenings? Won't you show me where to go? I don't know a soul but you, you know." She flashed her fine eyes up at him confidingly and he felt in duty bound to take her to the piazza. He went there rather than to the parlor, in a vain hope that Maria might soon come and redeem the situation. But time passed, the sunlight faded from the sky, the moonlight came over the water, and still the young woman by his side gave him no opportunity to leave, without absolute rudeness on his part. He was growing more and more uneasy, when Maria at last arrived, and if she had not been so engrossed with her own feelings at the sight of him and Nannette sitting together in such evident good fellowship, she must surely have noted the joy that broke over his face at sight of her, and the warm welcome he gave her. Be assured Miss Davenport saw it, and ground her pretty white teeth, that in spite of all the charms she had exerted she had not once been able to bring to his face that true pleasure which was there now. She resolved that before many days should have passed this should be different, and thenceforth Lone Point was no longer a desert island to her, for there was a man there who must be conquered, and added to the long line of conquered admirers in the past.

Maria, however, in spite of her mother's comforting words, was ill at ease again the moment she came into Nannette's atmosphere. If she roused herself to reply to Nannette it at once threw her back into a past which she did not like to feel had ever been hers, and with which she did not wish Mr. Fairfield to know she was familiar. If she should speak to Mr. Fairfield, what should it be about? Not Mr. Meyer's book! Not the Bible verse about which they had been talking so freely but yesterday, for what would Nannette think, and how could she drag sacred things into a conversation so filled with the froth of that young woman's remarks?

Mr. Fairfield finally settled back to wait till Maria should go home, thinking he would walk with her and they could have a little quiet word together after all, and he found his mind wandering out of the talk so that he was often silent. He was thinking what he should say to Maria.

Did Nannette read what was passing in his thoughts? Certainly she acted as though she did. When Maria rose to say good-night, she followed her to the steps and then, as if the thought had just occurred to her, she put her hand lovingly on Maria's arm and said: "Why, I guess I'll walk over with you, 'Ri, if Mr. Fairfield doesn't mind bringing me home. I should get lost, you know, if you didn't," she said, turning laughingly to him, and she looked him straight in the eyes in the full moonlight and saw that he was disappointed.

When Maria reached her room that night it was late, for Mr. Fairfield had determined that he would take his revenge upon the new arrival and therefore he proposed a walk. He knew that Maria was used to the sand, and could stand it well, and that to the young woman from the city streets it would be harder work. He hoped perhaps to tire her out and take her back to the hotel before Maria had been taken home, and still have his quiet half-hour with her.

He had reckoned without his host, however. Nannette possibly perceived his intention, or it may be that she was stronger than he had judged possible. She bravely waded through the sand wherever he led the way, exclaiming in delight over scenes which only half pierced to her mental retina at all, and still saying she was not tired. On he took them, this way and that, now nearer the bay now nearer the ocean. Not to the walks which he and Maria had taken together; they were full of pleasant thoughts and should not be marred by the memory of this walk. He grew quite gay in his effort to gain his point, and Maria wondered at him and grew more silent herself. And now he perceived that she was growing very weary, for there was a white droop about her mouth he had not seen there before, and for her sake he proposed that they go straight home.

There was triumph in Miss Davenport's eyes as she faced herself in the mirror of her room at a late hour, and her lips had a firm set. It had been a hard race, for she was very tired, but she had not given up, and she had gained her point. She would win him yet even if she had to be "good," as she phrased it, to get him.

Maria in her room, with only the moon to light her to her couch, threw herself on her knees beside her sleeping sister. She was tired out, soul and body. She was too weary to pray and too weary to cry. She felt as if it would be so good if the dear Christ could just come to her gently, as her mother had done, and tell her what all this meant and why she was so very unhappy. She did not want to try to think and reason it all out. She supposed there was an ugly feeling of jealousy in her heart. It must be that her trouble was because she wanted that young minister to admire her and be with her all the time. It was all very humiliating. She had not known before that she was so selfish. He had helped her to a better life, why did she not want Nannette to have the same opportunity? Was it possible that she had made that great decision just because she admired the man who asked her to do it? Had she fallen so low that her motive was only self-pleasure, after all, and that she did not give up to Christ but to a man whom she admired? Did she not love Christ? With this question came a surge of feeling. Yes, she did love Christ. She felt now as if her all depended upon him. She would give up everything for him. She only wanted his rest, his peace. He had promised it, she had accepted it. It was hers. No one could any more take it from her. Nannette could not touch it. The minister might turn his entire attention to Miss Davenport and forget her. It would be as well if he did, for evidently she was beginning to think too much of him. He might help to bring Nannette to Christ, and then perhaps have a deeper feeling for her, marry her, perhaps. It ought to be nothing to her. She was Christ's. Henceforth she would do as he bade, go where he sent her, live as he would live in her. What a glorious, what a precious thought that was! Would it last till morning? Could she trust it still to be there when she awoke, and could she go to sleep saying, "I am Christ's, I am Christ's. He is mine"?

Strangely, wonderfully, it seemed to her, came an answer from her inmost soul, "I can," and she fell asleep.

If the minister could have known her thoughts as he stood disappointedly beside his window, looking out on the now dark night with only a glimmer of light here and there of a belated cottager, for the moon had set, he might have prayed for her a prayer whose words he knew and loved, instead of wondering gloomily why everything seemed to have gone wrong:

> *Rest her, dear Master! . . . draw very near*
> *In all thy tenderness and all thy power.*
> *O speak to her. Thou knowest how to speak*
> *A word in season to thy weary ones,*
> *And she is weary now. Thou lovest her—*
> *Let thy disciple lean upon thy breast,*
> *And, leaning, gain new strength to "rise and shine."*

20

MR. FAIRFIELD, as he looked out over the sparkling waves the next morning, felt new life and joy come into his soul. What was the use in being downcast when the world was so lovely? He was a child of the living God. He would be given all that was needful for his good and happiness in life. Why should be begin to doubt and grow gloomy because he feared the Lord would take some pleasure from him? Surely it was not worth while to begin to fear anything until he saw it plainly before his eyes? What was it he feared, any way? Was his anxiety wholly unselfish? He recognized clearly that there was a danger menacing Maria's new-found joy in Christ, but could not he and she both trust the One to whose keeping she had committed herself? He remembered the words, "He is able to keep you from falling and to present you faultless," and knew that he was wrong to fear for her.

No, that was not all, though there had been a quick recognition of Maria's danger. What was this other feeling which came and went, a warm, rich, new current in his heart? Miss Hammond had grown to be more than a mere acquaintance; more than one to whom he was trying to bring a message from God, though that relation is a very precious one. There had grown up a personal tie. He told himself that she was the first really intimate friend he had had since his chum in college died, and tried to be satisfied with that way of putting it, but somehow he knew there was something not altogether sincere about that statement either. He decided to go for a quiet stroll along the beach in the early sparkling morning and think it out. There he would be quite alone with God. There was something serious here which ought to be settled at once, he felt sure. Strange he had not thought of it before! Was it possible that this girl, an acquaintance of but a few weeks' standing, was growing indispensable to him? Before he had walked very far, or turned that thought over many times in his mind, he knew that it was so, and that he loved Maria. He sat down on the sand and looked off at the ocean without seeing a single wave of it, to take in the wonder and the beauty of this thought. It fairly overwhelmed him. It was another day and another experience something like the one when first he had realized that he loved his Saviour. He remembered now to have heard Henry Drummond once say that an earthly love was the highest and best example of, and the only thing really approaching at all, the soul's relation with Christ. "Get acquainted with Jesus just as you would with an earthly friend," the great, simple man had said, and the young theologue had been rather inclined to call him irreverent then. But now he saw it in all its beauty, the earthly love, so real and warm and dear, a type of the heavenly, just as close and warm and dear and real, only infinitely more in every way than the human heart could comprehend. Was this what God had made earthly love for, that he might the better show us what his love for us must be?

The thoughts rolled past him, rather than were thought by him. He felt, as he sat there in the midst of the lovely morning, as if God spoke to him out of his grandeur and beauty, and was very gracious to him. Most gracious of all because of this wonderful gift of love which he found in his heart for another of his children. He felt that he loved his Heavenly Father more intensely, more intelligently than he had ever done before, because of the sudden blessed realization of another love.

He arose from his hour's meditation feeling that whatever came after, he should always be a better man for that sacred experience, and that he would be able better to preach of the love of God now that he could understand a human love, like the love of a man for a woman; aye, he would be a better man for having harbored this love in his heart, even though he might fail to win her— though, please God, he would *not* fail if he could help it.

As he walked back toward the hotel he suddenly remembered Miss Davenport and her proximity to him at the table. He wished that he had remembered sooner. It must be late. He would like to get his breakfast and get away before she came. He did not care for a *tête-à-tête* with her just now. He felt that her rattling conversation would be a desecration to his joy-filled mood. How hard it was to have to come down from the heights to every-day living, and every-day disappointments and perplexities! And yet, that was the discipline of life and must be cheerfully borne. He hastened his steps, hoping that she would be late to breakfast, as indeed she was, and he hastened his breakfast, to get out before she came. He did succeed, but little good it did him.

Miss Davenport awoke with a feeling that she had slept later than she intended, for she had business of moment on hand that day and must not let the enemy get any small advantage at the beginning. She found to her dismay that her watch had run down, and she had no means of telling the hour. Glancing from the window, she saw Mr. Fairfield, watch in hand, hurrying toward the hotel, and rightly concluded that breakfast must be ready. With unusual alacrity for a girl of her ordinary lassitude she hurried through a charming toilet prepared with much forethought and intended to deepen the interesting pallor of her supposedly grief-stricken face. Then she hastened to the dining room.

She found to her chagrin that the prize had already escaped her, and the maid was clearing the dishes away from Mr. Fairfield's place at the table. He must have breakfasted hurriedly, or else she had been longer than she thought. As she sat biting her red lips in vexation, she saw him through the opposite window at the other end of the long room, going with determined steps down the sandy path. One comprehensive glance at the landscape told her that he was going in the direction of the green cottage. She watched him a moment and saw that her guess had been correct, for he ascended the steps, knocked at the door, and then sat down in one of the big rockers standing on the piazza. Her purpose was taken in a moment. Taking a few swallows of coffee from the cup just set down beside her, she slipped up to her room for her parasol and hat and followed the path he had just taken.

Mr. Fairfield had felt during his brief breakfast that the thing he wanted most in life just then was to look upon the face of the one whom he had just discovered he loved. Not that he intended to tell of his love just now; no indeed! He saw instantly that it was too soon for that. She had not known him long enough. She might not love him—how could she?—and he would not startle her by telling her of it abruptly. No, he would teach her daily to love him. He would wait and see if there was any chance for him, before he told her. But whatever came of the telling, the fact, the precious fact, remained that he loved her, and he wished to see her in the light of the knowledge of that fact. He had hastened his morning meal that he might go to her home and ask for a walk, before Miss Davenport could be around to claim her time, and thus he had gone happily down the path, whistling a few notes of a popular song, then humming a line of a hymn, and so, joyously, scarcely knowing what his thoughts might be. Rachel answered the door and told him her sister had run in next door on an errand for her mother but would be back almost immediately. He sat down to wait while Rachel went on with the work she was doing, which she could not leave just then. The acquaintance between the Hammonds and Mr. Fairfield had grown sufficiently intimate for Rachel to feel privileged to go on working and occasionally come to the door to make some pleasant remark or answer something Mr. Fairfield called in to her.

Maria coming in the back door with the basket in which she had just carried some fish to Mrs. Parker, a present from her mother, who had purchased more than she needed, heard the minister's voice and answering Rachel's motion slipped into her room to change her dark working calico for her beach dress. Rachel, buzzing about in the kitchen finishing Maria's morning work that she might not be kept from her friend any longer, did not see the tall black-robed young woman who presently came up the steps, on the veranda, and greeted its occupant with such effusiveness, seating herself in the next rocker and entering into an immediate discussion of the morning and its charms.

It seemed to Mr. Fairfield as if some black cloud had suddenly been cast across his sky, but he tried to remember that this was Maria's friend, and while she was not in

the least like Maria, she might have a great many delightful qualities if one could only get at them. At least she
had a soul, and if he could not be interested in her in any
other way, he would try to remember that, and let his
courteous treatment of her reflect his Master's example.
If he had but known her heart he might have felt more
tempted to assume a scourge of small cords with which
to drive her out from the temple of that day, into which
she had set tables for her barter in hearts. If good was to
reach her soul, at least he was not intended to bring it,
not in the way in which he brought it to Maria. This one
was not capable of receiving the good word, not yet at
least, for the ground was stony and shallow and barren.

Maria, coming with a bright face to meet her friend,
found the two seated side by side. Nannette was bending
over the other's chair to inspect a tiny gold ring which
he carried on his watch chain, and which she had herself
asked about. That this action on Nannette's part was
greatly to the annoyance of Mr. Fairfield Maria could
not possibly be expected to know. She would never
have been willing to ask about a gentleman's personal
adornments, nor to reach out and handle them of her
own accord, and she naturally judged that no other girl
would so far forget herself, especially with an acquaintance of barely one evening. The natural inference was
that he was telling her the story of the charm, and had
invited her to examine it. Of course it was evident that
they had come together from the hotel to see her,
anybody would know that. She half wished in her heart
that they had gone off together, and not brought her in
at all, then her life and her troublesome feelings would
not perplex her so. Nevertheless they had come, and her
part was to be pleasant and polite. She hastily drew to
her the memory of the night before, as a child will reach
out its hand to its father when in fear and remind him of

his promise to protect. She understood the swift upward look of her soul to the Saviour, asking him to help her to forget all but that she was his, and her heart thrilled with the answering strength that came to her need.

Nannette instantly saw her advantage. Indeed she had hastened her steps and given up her breakfast, scarcely hoping she might succeed in gaining the porch before Maria came out, but wishing, if possible, to give her the impression that she had come with Mr. Fairfield. If Maria would draw off and leave the minister to her, her task would be more than half done. It was Maria's presence which hindered her own charm from working. It piqued her to think that Maria could be supposed to be more charming than she, but then Maria had been there first, and there was no telling what a man might not take a fancy to if he had nothing else at hand. Nannette's idea of a man was that he must always have a woman to amuse him, as her idea of a woman was that she could never be happy without an adoring man or two about.

"You were so long coming last evening, dear, that we thought we would run right over after breakfast and stir you up," said Nannette gayly.

It occurred to the minister that Nannette must have eaten her breakfast long before he had, or else had gone without. He gave her a searching look and decided for the latter theory. Then he wondered what was her object. He was not a conceited man, and therefore her real object had not yet dawned upon him. He took her merely for a disagreeably bold, worldly girl, and decided to keep away from her as much as possible. He did not know yet how much control this skillful coquette had over the possible when she chose.

Maria sat down clothed in her new strength. She tried to look at Mr. Fairfield merely in the light of a chance acquaintance in whom she had no interest at all, and to heartily enter into Nannette's talk, at least in so far as she conscientiously could. She did not talk to Mr. Fairfield this morning. It was easier for her not to do so.

Mr. Fairfield was disappointed at the way things had turned out, and solaced himself by retiring from the conversation, as he had done the evening before, except when absolutely pressed into it by Miss Davenport. He was studying the fair lines of Maria's face, and thinking how lovely she was, and wondering why he had never noticed her beauty as being so unusual before. He thought there was a new touch of gravity and earnestness about her too, which sat well on her countenance. As he watched her and noted her replies, he made up his mind that she was in no present danger from Miss Davenport's influence.

But Nannette perceived that the conversation, of which she had the monopoly, was becoming strained, and casting about for something to change the situation she discovered in the distance along the Spray View road a carriage containing the De Veres. She immediately began to dilate on the excellencies of that family, and remembering that quality in man, jealousy, which had often served her a good turn, she professed especial delight in the coming of Roland De Vere.

"We always were such good friends," she said, turning her eyes sweetly upon the minister; "we used to play together by the hour as children, and as we grew older our friendship was really something lovely till he went away to college. Don't you think he has a very remarkable mind, Mr. Fairfield?"

Maria, remembering Nannette's account of her quarrel with Roland De Vere, listened in wonderment. Nannette had omitted to state that her intercourse with Roland De Vere from their earliest childhood had been strictly upon a war footing. He had never been afraid to tell her of the shams and falsehoods he saw in her, and this had made her almost hate him. Nevertheless, it was sometimes expedient to seem to love your enemies, at least for a time. This was one of the unwritten commandments in Miss Davenport's code.

Maria felt greatly relieved at the appearance of the De Veres. So did Mr. Fairfield, and so did Nannette, but each for a different reason.

A sailing party was the order of the day, and the De Veres had driven over to secure their Lone Point friends to join them. The yacht was to be at the Lone Point wharf in an hour to wait for them, and they were to send the carriage back by the driver, and go out across the bar and fish in the open sea, returning by moonlight. It was a thoroughly delightful plan. Maria could not help but be happy, and forget all her troubles. Somehow they seemed to melt away in the light of the genial company. She hastened in to call Rachel, and consult with her mother about some additions to the ample lunch which the De Veres had brought with them.

"We'll go in and tell the Parkers," said Fannie De Vere, catching Rachel's hand in quite a girlish fashion, and starting off through the sand.

"The Pahkahs! And who are the Pahkahs?" asked Nannette, amid the pleasant hurry that prevailed. Nannette always used the Southern drawl when she wished to be interesting.

"They're nobodies, Nannette; just nice, pleasant people, not at all like you and me. You won't care for them in the least," answered Roland De Vere with a touch of the old rudeness which had characterized his conversation with her always.

21

MR. FAIRFIELD, during the preparations for the excursion, had been diligently studying how he might secure Maria's company on the way to the boat, and for as much of the day as possible. But although he made himself variously useful, offering assistance to Maria and Rachel in numberless little ways, and gladly taking upon himself all the burdens of wraps and lunch baskets that he could find belonging to the green cottage, he did not seem to succeed. Maria was busy and dignified. If he essayed to walk beside her she suddenly discovered an errand with another member of the party, or rushed back for her forgotten parasol. Laden as he was he could scarcely follow her, and when he waited behind the rest he was at once pounced upon by Nannette, who called him a 'poor, lone man,' and sweetly insisted upon holding her parasol over him and carrying Maria's blue jacket, in the possession of which he had taken especial delight. He could do nothing but submit, for he was helpless. There was nothing for it but to walk grimly on to the wharf as fast as possible and hope for better fortune. Maria did not seem to see all this. In fact she was remembering just then that Mr. Fairfield had never told her the story of the dainty little gold ring he wore, nor even spoken of it. He took her for a girl who did not care for such things. Well, it was as well. He had helped her, he was a minister, a—no, it would not do to call him her friend. There must be a more dignified name for their relation than that. The Catholics had a good name for it: "Spiritual adviser," that was what he was. As such she could enjoy his conversation, and feel that she did right to take pleasure in his company, but not when Nannette was about. Maria, therefore, walked forward and began to talk eagerly with the first unoccupied one of the group. This happened to be Marvie Parker, and Maria silently blessed her for her bright, girlish conversation, which in spite of her, cheered her thoughts and turned them in another direction from the one which they were constantly tempted to take.

George Parker at the last moment joined the group on the wharf. Nannette had given his sister a comprehensive sweep of her big, brown eyes, and ignored her beyond the slightest possible inclination of the head. When the brother arrived, tall, grave, somewhat diffident in his manner toward strangers, and with a rather homely face and figure, by some mischance she was not introduced. It was as well, perhaps, for she stood in the shadow of a sail, and curled her lip as she looked at him. Of the happy little party standing about and warmly greeting the new-comers only Marvie saw that glance. Instantly her warm, loving heart resented it for her dear brother, and her anger flamed up till she was ready to blaze out in a well-deserved reproval, for Marvie Parker was a girl of tremendous impulses. But fortunately her impulses were under the control of One wiser than herself. A moment more, a hasty prayer, and she was ready to look again at the silly, conceited miss, and forgive her, and say, "Poor thing." Then she set herself to see if she could not in some way do a kindness to the one who had smitten her so hard upon the one cheek. She knew her brother far too well to carry revenge in her heart for his sake.

Maria took care to place herself between Fannie De Vere and Marvie Parker when they seated themselves in the boat, and when Mr. Fairfield cast about to get near her he found no opportunity. Miss Davenport had not been so discreet. She took good care that there should be a vacant place beside her, but the disappointed young man for once got the better of her. If he could not sit beside Maria, at least he would not subject himself for an entire morning to the chatter of her disagreeable friend. He went to the bow of the boat and seated himself among the coils of rope. Here he could be quiet and think and watch Maria without being observed.

Roland De Vere swung himself aboard at the last minute and took his seat, without noticing, beside Nannette, and when he discovered her proximity he was fully as dissatisfied as she with the arrangement. He began to wonder what he had done to deserve such punishment, but as Rachel was at his other side, with George Parker next, he devoted himself as much as possible to them.

Like some beautiful, intelligent creature, the boat spread her white wings, and turning glided from the bank. There seemed something almost unearthly in the beauty of the day and the flying of the boat along the shimmering bay, swiftly, swiftly to the place where the soft, benignant blue of the sky came down to meet the water. Perhaps Mr. Fairfield was the only one who thoroughly enjoyed it all. He was by himself and with pleasant thoughts for company. The others were arranging themselves comfortably and answering one another, as bright shafts of sarcasm and bubbling mirth went from one to another. Nannette was cross. She had missed her aim. True, she had managed to separate Maria and Mr. Fairfield, though she felt pretty sure that Maria had done that herself, and she could not even claim the credit of it. But she had not gained his company. She had felt certain that a whole day by her side amid such lovely surroundings would surely fix her in Mr. Fairfield's good graces by night. Now she had no one but that hateful Roland De Vere, and she saw instantly that he was not disposed to be forgetful or friendly. She decided to show her pique by making fun of those ungainly Parkers. If the young man had been just the least bit better looking, or seemed at all to glance at her with admiration, she might have been driven to flirt with him, but with such a man as Mr. Fairfield by, unwon, she felt she could not stoop so low. She decided, however, that Mr. Fairfield must not see her making fun of that solemn looking Parker boy, for as he was a minister she supposed he would be obliged to disapprove. She had a theory that young ministers always disapproved of wrong things because their churches obliged them to do so, and not at all because they felt any strong convictions on the subject.

Her opportunity to practise on young Parker came soon, and for want of better material she fell to work at once. Roland De Vere as early as possible during the morning made an excuse to change seats with George Parker. He felt sorry for George when he did it, but George Parker was one of those people who always have the disagreeable people and places thrust upon them in this world, and who seem to be given the grace to accept them pleasantly. His sister watched him as he sat down and turned his keen, gray eyes upon Miss Davenport, with a remark about the beauty of the day. Nannette had fancied him shy, and was astonished to find that he had a fine voice and spoke with perfect ease and unusual grace of manner. She plunged into a conversation with him, her most disagreeable expression upon her face, determining to put him to embarrassment as soon as possible. She had found from the talk of the others that he was something of a musician, and fancying him wise in his own conceit as a superficial amateur, she thought this would be as good an opportunity as any to "take a rise out of him." Summoning all her slight knowledge of the truly musical world, which amounted in all to the names of a few leading performers, with perhaps the titles of a number of brilliant productions, though it is doubtful if she knew which piece was being played without her programme, she began.

"Did you say you lived in the city?" she asked him, turning toward him with one of the cold stares which was usually so disconcerting to the poor victim whom she chose to transfix with it. "Then I suppose if you are so fond of music you heard Josef Hoffman last month."

Her expectation was that he would hardly know to whom she was referring, but to her amazement his plain face lit up with joy, thinking he had discovered a kindred spirit. "Yes, I did," he answered at once. "I heard him both times. It was a treat I would not have missed for the world. I was unable to get a seat, to be sure, as I had to rush there just at the hour, and there was scarcely standing room left. However, I might have been standing on my head for all I knew about myself while he was playing. Wasn't it fine? What did you think of his rendering of Beethoven's E-flat major sonata? Wasn't that first movement absolutely perfect? Didn't he bring out the orchestral effects most marvelously in Liszt's transcription of the overture to 'Tannhàuser.'"

It was Nannette's turn to be embarrassed. She had not heard Josef Hoffman, and would not have understood him if she had, for she was not a musician. Worse than that she had not one atom of delicate appreciation of good music; it was a bore to her and nothing more, unless it was the accompaniment for dancing. Then, and then only did it find an answering chord in her soul.

She flushed slightly, paused, but rallied and tried again. Her malice was stirred. She never quite forgave any one who made her feel uncomfortable. She flew to a subject in which she felt more at home.

"Were you at the opera house last month? Did you see 'The Wife's Revenge'?" she asked, a wicked look flashing across her face.

The young man looked at her with instant comprehension of the mistake he had made at first.

"Yes," said he, "I was at the opera house last month; but I did not go to see a play. I was with Mr. Moody."

Now Miss Davenport was so utterly out of the religious world that she did not at first know who Moody was.

"Moody," said she puzzled; "who is Moody?"

"Moody, the evangelist. Surely you heard of the two weeks' series of meetings held in the opera house."

"What! Moody and Sankey Sunday-school songs?" she exclaimed with a disagreeable laugh. "Oh, you're good, are you?" The sneer on her face was decided this time; but to her disappointment it did not seem to have any effect whatever upon her listener.

He turned his grave, gray eyes full upon her.

"Just what is your definition of goodness, Miss Davenport?" he asked quietly.

Nannette was nonplussed. She had not expected to be answered like that. She had looked for a wave of color over his face, and immediate disclaiming of any right to the adjective she had applied, in the midst of which she would laugh scornfully and make him to feel that to be "good" was above all things else a thing for one to laugh at and disclaim.

"Oh, I never deal in definitions," she answered uneasily. "I leave that to the dictionary."

"The dictionary gives some ten or twelve different meanings to that word, if I am not mistaken," said he; "but the one I like the best was given years ago by Paul: 'For scarcely for a righteous man will one die: yet peradventure for a good man some would even dare to die.' If I might claim that sort of goodness, Miss Davenport, I would count it the highest honor.

After that, conversation between these two languished. Nannette had really nothing to say. She felt that she had been worsted from the first, and with weapons which were new to her. She took refuge in teasing the fish which they presently began to catch. Strange to say, she was among the successful catchers that day. The line she held was often taken by some poor unwary fish, and she would jerk him out of the water and let him down again, only to give the line a stronger jerk and keep the poor creature in agony. The girls protested once or twice, and at last Roland De Vere turned with sudden vehemence upon her:

"Nannette, stop torturing that poor creature. It will rise in judgment against you at the last day." He perhaps did not mean his words literally, but he was angry at the cruelty of her action.

Nannette laughed scornfully and gave the fish another jerk. "Your theology is all wrong. They don't have fishes in heaven," she responded saucily. "Mr. Fairfield," she called laughingly, "do set Mr. De Vere straight. He thinks we shall have fishes in heaven. Do tell him they haven't any souls."

"I leave it to you, Fairfield," said the young man,

turning toward the minister, "if some animals haven't more soul than some human beings."

Thus appealed to, the minister recalled his thoughts from their pleasant wanderings and answered: "Certainly, De Vere, I fancy animals will have some part in the future life. Whether they have anything answering to souls or not, I cannot say; but I surely do think they will have their part, with all of God's creation, in the heaven that is being prepared."

This statement aroused much discussion and many exclamations from the rest of the party, and Nannette and her fishes were left to themselves while the others contemplated the new thought. Maria, who was charmed with the idea, which was a new one to her, found herself looking at Mr. Fairfield with her old admiration and thinking what a delightful talker and deep thinker he was. She wished he would go on and tell more about this; but he was not inclined to say much. He seemed to be changed somehow from the genial friend she had known so well for a few weeks. She wondered what had made the difference, and if Nannette had been the cause. How pleasant it would be if she could have him by herself just for a little while, so that she might ask him some questions about her new life which were perplexing her; but she supposed that must not be, for it was better for her not to see too much of him. What if he had seen how much she had enjoyed his company and had drawn off from her on that account, to save her from the shame of showing him her heart. Her face burned at the very thought. How dreadful that would be! Surely she could not have seemed to care for him! How could she when she did not know it? Of course she did not really care for him, she only feared she might. But she would not, now that she saw her danger. That would be terribly unwomanly. It was bad enough to have to realize her own danger. If she had been more careful she would not have had to endure the humiliation of that thought. But then, she might have missed this blessed joy of finding Christ. And her heart was really happy with the feeling of the perfect peace she had with God. She could be willing to endure even to have him think humiliatingly of her for the sake of that sweet peace. But she would take care to show him in the future that she had no interest in him apart from the spiritual help he had given her.

What a happy day this would have been if these two could have looked into one another's hearts! But God knew best, and he had some wise end in view through this discipline.

> *I cannot say, beneath the pressure of life's cares to-day, I joy in these;*
> *But I can say that I had rather walk this rugged way, if Him it please;*
> *I cannot feel that all is well when darkening clouds conceal the sun;*
> *But then I know God lives and loves; and say, since it is so, "Thy will be done."*
> *I cannot speak in happy tones; the teardrops on my cheek show I am sad;*
> *But I can speak of grace to suffer with submission meek, until made glad.*
> *I do not see why God should e'en permit some things to be, when he is love;*
> *But I can see, though often dimly, through the mystery, his hand above!*

22

ALTOGETHER Nannette felt very much discontented and dissatisfied with her first week at Lone Point. The weather had been perfect, but what is weather when there is a storm within? The party had been a merry one, but somehow she felt utterly out of harmony with it. Perhaps they felt this inharmoniousness more than she did.

The fishing had been abundant and successful. What fishing party could ask more? The sea had been calm. The sunset was one of the most magnificent ever seen at Lone Point and the moonrise was equally resplendent. They had floated slowly home, drawn by zephyrs that seemed willingly to obey the hand that held the helm. But one thing had been lacking in it all for Nannette, the only thing that made fishing parties and moonlight trips home again filled with pleasure, and that was an adoring man at her side who would chatter nothings and feed her vanity by likening her eyes to the sparkles on the wave and her complexion to the dazzling whiteness of the moonbeams. Mr. Fairfield had persisted in keeping a dignified distance, at least as far as was permitted by the length of the boat. Once, during a change of places she had gotten beside him as they came back from supper at the hotel on the mainland and were re-embarking for their homeward ride, but he had after a few words abruptly excused himself and gone to the aid of one of the sailors, who she felt sure needed him not at all. It was all very humiliating to her pride.

Any one, even George Parker, would have been better than no one at all. She was absolutely tied down to the companionship of the girls, and to her that was as low as she could fall. She had never taken pains to make any true friends among the girls, and felt, what was true, that she was only tolerated out of politeness. This she cared not one straw for when she had plenty of men at hand. She looked over at George Parker and wished she had been less disagreeable to him in the morning. It would at least have amused her to subjugate him, she felt it would have been an easy task, and to have enjoyed the dismay of that pious little sister of his. Altogether, Nannette was as thoroughly unhappy and disagreeable as she ever had been in her life. All the way home there had been singing. She had asked for one or two songs, but no one seemed to know the airs she called for, most of them society sentimentalities, or if they did, they did not care to break the harmony of the evening by bringing them in. The songs they sang were old ballads mostly; soft, low, sweet strains which seemed to be in tune with the murmur of the waters. By and by some one started a hymn, and they sang on from one to another favorite. It was wonderful how much more the words seemed to mean when sung on the water.

> "Far, far away like bells at evening pealing,
>   The voice of Jesus sounds o'er land and sea."

Nannette had an uncomfortable feeling that there might be a supernatural voice going to speak to them pretty soon. The songs chosen seemed all to follow one thought:

"Jesus, Saviour, pilot me,
Over life's tempestuous sea,"

and as the last words died away Rachel's voice took up the words of another:

"Jesus, Jesus, visit me,
How my soul longs after thee.
When, my best, my dearest friend,
Shall our separation end?"

Then Roland de Vere started with

"My Jesus, as thou wilt."

and his sister took it up at the close with the lovely tune of "Dorrnance" in the words,

"Jesus calls us, o'er the tumult
Of our life's wild, restless sea;
Day by day his sweet voice soundeth,
Saying, Christian, follow me."

Maria sang the words, feeling every one in her heart. She was enjoying this service of song more almost than she was able to endure, for tears of deep, unspeakable gladness would come to her eyes now and then, as she said over to herself: "He is my Jesus. I can feel it. I know it. I love him." And she realized at that moment that all her Christian life she had been dissatisfied with herself

and longing for just this thing to come to her, only she
had not been willing nor known how to take the
necessary steps to bring it about.

As they neared the shore and the lights of Lone Point
began to shine out over the water, Rachel and Marvie,
sitting together, started the sweet strain:

> *One sweetly solemn thought, comes to me o'er and o'er,*
> *I'm nearer my home in heaven to-day, than ever I've*
>   *been before."*

Nannette felt the hush that hung over the little company as the boat silently slipped up to the dock when the
last words were ended, and she was reminded so strongly
of her mother's funeral that she felt tempted to jump
overboard in order to create some kind of an excitement. Just as the boat touched the wharf, Mr. Fairfield
repeated in the clear rich voice which had hushed a
congregation to instant attention so often:

> *"And I pray that every venture*
> *The port of peace may enter,*
>   *That safe from snag and fall,*
> *And siren haunted islet,*
> *And rock, the unseen Pilot*
>   *May guide us one and all."*

It seemed like a benediction at the close of a beautiful
meeting. They landed in silence and went toward their
homes with a hushed reverence upon them.

Nannette, seated before her mirror—she always made
a practice of sitting before her mirror after she had been
anywhere, that she might see just how she had looked
and what sort of an impression she had made—curled
her lip in intense scorn.

"I feel exactly as if I had attended a revival meeting and been sitting on the mourner's bench all the evening. I declare this is worse than reading to Cousin George. I have half a mind to go home. If it were not for making that stuck-up minister come down a peg I believe I would; but he must be conquered! If I could only catch Maria at a disadvantage when he was along! I must see if I can't work something up along that line. I see plainly, however, I shall have to try the pious dodge before I can do very effective work. Ah me! What a bore! I shall make up for this next summer!"

Then she went to her bed, but not to sleep. She lay there planning a campaign which meant victory and the downfall of the ministry in Lone Point at least.

The days passed by with much the same relation between the three, Maria, Mr. Fairfield, and Nannette, that there had been the first day of Miss Davenport's arrival. Nannette annoyed Mr. Fairfield not a little, asked services of him, and accepted them in a gracious manner, as if it were a favor to him to be allowed to run her errands. She circumvented his plans to meet Maria in the most ingenious ways, often making it appear perfectly natural that it should be so, so that he had not even yet begun to suspect how deeply laid was her plan.

Nannette had not forgotten her wish to show Maria off to disadvantage before him, and constantly her mind was trying to discover some means of doing this. She went about her work with an ingenuity which was worthy of a better cause. One day at the table she began a conversation with a view to ascertaining his views on certain questions.

"Mr. Fairfield, what do you think of cards? Aren't they awfully wicked? Don't you find they do a great amount of harm?"

She asked the question one morning at breakfast. Mr.

Fairfield turned in amazement from the contemplation of his plate. This was not a subject in which he would have supposed Miss Davenport interested. As for discussing the right and wrong of card-playing, he did not deem that it would be at all profitable. He supposed, of course, she must be a card-player, as indeed she was, though she chose this morning to pose as one greatly disapproving the folly of it.

"I find that card-playing among Christians, as a rule, leads to worldliness," he answered stiffly. He judged Miss Davenport's object in asking the question to be to force him into an argument, and he did not care to discuss worldly amusements with a person who professed to belong wholly to the world. He was a little surprised that she did not further pursue the subject, but thought no more about it. He had more important things to think of. There was to be a concert by a fine orchestra on the veranda of one of the Spray View hotels. The Lone Point young people were invited over to spend the evening and attend it with the De Veres. Mr. Fairfield was hoping that the evening would give him an opportunity for at least a few minutes with Maria, so that he might ask her to walk with him the next day. He had a new address by Mr. Meyer which he was sure she would like to see, and he wanted the pleasure of reading it with her for the first time. It must—it surely could be planned. It was absurd that he actually could not get a chance to speak to her alone any more. He would have to resort to writing pretty soon if things went on as they were going, though he feared that for him to write would appear strange in her eyes, and precipitate matters before the time was ripe. He wondered, with a sigh, how long Maria's friend would stay in Lone Point. Perhaps he could ask her and find out the limit to this, to him, most distasteful state of things.

The fact was, if it had not been that Maria was resolved that Mr. Fairfield should not imagine her anxious for his company, Nannette would not have been able to contrive so many separations as she did; but with them both at work to keep him from his object it was a difficult thing for him to gain his point.

It was about this time that Winthrop Hammond had remained in town continuously for some days, taking care of a friend who was alone in the city and was ill with typhoid fever. The young man's parents had at last arrived and Winthrop felt at liberty to leave him, and so had come to the shore for a few days to stay, without going up to the city, as he felt he needed rest after his many nights of nursing and wakefulness.

It so happened that this concert at Spray View was the first one of the gatherings of the young people at which Winthrop had been present, and therefore was the first time Nannette had met him. Strange to say they had never happened to meet in town.

Maria prayed earnestly before going out that evening. She asked Winthrop anxiously several times if he would not rather remain at home and rest, saying she would gladly stay with him; but as he seemed to be really anxious to go, she ceased talking about it. Perhaps Nannette was so interested in Mr. Fairfield that she would not set any snares for Winthrop. At any rate she had put the dear brother into God's keeping, and nothing more could be done. She hovered about Winthrop and tried to be as cheerful and interesting as possible. Indeed, Winthrop noticed how she had changed and wondered what it meant. It was pleasant to have her seem to care to be with him, though it was unlike her too, for she was one who always had plenty of admirers of her own.

Nannette's plans were not thoroughly made, though

she knew she meant to make some decisive move that evening. She had a shadowed outline of a plan which should depend upon circumstances, and upon this occasion circumstances favored her. Early in the evening, she met a company of young people with whom she was well acquainted. Among them was a particularly fast young fellow, whose face showed plainly what his life must be. Nannette took pains to introduce them to Maria. This young man in particular seemed to be greatly taken with her, and whispered in an aside to Nannette:

"I say, Nan, she's a 'beaut'! Where'd you pick her up? I like her style. She's not so slow as a 'looker,' is she? Say, give a fellow a chance to talk with her for a while."

"All right, I will," she agreed readily enough, "if you'll do something for me in return. Promise me to get up a set for whist or euchre with her in it in the small card-room to the left of the office, the one with the wide windows on the piazza, you know. I have a special reason. I'm setting up a little joke on some one, that's all. I think she knows how, all right, but anyway, if she doesn't, you offer to teach her."

"You're a jewel, Nan," he responded eagerly, glad of the chance to teach so pretty girl as Maria anything; "just command me and I'll obey."

"Well, you be in there with the girls in five minutes and I'll manage to send her in," and Nannette went airily on her way. She was by no means so sure of Maria, as she pretended, but she would do her best. Fortune favored her a second time as she walked back to the end of the piazza, where the De Vere party was seated. Winthrop Hammond met her near the parlor door. He stopped her and begged that she would send the others to him as he had secured better seats for the music, but could not leave them lest some one else would pre-empt them. Here was one more aid for her scheme. A few minutes' delay one way or another would make no difference about the seats, and Winthrop Hammond would never find out. Yes, she would try it.

"Maria, dear," she said in a low tone as she came up to the party, who had not noticed her absence, for she had only walked away with her old friends for a few moments, "Maria, I just met your brother and he wished me to ask you to come to him. You will find him over there in that small room to the right of the office."

Maria rose at once and went in the direction she had pointed, wondering what in the world her brother wanted, and feeling a glad little thrill of joy that he did want her instead of some one else. As she walked away, Mr. Fairfield broke off in the midst of a sentence to Marvie Parker and rose to go with her, but Nannette quickly stepped to his side and, in a tone which all could hear, said sweetly: "Oh, Mr. Fairfield, would you be so good as to help me find my friends again? I have lost them and I am very anxious to see them once more before the music begins."

Of course there was nothing else to do as a gentleman but to offer her his arm and march away down the wide piazza, inwardly fuming at his trying position and, let us admit it, at its pretty cause.

Now Nannette could not, for her own purposes, have better timed their coming to the part of the piazza where the little card-room window opened out upon it, if she had been gifted with supernatural powers.

"I think I heard them say they would be near here. Would you just look in that window, please, and see if you catch a glimpse of them?" With her quick eye she had already seen the forming tableaus within and knew that time and scene were ready for the intended auditors. A table stood in the center of the room, around which sat the company of young people whom Nannette had recently introduced to the Lone Pointers. One seat was vacant and the fast young man was just bowing and holding it ready for Maria to be seated as Mr. Fairfield looked in. From where they stood in the darkness, gazing into the brilliantly lighted room, he could plainly see the cards on the table and in the hands of those about it, and then a soft little hand stole quickly over his eyes and Nannette, in the gayest of shocked laughs, said: "Oh, please come away. I'm so sorry. I wouldn't have done it for the world if I had known. She wouldn't have you see her in there, I know; but you won't think hardly of her for it, will you? She has been having such a hard time keeping up, you know, and one can't be good always. One must have a little fun occasionally. Besides, Maria has done bravely. She isn't used to such a straight-laced life, you must remember. She has been telling me how hard it was for her. But she would be terribly broken up if you saw her. She has been telling me about your—well, perhaps, I would better not say any more, for she might not like it, you know," Nannette broke off hesitatingly. They had been walking on toward a secluded end of the piazza, entirely deserted now, for the guests were gathering for the music. Nannette determined to strike while the iron was hot, for she thought she saw that Mr. Fairfield was greatly taken aback at what he had seen. Here were seats and the loud dashing of the waves. No place could be better for confidences and a pleasant little flirtation. What if the music did go on and pass, no matter if she fought for and won this trophy.

"Let us sit down just a minute, please," she said as if out of breath, putting her hand to her heart; "I feel so upset by this; I am afraid she would blame me for it, and I should feel so sorry. She has been telling me all about it, you know, and well—excuse me, but I have these little turns with my heart ever since mother's death. It will soon pass away. There—oh, please sit down just a minute."

She leaned her head back against the wall and let it incline till it almost rested against her escort. Only just an instant did she let it remain, and then she seemed to come to herself and gain strength to sit up, and to beg his pardon. She had hoped, that he might feel impelled to do as other young men had done before when she had been attacked in a like manner, but as she saw no sign of any such movement on his part, she concluded to discreetly withdraw.

Mr. Fairfield, on his part, was startled almost out of his accustomed composure. He would not have thought it so great a thing to see Maria playing cards, for she had told him herself that she had lived a worldly life, and she would not be expected to have thought over all these questions and to have decided them, in so short a space of time. But to be told that she had thought about it, and had deliberately gone in there to play, planning that he should not know about it—that she was actually trying to deceive him and appear better in his eyes than she was, was another matter. Worst of all was it to know that the sacred words which had passed between Miss Hammond and himself about a better, nobler life, had been recited in detail to this worldly, unsympathetic listener. This was what cut him to the quick. He sat dumb for a few minutes with the pain of it.

23

ONE might have supposed that Howard Fairfield, a minister of the gospel for three years, had lived long enough in the world, and had experience enough of it, not to believe all that such a girl as Miss Davenport told him. Indeed he had never put much faith in anything she did or said from the first, but somehow the little that he had seen with his own eyes to-night had suddenly broken down his good common sense, and he began to doubt Maria. This was what Nannette had hoped for. She had thought that with his first doubts of Maria he might turn to her, and then she would have gained an influence over him which she well knew how to use. But Nannette showed in this that she was not a good judge of human nature. She did not understand the pure, high nobility of such a man's heart or she would never have thought to thus turn him to herself.

Miss Davenport, when she saw that the minister was sitting by her side and waiting, got out her little black-edged handkerchief and began to sob softly.

"It frightens me terribly when I get one of those heart attacks," she said in a soft, childish voice. She was a very good actor when the occasion demanded private theatricals. "I feel as if I were not good enough to die."

She paused. She thought if there was a spark of the true minister in him he would turn now and try to preach to her, but instead he sat quite silent beside her.

After a moment in which nothing could be heard but the beating of the waves, he spoke in a stern, controlled voice:

"Are you quite able to return to your friends now Miss Davenport?" It was all that he could bring himself to say. He had detected the false note in her voice instantly. He could not try to talk to her of spiritual things. He felt instinctively that it would be casting pearls before swine. "If you do not feel able to go back, I will go in search of assistance for you," he added.

Nannette rose hastily from her chair, stung by anger and defeat, and during the long walk down that piazza neither of them spoke a word.

It was a pity that Mr. Fairfield could not have lingered just an instant longer before that brightly lighted window and have seen Maria coldly decline the seat at the card table, and after a glance about the room as if she were searching for some one, and a dignified word or two of inquiry about her brother, leave the room again. He might have been spared the pain which continually surged back and filled his heart, for then he would have seen that the whole thing was manufactured in the fertile brain of Miss Davenport. Perhaps too, it might have dawned upon him sooner that the young woman in question had an end of her own to gain, namely, himself. But the man's nobleness of character cannot better be described than by saying that such an idea did not even occur to him. It was not until he was in the quiet of his own room, and remembered that head almost laid upon his shoulder, that he began to see what sort of girl Miss

Davenport really was, and a blush of shame mantled his brow for her sake, and for the sake of the womanhood which in his thought she, even in that slight act, had dishonored.

Meantime Nannette, humiliated and resentful, directed the party to where Winthrop Hammond was waiting for them, and disappeared for a while from the room as she saw Maria approaching.

Mr. Fairfield slipped away as the music began. His excuse was that he had promised to preach the next day, and needed the time for preparation. No one thought it strange, though all were sorry to lose his companionship. As he walked down the long piazza, intending to walk home by the beach instead of the road, he espied two people ahead of him. They were some distance away, and he could not see them distinctly. In the mingled, uncertain light of moon and dashing spray, he scarcely noticed them at first, except to know that the dark figure was a man, and the white draperies belonged to a woman. But as they turned out into the brighter moonlight to walk on the silver sand close beside the waves, his rapid steps gaining upon their lagging, lover-like ones, the man's dark arm stole out and encircled the waist of the white dress beside him; then in the settling, confiding, unresisting attitude of the woman he suddenly realized a familiar memory, and as suddenly became aware of two long, black sash ends, with fluffy little black chiffon ruffles about them, which he recalled noticing on Miss Davenport's dress as she walked before him on the way from the De Vere home over to the hotel. It had occurred to him as he first set eyes upon them that he had felt morally certain if her bereavement had not positively forbidden it, that sash would have been a bright red.

He was drawing nearer, and could see their faces now.

Nannette was looking sweetly up into the man's eyes so close above hers, and he saw that the man was the same one who had but a few moments before placed Maria's chair at the card table. At least it was a relief to know that Maria was not playing with that man. He half wished he had remained to see what became of Maria, but he would not go back now. Moreover he had witnessed all the flirtations he cared for in one evening, and he turned abruptly off over the sand and struck straight across the country to the carriage drive, regardless of hillocks or wire fences, or even quicksands.

It was not a pleasant walk, and he felt as if perhaps he had lost rather than gained strength for his work on the morrow. He went straight to his knees, and in communion with his Heavenly Father he by and by lost the heavy strain that the events of the evening had put upon him, and was able to think of what he intended to say on the morrow.

He had chosen for his text, "For me to live is Christ"; that verse had been deeply impressed upon his mind since the first evening when he had visited the Hammond cottage, and Rachel had asked her innocent, earnest question.

By the hour of church service, the rest of the night, the beauty of the morning, and above all the peace which Jesus Christ had given him, had lifted him above his troubled thoughts of the evening before, and he felt "in the Spirit on the Lord's Day" as he went forth to speak in Christ's name.

For just a moment after he was seated in the pulpit, while the congregation was gathering, he felt a disagreeable sensation as Miss Davenport came in and seated herself before him in her elegant black robes. Perhaps he was hard upon her, but he was a noble man with high ideals of womanhood, and his very soul shrank from the thought of what he had seen of that young woman the night before. He caught however a glimpse of Maria's face, on which unconscious loveliness sat so sweetly, and of Rachel's calm brow, and he remembered that there were women in the world who would not stoop to what was beneath them. He wondered, as he looked at the sisters, why he had never noticed before how much alike they were. Happily for him he forgot for the moment the trouble about Maria that had come to him the night previous, for the sight of her face in its Sabbath peace seemed so foreign to anything deceitful that it was not until his work for the morning was over that the occurrence suddenly came back to his memory. There is no time when God's servants need so earnestly to watch and pray as when they have just finished some special work for him which required attention, and nerves on the alert. The tension is over, and they feel no more need for the watching and prayer immediately, and Satan steals up unaware when they are all unprepared for attack and takes them in their weakest place, sometimes undoing or rendering useless all the work of the time of action.

So after the hour of exaltation, when Mr. Fairfield almost stood upon the mount with his Saviour, and face to face with him gave forth the message of life, when as he spoke he felt in his heart that though to live for Christ was glorious, yet to die for him would be better than all, and that he would welcome death at once if Christ should send it; after all this Satan stole upon him on his way home and told him his preaching was of no effect, that his dearest hopes were vain; that the woman whom he felt was the one of all the earth for him was vain and deceitful, and possessed a number of other qualities he could not bear to think of.

However, as Satan was busy with the preacher, he had

not time just then to go about picking up the seeds o‹
good that had fallen upon the open mellow ground, anc
when he did get back to that work he found that much
of the seed had already taken root and was growing.

It was only that which had fallen upon the rocks tha‹
he could pick up and destroy.

Maria felt the uplifting of the morning sermon. It had
helped her beyond anything she had ever heard before
It may have been because the preacher had written hi‹
sermon just for her. He had in mind her heart experience
and he seemed to have anticipated all her doubts anc
perplexities and answered them. He had been much
with God during the days when he had not been able to
talk with her as he had done before and perhaps thi‹
separation had been good for them both for this very
reason. They were learning each to first find help in Goc
and only after that in one another. She thanked Goc
over and over again that day for that sermon. She wa‹
not unaware that the preacher's face, in its high intellectual refinement, had worn a look of spiritual illumination which in her eyes made it more beautiful in a manly
way than any face she had ever looked upon. It troubled
her that the realization of the speaker's personality came
so often to her mind, but after several vain attempts to
put it away she decided to enjoy the day and the sermon
and not trouble herself about this part of it, which
apparently could not be helped.

There was just one speck of trouble on the bright
surface of the day to her. Her brother Winthrop had
walked beside Miss Davenport back to the hotel from
church, and after dinner had declined Rachel's earnest
request that he should attend her to the Sabbath-school
and gone directly back to the hotel. From the piazza of
the green cottage she had soon thereafter seen him
emerge from the hotel carrying Miss Davenport's shawl

and parasol, and with her by his side they had sauntered down the beach. She had evidently made up her mind that so spiritual a preacher would hardly be good material for a jolly Sunday afternoon and looked about for other prey.

As Maria had watched her during the past week or two, she had become more and more convinced of the shallowness and perhaps wickedness of her heart. She felt assured that she was an utterly unprincipled girl, and she could not bear to see her brother Winthrop walk into the net spread for him. In this fear she was evidently joined by Rachel, although neither said anything to the other; and Rachel stood by her side on the piazza, her calm brow for once clouded with trouble and the ready tears gathering as she watched their brother. Maria had turned and looked at her and as their eyes met she obeyed the warm impulse of her heart and kissing Rachel gently, said "Come with me." Almost in a daze, Rachel had understood, though up to this time there had no word of any change in Maria passed between the two. Rachel followed her sister to their room and together, hand in hand, they knelt down beside their bed. They spoke no word aloud then, nor after they rose, but Rachel kissed Maria this time and then slipped softly away to the Sabbath-school. Because of this little incident, Maria felt that the day had been a wonderful one, and so did Rachel. It had touched Rachel's heart beyond anything that had ever happened between them, to have Maria tell her in this way of her new deep feelings. She was a remarkable little sister or she might not have understood.

It may be that some little seed of the morning's word dropped on Miss Davenport's heart. She felt troubled. She was reminded unpleasantly again of her mother's death. She always avoided solemn things if she could, but that had been the one solemn incident of her life thus far that she had been unable to avoid. She did not wish to think about it, because while in her life that mother had not been so strong and faithful as she ought to have been, yet in her death she had aroused to the sense of her responsibility and had spoken a few dreadful words to her daughter, which by night and by day pursued her, unless she could keep her mind occupied with worldly things. However, her mind was shallow and she easily turned the tide of her thoughts to light things.

She had not been without some recognition of the illumination of the minister's face as he preached that morning, though in her words he was judged "decidedly handsome and *distingué.*" She remembered his severity of the evening before, and a blush of actual shame crept over her face, unused to such blushes as it was. Then to drive out this unusual feeling she began to wonder if after all there was not yet hope that she might conquer this man. He had held out so long that it would really be quite interesting if she could bring him to her feet now. She might even fall in love with him. She really felt nearer to falling in love than she had for four or five years. And if he had a good church and large salary it might not be so bad a "catch" after all. She began to speculate upon just what the position of a minister's wife was, and how much would absolutely be required of her, for propriety's sake. The only drawback she could think of would be that she might be occasionally called upon to attend funerals, and *that* she *would not do*. She would never do it to please any one! Horrid places! She shuddered involuntarily and took up her fan, deciding that she would put her foot down upon that at once and declare she would not go. After all, as she had plenty of money, and probably would have more than he, there would be no danger but that she might have her own way about everything. Thereupon she looked up to the minister's face to see how it would seem to look at him in the light of a possible husband, and perceived that he had hushed the audience into tears by a simple story of pain and loss and love and loyalty to Christ which he was telling. She took up her handkerchief and tried to listen with the others as he recited impressively, the words:

> "When his steps
>   Were on the mighty waters—
> When we went with trembling hearts through nights of
>   pain and loss,
> His smile was sweeter and his love more dear;
> And only heaven is better than to walk
> With Christ at midnight over moonless seas."

During the prayer that followed the sermon's close she formulated the plan which she carried out that evening, her final plan for his capture. Then with the benediction, she rose, satisfied with her morning's worship, and turned to Winthrop Hammond with her sweetest smile. If the plan should fail, there was this one left, and he was handsome and of a good family, and not very hard to subdue as she could easily see.

As Mr. Fairfield passed down the aisle, his exaltation yet upon his face, his thoughts hardly called back to earth from the message he had delivered, she stretched out her daintily gloved hand and just touched his coat sleeve with the tips of her fingers:

"Oh, Mr. Fairfield," said she with a sweet and re-minding quiver in her voice, "thank you for that sweet sermon. It was just perfectly lovely. I did enjoy it so much."

And the minister suddenly remembered that he dwelt yet upon the earth.

24

MR. FAIRFIELD received two letters of note in the Monday morning's mail. One had no postmark. The other was from his city home, telling of the severe illness of a woman who belonged to his church. He read this first, naturally anxious to know the home news, and sat with it in his hand pondering whether his duty did not call him home, at least for a day or two. Then he suddenly remembered the other letter. It was written in a high, angular hand on a thick cream, violet-scented paper, and as the handwriting was very "high" indeed, and the letter long, it was consequently bulky. It read as follows:

MY DEAR MR. FAIRFIELD: *My heart is filled with conflicting emotions as I sit down to write you this note. I feel as if I had come to a crisis in my life. The moment that I met you I realized that you were one who was to wield a great influence over me, and have something unusual to do with my life. This morning when I sat entranced listening to your words of eloquence I realized this still more. More than any one I have ever met, I believe you have influenced me. I was deeply affected. I have been thinking the matter over, and have decided to ask your help and spiritual advice. My dear mother used to tell me that some day I would meet with some one who would have the power to reach my stony heart religiously, and I now see that she was right. Oh, I am very wretched and miserable! If you can bring me any consolation from the religion which you so beautifully preach, I shall be forever grateful to you. I know you will not leave a poor girl who has no one else to whom to turn, comfortless. You will come to me and let me tell you the story of my life, and you shall teach me how to be good like yourself. I cannot endure yet to have any of my friends know that I have taken this step. It is too new and too sacred a thing to me. Therefore I ask you to meet me by the inlet, up toward the lighthouse, where the old mast is buried in the sand. There we can sit and talk to our heart's content without being observed. I shall be there at half-past ten in the morning, and I know you will not fail me. Until then farewell. Yours penitently,*

NANNETTE M. DAVENPORT

The minister felt a cold chill creeping over him as he read this letter. He was more and more convinced of the insincerity of the writer as he thought over the matter, and read and re-read the letter. There was not in his heart one particle of response to that summons for help. He tried to examine himself and see whether it was his prejudice which made him feel so; but no, he could not think of any one else, no matter how humble, whom he would not gladly have gone to meet and help. He could not feel that the Spirit of God was sending him to this one. Saturday night's experience stood out too plainly in his mind, and the horror that he felt, grew as he thought about it. If there had been no one to talk with her, the case would have been different. He would have risked all on the mere chance that she was in earnest. Or if she had not worded her letter so strangely, and chosen so secluded a spot for their talk, he would not have been half so suspicious. What should he do? He felt strongly that this letter was written in much the same spirit as one a tramp had brought to him some months before, poorly spelled and ungrammatical in wording, purporting to be from a scholarly member of his church. It was to the effect that if he, the minister, would give the man some help from the church funds, this church-member felt sure that they might win the man to Christ. He was disposed to beware of this letter in the same way that he had been of that, for in the former case his suspicion that the man was an arrant fraud and the letter a forgery had proven entirely correct.

He felt now that for the sake of the love he bore Maria he ought not to meet this strange young woman. What if Maria should be walking upon the sand, and come upon them? Perhaps Miss Davenport meant to plan just such a *rencontre*. Now that his eyes were open there were no depths to which he felt she might not descend to gain her end, whatever it was. Then the letter had no genuine ring. There was too much talk about himself and his influence on her. There was no confession of having sinned. Why had she seen it necessary to write at all? Why had she not boldly asked him to talk with her upon the porch or anywhere? There were plenty of opportunities. Why, if she wanted religious help, had she not gone to Maria who, according to her own statement, had talked with her on these topics? He went to his room and asked his Heavenly Father's advice. This was a matter too important for his own inclination to decide. He could not easily refuse a call for help, even though he did doubt it. He prayed, trusting that an answer would come, and it did.

As he rose from his knees the other letter, the one about the sick woman, fluttered from his hand upon the floor, and on the back of the sheet where he had not noticed it before he saw a short postscript, asking him, if possible, to come home, as the woman had wished for him and seemed to have something on her mind to tell him. Quick as a flash he felt that this was his heaven-sent answer, and he must obey. A glance at his watch told him that the next train was due at the station in one hour, just ten minutes before the time set by Miss Davenport in her letter for him to meet her at the inlet. He would go home. He certainly ought to go home, for his church was his first duty, and this woman was dying. Hastily he gathered together his belongings, and settled up the few matters which had to be attended to before he left, trying all the while to think what to do about Miss Davenport's request. He might ask some one else to meet her. He thought of a dear old Christian woman at home and wished she were here, but she was not. He thought of Maria, but disliked to ask her to go on such an errand to her own friend, lest she might suppose he had formed an intimate friendship with Miss Davenport, the circumstances of the past week well bearing out such a supposition. Nevertheless, he at last made up his mind that Maria was the only one to whom he could turn now. He went at once to the green cottage, leaving his orders about baggage at the hotel, so that he would not have to return.

Nannette was far up the beach practising pretty little maneuvers with her deepest bordered handkerchief, and thus failed to see him go. But when Mr. Fairfield reached the green cottage he found to his dismay that Maria, with her mother, had been driven over to Spray

View in Mr. Higgins' green wagon to do some Monday morning marketing, and would not be likely to return before the city train left. His heart was filled with a great regret when he thought of leaving her so abruptly, so that for a few minutes the thought of Nannette in her self-appointed trysting-place did not come to him. Rachel was at home and had given him writing materials, and he was trying to construct a note of farewell to Maria. Perhaps he ought to write a note to Miss Davenport. It was only courteous to do so, but when he started he found that in his inmost soul he shrank from addressing a word to her. He glanced up at the earnest face of Rachel as she sat shelling peas on the upper step of the piazza. Her far-away, dreamy expression told that her thoughts were upon high and lovely things.

Suddenly a new idea came to him. It would be late when Maria returned, too late for her to reach Miss Davenport at the inlet before she had left there. Here was Rachel. She would know how to help that girl. There passed through his mind the verse about how the Lord had kept some things from the wise and prudent and revealed them unto babes, and while Rachel was no babe, still she was a child at heart. He remembered how well she had taught the little boys upon the sand. She had the root of the matter in her, and could surely bring the message of salvation to another soul. He would send her. In a few words he explained the situation to Rachel, telling her only what was absolutely necessary, that Miss Davenport had been affected by the services of yesterday, and had written him a note, in his capacity as a minister, asking his help spiritually. He was called suddenly to the city by sickness in his congregation, and might be detained he knew not how long. Would she go and meet Miss Davenport, and help her to find Christ?

Rachel's face beamed with a holy light to think she was to be sent on an errand of mercy. She was genuinely glad that Nannette wanted to be a Christian. She had been secretly praying for her ever since her arrival, she seemed to Rachel to be so much in need of a Saviour. She promised eagerly to go at the appointed time, and immediately went away to get ready, such a joy upon her face at the thought of the work before her that the minister was put to shame and felt he ought not to have shrunk from it. However, he reflected that as Rachel had no such doubts of the would-be inquirer as he held, she might be able to do much more good, for she was going trusting that her mission would be blest, and perhaps it would. He pledged himself to pray for this.

Then he found to his dismay that he had very little time left and could only write a line to tell Maria he was sorry to leave without seeing her. He left the Meyer book for her, asking that she would read it with him on his return, if he was able to return that summer. Then he heard the train whistling at Spray View, and hastily bidding Rachel good-bye went to the station, feeling that he was leaving behind him all that was precious in this world. It certainly was very hard for him to go. If only he could have had a little word with Maria and one of her lovely smiles to light him on his way!

Rachel, with exalted expression and her little Bible in her pocket, walked swiftly up the beach. She was praying as she went that she might be led to say the right words.

Nannette was seated on the sunken mast, her back turned toward the entrance of the secluded amphitheatre-shaped place she had selected for her morning's confessional. Her idea was to be deep in meditation of an affecting character when the young man should arrive, and thus make a good impression at first. She reasoned that if any one else came by and saw her sitting thus they would think she wished to be alone and pass on.

Rachel came with eager steps almost up to Nannette before she realized that any one was near, and then hearing the rustle of a dress, Nannette turned quickly to see who was there.

"Oh, Nannette! I am so glad!" exclaimed Rachel, stooping down and kissing the astonished girl on her forehead. "I am so glad for you, but I wish there was some one better than I to help you."

"What do you mean?" said Nannette coldly, pushing her back and looking at her strangely. It had been so long since any girl had cared to kiss her that it made her feel queer.

"There! I have done just as I always do, and plunged into the middle of things without any beginning," said Rachel distressed.

"Why, Mr. Fairfield had to go away to the city this morning. He was called suddenly to a woman who is sick, and he stopped at the cottage and told me you were troubled, and you wanted to know how to be a Christian; and he asked me if I would come and tell you the best I could about it. I am sorry it is only I. If Maria or mamma had been at home one of them would have come; but he was anxious some one should come to explain at the hour, why he was not here, so I have come and I'll do my best, dear. I do love Jesus, and I think I can tell you a little about him," she said sweetly; "and oh, I am so glad you are going to belong to him too."

Nannette looked at Rachel blankly.

"And so he is gone!" she exclaimed, and broke into a harsh laugh. "Well, I have taken a lot of pains for nothing. It was awfully good of you, Ray, to travel way out here in the sand and sun, and you are doubtless just as good a talker as any one else, so don't worry your righteous little soul about that; but indeed you needn't trouble yourself to talk religion to me. I'm not in the mood for it, and it really wouldn't pay you. You'd better keep it for the fisherman's children. I hear you are quite converting them." Nannette arose to go back, a disagreeable look on her face. She felt that she was foiled again, and this time pretty badly. There was no longer any hope of reducing the minister to admiration of her charms; he was gone. He had evidently run away. She laughed aloud again. "Rachel, I have driven him from the ground. He didn't dare to stay and fight. It is a sort of victory, after all."

Rachel, who had been watching her in puzzled silence, was now completely mystified, and began to wonder if Nannette was losing her mind. "What do you mean, Nannette?" she asked.

"Oh, you dear little goose," laughed Nannette. She had not the energy to keep up her "pious dodge," as she called it for the benefit of a girl; what would be the use? She told herself it would make her no end of trouble, so she frankly admitted the part she had been playing.

"Did you really suppose I was anxious about my soul? Well, you must have known very little, indeed, about me. Don't look so worried, I was doing no harm. Your nice little words that you had all fixed up, will come in quite handy for some one else. If you were not such a blessed little goose, I would be very angry that he had dared to send some one else in his place."

"But, Nannette, he couldn't come, and I was the only one at hand he could send," said Rachel, with her troubled eyes looking earnestly at the other girl. "Perhaps he had not time to explain it all out to me. What was it you did want of him? I don't understand."

Nannette was very much amused, indeed. She laughed and laughed, using the black-bordered handkerchief to wipe away tears, genuine for once, even if they were born of mirth instead of grief.

"Well, I would have been a fool indeed if I had lured the minister out here just for the sake of talking religion at me, my little innocent," she said when she could control her laughter sufficiently to speak. "My dear, I wanted to bring him out here for a nice, little, harmless flirtation, that's all. Don't be so shocked. I wouldn't have hurt the poor man for anything."

"Oh, Nannette!" exclaimed Rachel in a horrified voice, "don't say that; you surely don't mean it, that you would plan such a flirtation with a minister?"

Nannette fairly shrieked with laughter now. "And did you suppose, my dear, that because he was a minister he had no heart?" she said between her peals of laughter.

Rachel was silent for a moment, taking in the meaning of what had been told her. "But, Nannette—" she hesitated as a new thought came to her. "Aren't you engaged to that other man? The one we met last night? Excuse me, but I couldn't help seeing. I stood on the piazza with Fannie De Vere as you went down the beach and I saw—him—put—his—arm—" She stopped. She could not bring herself to say more, and the tears were coming to the surface now with the effort she was making to do her duty.

A blush of as much shame as this girl could feel stole suddenly upon her cheek as she saw her own act, which had seemed to her an every-day affair, standing out in the light of this sweet, pure soul's ideals. It was perhaps the first time that Nannette had ever felt any real shame in allowing such familiarity with comparative strangers.

"Oh, little Ray! You are good fun!" she tried to say carelessly. "Why that was nothing. Any nice man would do that and think nothing of it. Just wait till Roland De Vere tries it with you and you'll understand."

And then Miss Davenport was treated to a touch of such righteous wrath as made her see that the gentle-hearted Rachel Hammond had more spirit in her than she had thought.

"Mr. De Vere would never do such a thing!" said Rachel, her bosom heaving and her face flaming, and then, her eyes flashing, she added, "But if he *did,* he would never try it again." She turned and walked a few steps with dignity. But Nannette rebuked, and not wishing to show it, sprang up.

"Oh come, now, Ray, don't be too hard on people who haven't risen to your heights. We can't all think alike, you know. I guess you're right about Roland. He's too much of an old granny to do anything of that sort. Come, let's be friends and go home, this sun is broiling. Don't tell your good mamma about this escapade of mine, I beg of you, or else she might write to my prim old auntie and have me sent home in disgrace."

Rachel walked along in silence. Of her in her everyday life it might be said:

"Other hope had she none, nor wish in life, but to follow meekly, with reverent steps, the sacred feet of her Saviour." It was not often that anything stirred her soul to the depths as this experience of the morning had done. And yet, as she grew calmer she realized that the girl beside her did not know Jesus, and that she had started out on a mission to help her to find him. She remembered how she had committed her cause to her Master before starting, and that she had confidently trusted in him to bless what she should do. And now she was going home without even having said one word that could make this other girl think more of Jesus Christ. Was the fault in her? Would it be casting pearls away to speak now, after what had passed between them? And yet could she in conscience leave her without having at least tried to fulfill her trust? All the way along the beach she was silent, letting Nannette talk as rapidly and vapidly as she would. Suddenly, as they came in sight of the hotel, Rachel paused beside a little side path that turned off from the beach and went down toward the green cottage, a shorter cut than going around by the hotel.

"Nannette," she said, putting out her hand gently to detain her companion, "I came out this morning to bring you a message from Jesus. I thought you were waiting for it, and would be glad to get it. I found you were not. I am very sorry. But I believe that Jesus sent that message to you all the same, even if you did not want it, and I must give it to you. Nannette, Jesus loves you, and he wants you to love him." The tears were in Rachel's eyes, and she felt that she could not trust herself to say another word, so she turned and sped swiftly down the sandy path toward home, and Nannette stood still looking after her, a strange smile upon her face, half of wistfulness and half of ridicule. As Rachel disappeared from sight behind the sand dunes she turned toward the hotel again, murmuring to herself, "She's a good little thing."

And who shall say but that Rachel's words were as the seed that often lies long in the cold, black earth before it gives sign of life? But at last it bursts and grows and brings forth fruit.

25

AFTER that Nannette plunged into a mad flirtation with Winthrop Hammond. She kept him by her side morning, noon, and evening. He was certainly devoted enough to make up for all the chagrin she had felt in the lack of admiration she had found in Mr. Fairfield. He bought her candy, and flowers whenever such were procurable in Spray View, regardless of the fact which he had heretofore kept before him that money was an article not to be carelessly spent by any member of the Hammond household just now. Nannette discovered a company of friends at Spray View who were altogether gay enough to suit her. There were little private gatherings for card playing and dancing, and Nannette, unrestrained by onlookers, took her part now and again, and began to feel that the summer was not such a bitter failure after all.

Having reduced Winthrop Hammond to subjection she set herself to make him drink wine. The young people with whom she went always drank it at their gatherings. She took him among them on all possible occasions where it was forthcoming. She ridiculed him when he declined it, and when he allowed his glass to be filled she dared him to drink with her. He had been brought up with a strong feeling against the use of wine, and he did not readily overcome it. Once or twice he drank to please her, because she made such a point of it. He was out very late at night these times, and his mother was troubled about him. His father even went so far as to suggest that it might be as well for him to return to his business, if he was going to use his rest hours to so poor an advantage. But he answered them all laughingly, and went on.

It was evident to the family that he had fallen in love with Nannette Davenport, and each wondered at it. They did not know how very charming she could be when she chose, and they could not know that she was choosing just now to very good purpose. Having been foiled in her first attempt she was angry, and determined to take her revenge out of the next victim. She appeared to think a great deal of her admirer, but in truth Mr. Fairfield's intellectual face and severe eyes turned full upon her, often rankled in her soul, and she felt deeply ashamed of herself and her whole life.

Things had been going on in this way for about two weeks. No word had come from Mr. Fairfield save an occasional paper or book addressed to Maria, and once a large box of beautiful flowers, which came by express and contained no card. Maria treasured all these things, but of course said no word to Nannette concerning them. Maria's life just now was a little hard. She worried daily about her brother, and prayed often. She tried to make a friend of Nannette, that she might, if possible, prevent the intimacy between her and her brother. Nannette apparently had grown quite discreet. She asked one day as they were walking together: "Say, 'Ri, you wouldn't write to that minister, would you, if you were I? I should hate to hurt his feelings, but really I don't like letter writing, and when a man's gone, why he's out of it, you know. If he should come back, of course I'd be nice to him, I suppose, but I hardly like to go so far as to correspond, it seems to mean so much, you know. A man always means a good deal by asking for the privilege, especially a man like that. I haven't written him but once, and I don't believe I shall again, would you?"

And Maria answered, "I should do as I thought best," and turned the conversation to other topics, but she could not help thinking that Mr. Fairfield had never asked her to correspond with him. And she never knew that Nannette had been prompted to these remarks by a chance sight of the box of flowers at the express office addressed to Maria in a handwriting she recognized.

Winthrop Hammond was to return to the city to his business the next morning. He was out, and it was very late. Both his sisters had silently kept the watch, which was also being kept by the anxious mother in the next room, for his footsteps. Rachel, as she lay quiet, lest she should rouse her sister from what she supposed was a happy sleep, wondered if her brother could ever fall so low as to treat Nannette in the way that other young men had done. She shuddered at the possibility, and yet she had seen enough in the face of that daring girl on the day when she met her at the inlet, to feel that her influence over any man would be a tremendous power should she choose to exercise it.

She and Maria had both spent much time in praying, during the past few days, for their brother. Rachel felt that an answer would surely come soon.

Winthrop came at last, but his steps were slow and lagging, and did not sound like him. He came into the sitting room, and instead of going directly to bed sat down heavily in a chair. Once Rachel thought she heard a groan, and then, as all was still, she waited. Presently her brother threw himself upon the couch and groaned again, this time quite audibly. Rachel sprang to her feet, and, throwing a shawl about her, hurried out to the sitting room, but she found that her mother was there before, and Maria not far behind her. There was no mistaking the fact that their brother was ill. He was suffering too much pain to talk or give them any idea of what was the matter, but he had a high fever, they could tell that for themselves. The father started almost immediately for the doctor, while the mother and sisters got him to bed, heated water, and gave various simple home remedies. They then waited anxiously the coming of the physician.

It was as they feared—typhoid fever. The evenings of pleasure following the nights of nursing had told upon him. The doctor warned them that it was likely to be a severe case. Then the household settled down into that forced quiet where there is the dread anxiety of critical illness. Maria insisted upon staying with her brother night and day, and, strange to say, though Rachel had always been his favorite, he seemed best satisfied with Maria in the room. During the nights and days of waiting and watching and breathless anxiety, Maria had no time to think of herself. Whenever she had a moment to herself she spent it in prayer. Her life now was one long prayer.

She sometimes looked back on the days when all was bright and happy and she had been unhappy and unreasonable, and wondered at herself. Then she thought gratefully of Mr. Fairfield and the change he had been the instrument, in God's hands, of making in her. She wondered how she could have gone through this long, tedious trial without Jesus as her friend. She seemed literally to be living in his presence now; to be bearing all she bore with his strength, not her own; to be watching his face to see if her brother was to be spared to live more years with them, or to be taken away. She felt an assurance that if God took him he would at least first give him time in which to take Jesus as his Saviour. He was delirious now for days, did not know one of them, and then lay in a sort of stupor. The time of the crisis had come. Maria was sitting by his side, while her mother rested near at hand, to be called should there come a change. She scarcely dared to breathe lest she should disturb the one so dear, who lay hovering between life and death. Her every breath was a prayer for him. Suddenly he opened his eyes, and in a feeble voice that was scarcely audible, whispered, "'Ri, can you pray?"

Maria thought he must be dying, but without daring to wait, so momentous seemed that instant, she dropped upon her knees, and in low, controlled tones, prayed that Jesus might stand by her brother, and loving him, might take his hand and hold him in that moment, for life or death, for time or for eternity. She scarcely knew what she said, as with upturned face and eyes that seemed as though they saw the Lord, she prayed on. The burning, unnaturally bright eyes upon the pillow watched her, drinking in every word eagerly, as though thirsty, while Maria, praying, pleaded promise after promise from God's word. By and by the restless look faded from his eyes and there came a calm like a shadow of peace, and at last the eyelids fell, and Maria knew by the soft, natural breathing that he was asleep. By and by she dared to rise and call the others, and the doctor coming in told them that the crisis was past and the young man would live. Then the sister went away and thanked God.

But her work was not yet done. As the invalid grew able to talk he wanted Maria, and long converse he held with her about the things of life. Maria felt that she was having her reward for the days and nights of watching, and her soul rejoiced in God her Saviour.

All this experience had been so hard that it seemed to put the summer, with its pleasure and brightness, and its disappointments too, far behind her. She looked back to those days when she and Mr. Fairfield had walked and talked together beside the sea, with a wistfulness sometimes, but still with all the sting gone from heart. Nannette, as soon as she learned the nature of the malady that had now befallen her devoted admirer, in dire dread and haste, picked up her belongings, tumbled them into her trunks, and fled. She had a horror of sickness at all times, and a superstitious fear that she would take typhoid fever if she were exposed to it. Besides her conscience troubled her. She knew that it had been her fault that the young man had spent so many evenings out late and had been drinking wine, a thing to which he was unaccustomed; and she began to fear that this had been partly the cause of his illness. Rachel was grateful that she was gone, yet indignant to think that the girl to whom her brother had devoted his entire attention for three weeks should depart at once without so much as a good-bye or an inquiry for him when she heard of his serious illness. The rest of the family felt nothing but relief.

The De Veres came daily to inquire and to offer aid, and in many ways showed their true friendship. Rachel often wondered that no word came from Mr. Fairfield, and felt sorry on Maria's account, for she recognized that he had been the means of making a change in Maria, and she was disappointed that he had left so suddenly, for she had liked him. She laid it all at Nannette's door, however, and tried to forget it.

One day in September, when Lone Point was almost deserted and only one guest left at the hotel, Maria was sitting on the piazza reading aloud to Winthrop, who was convalescent. The city train stole softly up the length of the island, its line of smoke, black against the sky, the only warning of its coming till the whistle blew near-by, for the sand seemed to dull all sound of rushing engine and whirling wheels. The two on the piazza were so deep in their reading that they did not stop to glance at the train, though they could easily have seen from the piazza who arrived or departed. It was the morning train too, and few ever came at that hour so late in the season.

Presently a step was heard upon the walk, and looking up they saw Mr. Fairfield standing before them. The pink rose to Maria's cheek, and the instant flutter of her heart told her that she had not forgotten, as she had hoped. Her embarrassment was heightened by his steady, earnest gaze, which seemed to be searching her face for some answer to an unspoken question. He took his eyes from her long enough to shake hands with her brother, who welcomed him most heartily, and then he looked back at Maria once more, with a glad, hungry look. Something, perhaps it was her downcast eyelids and the color in her cheeks, brought a half-satisfied expression to his face.

Explanations followed. Mr. Fairfield had suddenly gone to Europe, as much, perhaps, to his own surprise as to theirs. When he reached the city he had received word by cable that his sister was to be married at once in Berlin, and earnestly beseeching him to come over, if only for a few days. It was a sudden change of plans, for she was not to have been married for another year, but her intended husband was about starting on a trip through Palestine, Egypt, and the Mediterranean, and she and her mother were to accompany him. He had decided hastily, having very little time for choice as the only steamer which could possibly bring him to the other side in time for the ceremony sailed the next day, therefore he had had no time to send them a message telling them where and why he was going and for how long.

It occurred to Winthrop Hammond that it would have been rather an unnecessary proceeding to send them word, and he did not understand why Mr. Fairfield thought he should have done so. Then, as he looked at the young man, and beyond him at his sister's pink cheeks, a new idea began to dawn upon him. He whistled softly under his breath and drew his brows down. He did not want to lose this sister now that he had just found out what a sister she could be, but then—here he looked up at the minister—if she must marry, Fairfield was a fine fellow. He could remember some things in that sermon he preached just before he left. They had come to his mind during those awful days of fever and he had wished then that he had taken heed to them before. His face brightened with the thought that Mr. Fairfield would be one who would help him in that way now, and he was glad in his heart that he had come, whether he meant to take away Maria or not.

Then it was Maria's turn to explain how things had gone in Lone Point. She told in a few words the story of her brother's illness, and he, with a voice full of tenderness, added words in praise of her which brought a still richer color to her cheeks and made Mr. Fairfield look steadily at her once more, till she invented an excuse to slip into the house and bathe her burning face.

By and by Mr. Fairfield went to the hotel, and when he returned he asked Maria to walk with him. All the long afternoon Winthrop was left to the tender mercies of his mother and Rachel, who did their best to fill her place.

Maria had taken out with her the much-read and treasured copy of Meyer which Mr. Fairfield had left with her when he went away, thinking to grant his request and read it to him, but though they walked or sat upon the sand the whole afternoon, they did not read Meyer. They had something even better and brighter and more delightful than that to read—and they read it in each other's eyes.

As once before, they lingered long upon the sands, till the sun went down and the moon came up, and when they rose and started toward the green cottage they understood one another.

> *There comes a day when Love, that lies asleep,*
> *The fairest island in the mighty deep,*
> *Wakes on our sight;*
> *There do we stay awhile; but soon again*
> *We trim our sails to seek the open main;*
> *And now, whatever winds and waves betide,*
> *Two friendly ships are sailing side by side.*
> *In port of Love 'twas happy to abide,*
> *But, oh! Love's sea is very deep and wide.*

Maria thought something like this as she stood that night, somewhat later, out on the piazza alone, and looked up into the quiet starlit night. She did not put it into these words, but her heart felt it all and more. She was very happy. Her whole soul went out to God in thanksgiving for the wonderful beauty he had suddenly put into her life. It occurred to her, as it had done before, only more forcefully, to thank God that he had not permitted her to have her way and go somewhere else for the summer, but had set her just here. How otherwise could she have been brought to know Jesus Christ as a dear personal friend? And, oh, suppose she had never met the minister—*her* minister!

26

RACHEL HAMMOND sat in her room by the open window with her Bible on her knee once more. It was summer again, and they were in their own home yet. Maria's door was open and a light breeze stirred the muslin curtain just a little and blew the breath of honeysuckles in, but Maria was not seated in the other room, for Maria was gone. It was just yesterday that she stood in that open doorway in her white robes and bridal veil and kissed Rachel. Upon her bed lay the identical white sailor, whose wings and ribbons had been such a trouble a year ago. By some mischance in the packing it had been left lying there, for Maria did not want to take it with her. Rachel looked up, saw it, and remembered their talk of a year ago.

Perhaps it was because she was used to opening her Bible at that place that the leaves that morning had fallen open of themselves to the very verse she had been reading when Maria began to grumble about the summer arrangements and she had left her reading to try and brighten her up. "For me to live is Christ." How strange it seemed to Rachel as she mused. She remembered just how she had longed, as she laid by her Bible with a sigh that morning, that Maria might feel that verse in all the depth and beauty of its meaning. Now, it seemed to Rachel, that in all the list of her acquaintances there was not one who could so nearly truthfully say that verse as her sister Maria, unless it might be her brother-in-law, Howard. How strange it seemed to call him Howard! A real minister in the family! She remembered how she had wished she might know one well enough some time to ask him some questions and now she had not only a minister but a minister's wife, to whom she could go with all her little perplexities and doubts.

A tear stole out and down her cheek as she remembered that Maria's room was empty and Maria would not occupy it any more, nor be near-by as of old as her companion, but she laughed and brushed it away. God had been very good. She must not weep. She had tried to claim that promise, "Delight thyself also in the Lord and he shall give thee the desires of thine heart," and surely he had kept it and given her more even than she had asked or desired. She was glad and thankful, even though Maria was gone.

Then too, there was something in the fact that Maria lived down-town, only a half-hour's ride away. And was she not going down in a few minutes with Roland De Vere behind his beautiful span of horses to the new parsonage that the church had built for their pastor, to put in place several articles and hang a wonderful picture, the gift of Roland De Vere to the bride? And was there not something about this even more personal and more wonderful still for her? Oh, life was not shadowed much after all!

Rachel rose and went about her room singing, and knew not how appropriate to her life the words were, and were yet to be:

Judge not the Lord by feeble sense,
  But trust him for his grace;
Behind a frowning providence
  He hides a smiling face.

Blind unbelief is sure to err,
  And scan his work in vain;
God is his own interpreter,
  And he will make it plain.

THE ESSELSTYNES
OR, ALPHONSO AND MARGUERITE

Recognizing young Grace's talent as a story teller, her Aunt Belle took the 12 year old girl's first manuscript and had *one* book printed. This one-of-a-kind book has been reproduced from the original; including wood-cut illustrations and the signature page stating that the book is from her private library and her first book.

A Story written on purpose for "Mother's Boys and Girls," by one of the Girls, who is just 12 years old, and whose name is GRACE L—.

1879

Private Library
        Grace Livingstone Hill

My first book.
Published by Christie Belle to
surprise me.
                G. L. H.

At the Breakfast Table

"FRANK," said Mrs. Esselstyne, "I do wish there were some children in this house."

"So do I, Laura; suppose we adopt one or two; eh; how will that do?"

"Oh; do you really mean it! That will be perfectly *splendid.*"

"Yes, Laura, I really mean it; would not you like to begin this morning? I mean to hunt up some child, and—"

But no knowing what was going to be said, for the servant, who had just stepped out, returned, and having overheard the previous talk, and being very fond of children, thought this would be a good chance for getting some. She told her mistress that there were two of the prettiest little darlings out in the kitchen that she ever in all her life saw.

Mrs. Esselstyne gave a look at her husband that said as plainly as words could say:

"I think God has sent them here, don't you?"

Her husband nodded assent, and they both got up to go and look at the children.

"Jane," said Mrs. Esselstyne, "take these children to the bath-room, and give them good baths, and dress them, and bring them to my room."

"Yes'm; but what shall I put on them?"

"Why, sure enough! Well, wrap them in blankets, and bring them down to me."

"Yes'm," said Jane, and she went off delighted.

Here is a picture of Mrs. Esselstyne, waiting in her sitting-room, for the children to be brought to her.

The Question Decided

"WHERE do you live, children?" asked Mrs. Esselstyne, when Jane had brought them to her room.

"Nowhere."

"Where are your father and mother?"

"We haven't got any."

"What are your names?"

"We haven't got any names either, unless 'Ragbags' is a name; that is what the boys on the street call us."

"But what do you call each other?"

"We are brother and sister."

"Is that all the name you have for each other?"

"Yes'm."

"That is strange! Well, would you like to come and live with us, and be our children?" (Mr. Esselstyne had come in the room while they were talking.)

"Oh yes, ma'am, so, *so so* much! *Can* we?"

"Why, I think so, if you are good children."

"Oh, goody! goody!" and the poor things clapped their hands, and jumped up and down.

"Jane," said Mrs. Esselstyne, "take the poor darlings out, and give them some breakfast; they look very hungry, and I will see at once to getting them some clothes."

Here is a picture of the little girl, as she looked when Jane saw her out of the window. She was begging a penny of Miss Helena St. Marks, who was passing by. You will see the ragged little girl again, one of these days.

Getting Dressed

"OH! here are my darlings!" said Mrs. Esselstyne, as she came into the nursery. "Now, my little girl, I am going to give you a name; you shall be my Marguerite. And my boy, your name is Alphonso; you may call me mamma, and the gentleman whom you saw down stairs, you will call papa.

"Now, I am all ready to have you dressed. Alphonso, we will dress you first."

Now I will tell you how he was dressed; first his hair was combed and curled, then his dainty under-clothes were put on; the way his hair was combed was this, it was parted at the side, and rolled over in a lovely roll on top of his head, and the ends behind were arranged in wavy curls, (I forgot to tell you that his hair was quite long); then his pretty little brown pants and coat were put on, of course he had on a pretty little shirt, and last of all, a white rolling collar, and a lovely blue necktie. He had bright buttons on his coat and pants.

"You shall have a tiny gold ring for your finger, when we go down town," said his mamma.

And Marguerite said to him:

"Oh, brother, how lovely you *do* look!"

Then she danced up and down, as she always did when she was pleased.

Here is a picture of Alphonso as he looked after he was dressed; he is waiting for Marguerite to be dressed, and he is at the window with Mrs. Esselstyne's sister, watching the birds.

A Talk

"OH, how lovely we will look, won't we, mamma?" Marguerite said.

"You will look very nice, my darlings; but you mustn't be vain and proud. Did you know that God wouldn't love you if you were proud?"

"Yes, mamma, Mrs. Brown told us that; she told us a good many things about God, and she was talking about Him the last thing before she died."

"Who was Mrs. Brown, my dear?"

"She was a nice woman, who took care of us, and when she died, we didn't have anybody to care a bit about us any more."

"I used to have a washer-woman by the name of Mrs. Brown, that I thought a good deal of."

"Oh, mamma, I do believe, maybe you are the very one she told us about, that she used to work for; she said she wished we could find her; but that it would be no use to try, for she went to Europe to stay two or three years. She gave us a card, with her name on, so that if we should ever come across her, we should know it was she; but I can't read the card."

"Run and get it, darling, and let mamma see it."

So Marguerite went to her room, and returned in a moment with a card, which read as follows:

Mrs. Edward Frank Esselstyne.

"That is the very card I gave her," said Mrs. Esselstyne; "and that is my name. So you see, my darling, God has heard Mrs. Brown's wish, and brought you to me. Now get dressed dear, as soon as you can, we are going to ride, you know."

This is a picture of Marguerite as she looked after she was dressed. She doesn't look much like the girl that Jane saw from the window, does she?

A Morning Ride

THE CARRIAGE rolled to the door, and Mrs. Essel-styne, and her son, and daughter, came out, and were handed in; Alphonso had on a seal-skin overcoat and cap, and brown kid gloves; Marguerite's furs were of ermine, and her kid gloves were a lovely shade of lavendar.

"Oh! oh!" she said, as they rolled down the broad, handsome street; "what a lovely, *lovely* place; I didn't know there was any such street as this in all this large city. Oh, mamma! are we going to stop at this store? Won't that be splendid!"

"This is a bookstore, dear," said Mrs. Esselstyne. "I am going in to see about a book; you may both come with me, if you like; it is a very interesting place to go; you will see more books there, than perhaps you thought there were in all the world."

So they were helped out, and all went into the great handsome building, and the brother and sister wandered up and down the wide aisles, looking around in wonder and delight, while their mamma made her purchases. *On the other page is a picture of the great store where they were.*

The next place they stopped at, was a very large dry-goods store.

"Would you like to get out, and pick out some dresses, or would you like to sit in the carriage and watch the people pass by?"

"I think we would like to get out; wouldn't you, Marguerite?" said Alphonso.

"Well, perhaps you had better," said Mrs. Esselstyne. "There comes papa now, and he will take you with him to see about your new clothes, then Marguerite can come with me; help them out, James."

"Yes ma'am," said the coachman, touching his hat.

"Margie," said her mamma, "how would you like this suit of navy blue, trimmed with silk?"

"O mamma, it is perfectly lovely."

"Well, then we will take it; I have bought a bottle green, and a dark brown, now you want a cardinal red, and then I think you will have plenty of cashmeres. Now we must look at these white embroidered suits, and at sashes and hair ribbons to match your dresses, then from here we must go to the milliners to see about your new hats; you will need one to match every suit; I saw a white felt, trimmed with blue silk, and plumes, that will match the blue suit nicely."

"Oh, mamma!" said Marguerite, "how perfectly splendid you are!"

The Birthday Party

A WHOLE year rolled by; it was the children's birthday; they were to have a party. They were dressed and waiting in the parlor for their company.

"Ting aling-aling-aling" went the door-bell.

"Oh, there are Fanny and Cornie Monroe!" said Marguerite; and almost in the same breath, Alphonso said:

"There comes Fred Burton."

And after that, the bell rang every minute until the company were gathered. At seven o'clock they went out to the elegant dining-room to tea. *What* a table it was! Oh, I couldn't *begin* to tell you of all the elegant things there were on it; it looked just *lovely!* Then they had more games, and pretty soon, when all were gone home except two or three particular friends, whose mammas were coming for them, they went into mamma's room and sat around the fire in the grate, and mamma came and leaned over Alfie's chair and told them a splendid story; it was about a little boy and girl who were out in the cold, and the snow; it made Margie think of the many days that she had wandered up and down in the cold, with hardly anything on her feet to keep them from freezing; and she pushed up her hand softly, and took hold of her mamma's, and put loving little bits of kisses on it; but Alphonso couldn't realize that he had ever been a poor little boy; it seemed to him that he had always lived in this elegant home, and worn just such fine clothes. *You can see by the picture that he is a very handsome boy. It is he in the large chair, on which his mamma is leaning.*

Trouble

"NOW you have heard all about the young lives of this brother and sister; I have only told you this, so that you would know about them. They are several years older now. Alphonso has not improved in every respect. He had a friend, Fred Burton, who did him no good. One day he met him down by the wharf, where he was talking with the mate of one of the boats. His going to the wharf worried Mrs. Esselstyne.

"He is getting reckless, I fear," she said, with a sigh; "Oh, dear me, I *did* try to bring him up right!"

Well, to go back to Alphonso. He was talking with Fred. "I don't know Fred," he said, "whether I can go, or not."

"Oh, pshaw! of course you can go; we don't start till nine o'clock; will you go?"

"Well, y-e-s, I guess maybe I will."

"I wan't you to *promise.*"

"Oh, I can't do that."

"Yes you can; promise now, and then it will be done with."

"Pshaw! well, I'll go if something doesn't happen to hinder me, and that's all I w-i-l-l say."

"All right—that's enough; I can trust you. Good-bye."

"Oh, dear!" said Alphonso, the minute he turned away; "I wish I hadn't promised him; I don't want to go; at least mamma would rather I wouldn't; but after all, I don't see what harm there is in it; they needn't be so dreadfully afraid of a fellow."

Here is a picture of Alphonso, and Fred, and the Captain. Alphonso is the one who is sitting down.

The boys have been wading, and Alphonso has his pants all tucked into his boots; he is very fond of making himself look rough and dusty.

8

Plans

MARGUERITE had improved very much; for one thing she was a Christian; nobody knew it yet but mamma and papa, and Jesus. That same afternoon that Alphonso was at the wharf, she was out walking; she saw her brother with Fred Burton, and it troubled her.

"Mamma," she said, when she came in, "don't you think Alphonso goes too much with Fred Burton?"

"Yes, my dear," said Mrs. Esselstyne with a sigh; "I know he does."

"Mamma, some of the boys are going riding to-night, down to the willows, and are going to have supper; and I think they are going to have wines, and—a-n-d—"

"Yes, daughter, I know what you mean; and you are afraid our Alfie will drink wine; so am I. My daughter, you must pray for him."

"I do, mamma; but I can't bear to have him go to-night. There he is; I would rather not see him just now."

So she left the room and ran up stairs.

"Mamma, where is Sis?" said Alphonso, looking in.

"She just went to her room, my son."

Her brother wanted to see her about something, so pretty soon he followed her. As he was about to knock at the door, he heard her voice, and stopping to ascertain if any one was with her, this is what he heard:

"Dear Lord Jesus! please make my dear brother a Christian; *do* help me to keep him away from that supper to-night; I don't want him to go; I want him to go to the prayer-meeting with me; please make him want to. Please keep him away from places where they drink wine, and don't let him want to smoke any more. Hear me for thine own sake. Amen."

Her brother was dumbfounded! He did not know what to do. Just then, the bell rang, and off he went to his room to dress for dinner. After dinner he went back up stairs and stayed in his room until his sister came to ask him if he would not go to the young peoples' meeting with her; he said "Yes," very pleasantly. After meeting, several of their young friends came home with them, as Margie had invited them to do. She knew that Fred Burton was coming at nine o'clock to call for her brother; she had a plan for that; she told the coachman to be on the watch for Fred Burton, and let her know when he drove up; at nine o'clock, James, the coachman, knocked at the parlor door, and said in a low voice:

"Miss Margie, he is driving down the avenue."

Then Margie went to the door. *I have a picture for you, of Marguerite as she looked when she went for her walk that afternoon; look at it and then at the little beggar girl, in the second chapter, for they are the same.*

An Important Decision

"WON'T you come in, Fred?" said Margie, as she stood in the hall with Fred Burton; Alfie and I have a little company; I should have invited you; but you were not at meeting; we brought the boys and girls home with us from the meeting. Please come in."

"Well, I don't know," said Fred, very much embarrassed. "Alf promised to go out with me this evening, and I called for him; I didn't know that you were to have company."

"*He* didn't, either; it is mamma's and my surprise; please come in, Fred, your sister Annie is here."

"Oh, I don't think I can, thank you; I have my horse with me, and must attend to him."

"Why, James will attend to him; there he is now. James, take Master Fred's horse and take care of him, please; now Fred, come in. You see, I took your affairs into my own hands," she added, laughing, as she waited in the hall for him to lay aside his wrappings. So, very much to his surprise, Fred Burton found himself attending a delightful little party in the Esselstyne mansion, with a supper very much nicer than any that could have been had in the Hotel at the Willows.

Alphonso did a good deal of thinking during the next few days; he could not forget that prayer that he had heard from Margie's lips. He was half vexed at himself for thinking so much about it; he said to himself, that he hadn't been good for anything since "that night," as he phrased it. Finally, one afternoon he shut himself into his room, and said:

"I will *decide* this thing, one way or the other, and I will decide *now.*"

On his table lay the handsome big Bible that his papa had given him for his last birthday present; he hardly ever opened it, but this afternoon he did; and the first words he saw were: "My son, give me thine heart."

"I will," said Alfie; "I *will* do it."

And he *did*. After that you do not need to have me tell you that he became a splendid boy. *Here is a picture of him, as he looked when he read that verse in his Bible.*

THE END.

About the Author

Grace Livingston Hill is well known as one of the most prolific writers of romantic fiction. Her personal life was fraught with joys and sorrows not unlike those experienced by many of her fictional heroines.

Born in Wellsville, New York, Grace nearly died during the first hours of life. But her loving parents and friends turned to God in prayer. She survived miraculously; thus her thankful father named her Grace.

Grace was always close to her father, a Presbyterian minister, and her mother, a published writer. It was from them that she learned the art of storytelling. When Grace was twelve, a close aunt surprised her with a hardbound, illustrated copy of one of Grace's stories. This was the beginning of Grace's journey into being a published author.

In 1892 Grace married Fred Hill, a young minister, and they soon had two lovely young daughters. Then came 1901, a difficult year for Grace—the year when, within months of each other, both her father and her husband died. Suddenly Grace had to find a new place to live (her home was owned by the church where her husband had been pastor). It was a struggle for Grace to raise her young daughters alone, but through everything she kept writing. In 1902 she produced *The Angel of His Presence, The Story of a Whim,* and *An Unwilling Guest.* In 1903 her two books *According to the Pattern* and *Because of Stephen* were published.

It wasn't long before Grace was a well-known author, but she wanted to go beyond just entertaining her readers. She soon included the message of God's salvation through Jesus Christ in each of her books. For Grace, the most important thing she did was not write books but share the message of salvation, a message she felt God wanted her to share through the abilities he had given her.

In all, Grace Livingston Hill wrote more than one hundred books, all of which have sold thousands of copies and have touched the lives of readers around the world with their message of "enduring love" and the true way to lasting happiness: a relationship with God through his Son, Jesus Christ.

In an interview shortly before her death, Grace's devotion to her Lord still shone clear. She commented that whatever she had accomplished had been God's doing. She was only his servant, one who had tried to follow his teaching in all her thoughts and writing.